A Man of No Moon

A Man of No Moon

a novel

JENNY McPHEE

COUNTERPOINT

Excerpts from *The Second Sex* by Simone de Beauvoir, translated by H. M. Parshley, copyright 1952 and renewed 1980 by Alfred A. Knopf, a division of Random House, Inc. Used by permission of Alfred A. Knopf, a division of Random House, Inc.

Excerpts from *A Centenary Pessoa* by Fernando Pessoa, edited by Eugenio Lisboa and L.C. Taylor, translated by Richard Zenith, copyright 2003, used by permission of Carcanet Press Limited.

A selection of the excerpts by Fernando Pessoa are reprinted with the permission of Sll/sterling Lord Literistic, Inc. Copyright 1999 by Richard Zenith.

Library of Congress Cataloging-in-Publication Data

McPhee, Jenny.
   A man of no moon : a novel / Jenny McPhee.
      p.   cm.
   ISBN-13: 978-1-58243-375-2
   ISBN-10: 1-58243-375-5
    1. Poets, Italian—Fiction.   2. Americans—Italy—Fiction.
3. Triangles (Interpersonal relations)—Fiction.   I. Title.
PS3563.C3887M36 2007
813'.54—dc22
       2007017929

Paperback ISBN: 978-1-58243-462-9

Cover design by Nicole Caputo
Interior design by Brent Wilcox

Printed in the United States of America

Counterpoint
2560 Ninth Street, Suite 318
Berkeley, CA 94710
www.counterpointpress.com

For Massimo

The artistic life is a long, lovely suicide.

OSCAR WILDE

I balanced all, brought all to mind,
The years to come seemed waste of breath,
A waste of breath the years behind
In balance with this life, this death.

W. B. YEATS

There is no hope, desire being spent.
Rest forever. So many
Palpitations. Your flutterings
Serve no one, nor do you dignify the earth
With your sighs. Life is bitter and empty,
Nothing more. The world is a slough.
Calm yourself now. Despair
for the last time. Fate gave your kind
No gift but death.

GIACOMO LEOPARDI

PROLOGUE

At the risk of waking her, I ran my finger along the perfect little bumps of her spine, down into the small of her back, then up the gentle rise, until finally I sank it deep into the fissure between her supple, tender cheeks. I had traveled there earlier with my tongue and knew her heat, her smell, her geography. In my mind, I already had an intimate map of her drawn, all the dark, hidden places where I had strayed. She was lovely asleep, naked, quiet, her yellow hair tangled behind her ear, her thin lips slightly parted. She stirred and I removed my finger, replacing it with lire notes tightly rolled into the shape of a cigarette.

I left the bedroom and went into my office. I neatened up my desk to the tip-tap of raindrops on the windowpanes. I glanced at my agenda for that day—Wednesday, March 15, 1948—and whispered to the room "Beware." I considered destroying the stack of unfinished poems and stories but decided that would be treating them better than they deserved. The matter of leaving a note I rejected as inelegant, and what would I write—*I've finally done it. Hurrah.* I walked around the apartment for the last time, pausing before my favorite of Aunt Pia's paintings, a scene with nuns strolling along a row of cypresses on a lawn flaxened by heat, the sea shimmering in the distance like an unraveled bolt of silk.

I left the door unlocked. On my way down the stairs, I kept an eye out for who might see me, if a neighbor opened a door, or the concierge came out from his office to wish me a good evening. But I saw no one, and by now the concierge was eating his dinner or at the bar with his cronies discussing our ever-tumbling government, the chronic instability a welcome relief after Fascism's dreadful permanency.

I walked along the via Giulia towards the Ponte Sisto, the rain tickling my neck and ears. I considered going back to the apartment to get an umbrella, then appreciated the perversity of my thinking. As I arrived at the Lungotevere, I was momentarily blinded by the headlights of cars whizzing past. I could walk in front of one, like Germana, but I didn't like the idea of splatter. I made my way onto the bridge and halfway across. A man under an umbrella passed by without looking at me. The water of the Tiber, usually golden brown, was dark gray and colorless. I hoisted myself up onto the stone wall, proud I had gotten this far. Death brings freedom, I reminded myself, as I felt hesitation's familiar stranglehold close around my will. The scourge of ugly doubt could never torment me again. The Tiber's nectar would fill my lungs, and my inadequacy in all things would disappear with my last breath. A car honked. I moved closer to the edge, my feet dangling heavily. Why should killing myself be more difficult than killing someone else?

The first time I ended a man's life the sensation brought terrified confusion. By the third death the adrenalin of cruelty, the success of staying alive, and the endless rhythms of self-justification vibrated together into a crescendo of physical satisfaction. As hard as I tried, though, I never could make the severed body parts erotic. Guts spilling from stomachs, brains oozing from skulls weren't pretty, but they didn't get to me like the body parts. A lopped-off hand, the fingers still twitching; a head with lips still trembling; an arm and shoulder ripped from its torso; no matter how many times I saw these things, I felt I was being turned inside out like a glove peeled off a hand.

The lights of Rome filtered through the rain, sparkling intermittently. How seriously I took myself. Would the water be cold? Thick with filth? Would I struggle to survive? My questions were stepping stones to the oblivion of nevermore. So many others had gone easily before me, yet I hesitated. Time assured me of the meaninglessness of my gesture. I wanted to be rid of the present, an overrated tense. I pushed my palms into the rough damp stone and lifted my weight up onto my arms. I placed the soles of my feet hard against the wall. Dive or belly-flop? A raindrop landed on my eyelash and for a moment the city erupted into a kaleidoscope of possibility. Now, I thought, now.

Someone grabbed me around the waist and pulled me roughly to the ground. "Not on my watch," a negro American soldier said in English. "Unless I could trade your dumb ass for one of the dead in my platoon." He shook his head. "Anyway, the promised land's a ghetto these days, buddy."

He helped me back to my feet. "I am a poet," I said.

He laughed. "Aren't we all. I'm going to give you a military escort to wherever you're headed in this particular world."

I gave him Tullio's address. When he dropped me off, I asked him, "Your name wouldn't happen to be Clarence, would it?"

"More like Charon," he said.

1948

one

Rome

We spoke Italian at first and I relished hearing my language reinvented by that plump tongue, those tinted lips. Her name was Gladys Godfrey and she was an American actress. She had recently arrived in Rome and was eager, it seemed, to find the right bed. She was not a great beauty, and given her trade, she'd heard that said about her as often as she looked in the mirror. I wouldn't be able to do much for her directly, since I was in a different profession, but she must have decided I had something to offer. I finally interrupted our conversation about the recent Academy Awards—Rosalind Russell's surprise loss to Loretta Young and Vittorio De Sica's special award for *Shoeshine*—and, in English, said, "I speak English. I'm a translator."

She looked as if she might slap me, then her face relaxed.

"You're a cad," she flirted, "but I forgive you. I should have guessed you were a translator. You boys are a dime a dozen, like actresses in Hollywood. Do you get paid well, or do you live on the glory of your experience too?"

Her hair was standard starlet, light brown, shoulder-length, with a permanent wave. It suited her. She had brown eyes flecked with gold, creamy, powderless skin, and a too perfectly upturned nose, though I doubted it had been fixed. It was a forgettable face. She, however, was anything but.

"I get by," I said.

"Whom do you translate?" she asked.

"Hawthorne, Melville, Steinbeck, Whitman, Hammett, Fitzgerald, Hemingway, Faulkner . . . you name him, I've translated something or other of his."

"Americans," she said, her tone disparaging, "and all men to boot."

She wore a sleeveless blue dress and a matching cardigan that kept slipping off her shoulders. She smelled of hibiscus. I loved the assortment of scents women offered. When an appealing woman moves in my direction on the street or in a restaurant, anywhere, it is my custom to exhale through my mouth, then, just as she passes, to breathe her in. I have always been captivated by the scent, no matter how unexpected. But smell is a sensitive subject with women, one I often couldn't resist mentioning. I once told a lover her scent reminded me of asparagus and she never spoke to me again.

I said, "I don't exaggerate when I claim the Americans were our saviors."

"Oh, that dreadful war," she sighed. "You Europeans won't ever get over it, I'm sure."

The party going on around us was taking place in Tullio Merlini's sprawling apartment just off the via del Corso. Tullio was a kind of film industry ambassador maintaining diplomatic relations between the various players, mostly producers and talent. He also dabbled in international relations as he had friends at Ealing, Epinay, and, having spent the war years in Los Angeles, in nearly all the Hollywood studios. I believed he either took money from everyone, or no one. I never did know where Tullio got his money.

Like most of us in Italy, he was devoted to America, but it was difficult to be eternally grateful for something we should have done ourselves. So the exalted was also hated, the way a man obsessed with a woman can despise her too. Still, superficially at least, Americans, things American, were adored, and Tullio's apartment was a den of idol worship. Bottles of Jack Daniels and Coca-Cola, packs of Lucky Strikes and Chesterfields, the music of Glenn Miller, Art Mooney, and Dinah Shore, all in abundance, mocked their wartime prohibition while annihilating memories of shortages and black markets. The scene might have been perceived as a flaunting of the spoils, only Italians, perpetually in a state of decadent denial, refused to acknowledge that we were the conquered, not the conquerors. Evidence of our downfall lay everywhere just beyond Tullio's walls.

"I actually meant the American writers were our saviors more than the soldiers," I said. "Their work gave us hope for the future of civilization, not to mention literature. And translating them did earn me enough money to get by."

"Oh, them again. Well, I'd rather read a long-dead Brit like Dickens or Austen over any of them." She examined her crimson nails. "I mean, they're so fixated on manhood, it's boring. Poor Hemingway beat the poor thing so badly he finally just had to cut it off in one of his books."

She pulled a silver cigarette case from her handbag, extracted one, then glanced across the room toward a woman alone in a corner watching us. A wry little smile lit up Gladys's face.

"No, I'm not a fan of those guys," she said, turning her attention and body back to me. "What are you working on now?"

"Cornell Woolrich stories." I lit her cigarette.

"Well, that's better. At least the pulp writers know they're obsessed with themselves." Her mouth folded into a pout. She shrugged her shoulders.

"I've never met a writer of any kind who wasn't obsessed with himself," I said. "And I speak from experience."

"So you're a writer as well as a translator? That's like being an actress *and* a model, like adding insult to injury, *n'est-ce pas?*" A spiral of smoke snaked from between her lips.

The door to Tullio's apartment opened and there was some fanfare and loud exclamations. Gladys craned her neck to see who had arrived. Tullio had mentioned earlier that Katharine Hepburn, having recently made the crossing on the *Nieuw Amsterdam* for a European holiday, would be attending his soirée.

"Still no Kate," Gladys said, turning back to me.

The woman from across the room was now standing next to me and in front of Gladys.

"So you found him," she said. She wore an olive green suit that matched her eyes. They were chameleon eyes, as if they might change color at whim. "I'm impressed," she said.

These remarks were directed at Gladys. She spoke as if I were either invisible or deaf. The lingering smoke from Gladys's cigarette made it impossible for me to detect a scent.

"I'm smarter than you think," Gladys said to her.

"And I'm the better actress," the woman said.

Something very familiar about her gave me the sensation that I had known her all my life. I then noticed her uncanny resemblance to Gladys.

Gladys turned to me. "This is my older sister, Prudence Godfrey. She told me there was one man in this room worth talking to and challenged me to find him in under ten minutes. It took me three. Evidently you are he, but I never did get around to asking your name."

Prudence's eyes met mine directly for the first time, and for an instant I was afraid.

She said, "Dante Omero Sabato."

I liked the way she said it.

"He's Italy's most famous living poet," she added.

I even liked the way she said that. Her amused disdain held a kernel of awe. She *was* the better actress.

"I've heard of you," Gladys said. "You write film criticism for *Cinema*. No one agrees with you but they're all scared of you." She stubbed out her cigarette. "Let's skedaddle. I heard Kate Hepburn and Anna Magnani were coming but I'm hungry and sick of waiting around."

"I'm only leaving if he comes with us," Prudence said, apparently meaning me.

"Oh, he's coming," Gladys said, her arm slipping through mine.

"I would rather end my life right now," I said, "than let the two of you walk out of Tullio's door without me."

"Strange," Prudence said, still speaking to Gladys as if I weren't there, "he says it almost as if he means it."

It was the "almost" that made me fall for her. She was on to me, and my lack of conviction, from the start. She had intuited my suicide habit. I played with the idea continuously, like a cat with a mouse. I entertained killing myself with more zeal when I was between books—which was presently the case. To distract myself from the vacuum that followed the end of a piece of writing, I translated. When I called the American writers "our saviors" I was being quite literal in my own case. I didn't exactly know why I wanted to die. I didn't think it was solely because I couldn't bear the pain and humiliation of being alive, although that certainly was a challenge. Perhaps my obsession with suicide derived from a desire to conquer uncertainty. Although the certainty of death put a limit on every joy, it did the same for every sorrow. But the explanation was probably simpler. I wanted to die because I could. Choosing to live or die was a fundamental part of being human. There were those who never thought about the option, and others, like me, who were enslaved to contemplating it. Ultimately, it was my belief that if you wanted to get off the bus, by all means get off. It was a popular stop: Socrates, Codrus, Charandas, Lycurgus,

Cato, Zeno, Cleanthes, Seneca, Paulina, Dido, Demosthenes, Lucretius, Lucretia, Lucan, Artistarchus, Petronius, Hannibal, Boadicea, Brutus, Cassius, Mark Antony, Cleopatra, Cocceius Nerva, Statius, Nero, Otho, King Ptolemy of Cyprus, Samson, Theodore, St. Basil, St. Julia, St. Pelagia, Dominiana, Berenice, Prosdocia, had all gotten off there.

"'Whensoever any affliction assailes me, me thinks I have the keyes of my prison in mine owne hand,'" I said, taking hers and bringing it to my lips, "'and no remedy presentes it selfe so soone to my heart, as mine own sword.'"

"You poets," Gladys said, pulling her delicate hand away, "have always given an inordinate amount of thought to 'thine own sword.'"

Gladys, at the moment, was giving the most thought to my munitions as her fingers were stealthily making their way deep into my trouser pocket.

I discreetly shifted my body, hindering her excavation. If the intention of these women was to gain my attention, they had it. What else they might want, I was dying to know. That I would kill myself was a surety. I had decided long ago that I did not like it here and that sooner or later I would find a way to leave. The Godfrey sisters, it seemed, might cause a further delay.

We collected our things and said goodnight to Tullio, who fawned over the sisters. "You have become even more beautiful than when I last saw you in California. What the Mediterranean has to offer evidently agrees with you both." He then turned to me, saying, "Kate will be so disappointed not to meet you." I nodded, both Tullio and I fully aware that Katharine Hepburn had not the remotest idea who I was.

Outside, it was raining. Both women tied their raincoats tightly around their waists and pinned caps to their heads. We took a cab to the Portico of Octavia in the old ghetto, which had been slowly coming back to life. We passed kosher food shops, jewelry, furniture, and textile shops, *pizzerie, trattorie,* bakeries, and bars—some back in business, some still boarded up. Gladys had placed herself between me and Prudence in the back of the taxi.

"Oh, look, there's the Pasticceria Boccioni," she said, her leg firmly pressed up against mine. "I've tasted their rugulach and it's divine."

I wondered who had fed it to her.

We went to Da Gigetto, a restaurant tucked underneath what remained of the once splendid portico, built by Augustus as a tribute to his sister Octavia, the neglected wife of Antony. As the waiter was seating us, he shook his head and said, "Some guys get all the luck. God might have given you one American girl, but two? Two means you're dancing with the devil."

"I've had to do a lot more than dance with the old Beelzebub," I said. I asked him to bring us a carafe of wine and a plate of fried artichokes straight off as the girls were ravenous.

"You see the war everywhere here," Prudence said. "For us, the war was a distant disturbance, like a tornado on the plains—a long way off you see the dark, purple funnel and know it is wreaking havoc on all those in its path, but you hope the damn thing stays over there."

"Instead of excited, Prudence becomes hopelessly morbid when she gets a new part," Gladys said, taking another cigarette from her case. "She's going to be the lead supporting actress and the director is some kind of legend."

"It's the angles, Mr. Sabato," Prudence said. I had no idea what she was talking about.

"Dante," I said, offering Gladys a light.

"Joan Fontaine and Olivia de Havilland we're not," Prudence went on, "nor will our handprints ever disfigure the sidewalk in front of Grauman's Chinese Theater—but we have made it as far as we have because we don't have a bad angle."

It was true. They were wonderful to look at. Each of their features was peculiar and unique. The amalgam, depending on your perspective, went from exotic beauty to plain Jane and back again. Women were like two-way mirrors, peering at others and into themselves, on display all the while. Although I treasured them, I couldn't imagine spending an extended time with one exclusively. Tullio once told me I didn't find a woman to love because I idealized all women and couldn't bear the disappointment of having that ideal shattered by any one of them. Tullio always saw the best in me, but the truth had more to do with their reflective capabilities. If ever I looked at a woman long and hard enough, the layers of beauty and poetry and knowledge flaked away like eczema-afflicted skin, leaving the raw, red, pustulated image of my own self.

The radio was playing in the restaurant and Dean Martin sang, "Once in Love with Amy."

———

11

"His voice is so seductive," said Gladys, "it makes me wish my name were Amy." She sighed, then frowned at her sister. "We should have changed our names. As long as we're saddled with these, we're doomed."

"It's too late," said Prudence. "We've worked too much already using ours."

"You never let me get my way, ever," said Gladys, "and it will be the ruin of us."

Over a generous serving of fried codfish and chickpeas, I asked Gladys and Prudence what had brought them to Rome. The answer I got was evasive.

"We left Los Angeles because Prudence got fed up with the grit blowing in from the desert," Gladys said. Her lipstick had faded, and I preferred her lips unpainted and fleshy, having the texture and tint of a peeled grape. "She's annoyingly clean."

Prudence wasn't eating much. She didn't appear to be listening to her sister. Her skirt had slid up her leg to reveal the swell of her thigh. If it had happened with Gladys, I would have been sure it was intentional. With Prudence, I knew it wasn't, increasing my desire.

"It's true," Gladys emphasized, as if someone had objected. "The sand slipped into everything like a dirty old man. No matter how much Prudence cleaned, there it was, the light brown silt, in her glass, in the pages of her book, in the bathtub, in her sheets, on her skin." Gladys abandoned her fork and ate the pieces of fish with her fingers, then licked them free of grease. "It stuck to things and wouldn't move on. In the end, it started to really get to her, so I suggested Rome."

———

Prudence gave me a noncommittal smile, her green eyes flat.

Gladys took a sip of wine, its dark red color newly tingeing her lips and tongue. "Of course, I warned her that Rome might not be much better. I said to her, if the sand getting into everything bothers you, you'll never survive Italian men."

Prudence stared out the window, as if she wished to be hidden in the dark night, not exposed by the warm light of the restaurant. It seemed the evening was not going the way she would have liked. Finally, she said, "We came to Rome because Gladys had some trouble with a man. And Cinecittà's system of dubbing made the move here favorable in terms of work. We'll see how it goes." Prudence sighed. "In time, you will learn, Mr. Sabato . . . Dante . . . that what motivates me is some physical or psychic or spiritual discomfort. With Gladys it is always a man."

Her assumption that I would know her and her sister long enough to learn anything much about them was intriguing. They say curiosity killed the cat, but it was keeping this one alive. We gossiped about the actors Prudence would be working with on her upcoming picture *Bitter Rice*—Vittorio Gassman's relentless womanizing and his disintegrating marriage, Silvana Mangano's secret affair with Marcello Mastroianni.

"If *we* know about it," Gladys said, "it can't be *that* secret."

We moved on to books and Gladys asked me if I'd read Truman Capote's *Other Voices, Other Rooms*, which I had.

"A refreshing take on manhood," she said. "And the cover is sublime. He's such a dish in that photograph—makes me want to try to get him to switch sides."

If anyone had a fighting chance, Gladys did. "And what are you reading?" I asked Prudence.

"Sartre's *No Exit*," she said.

"No translator needed," Gladys said.

Prudence explained, "Our mother taught English and French and was a musician. She loved to read and she loved opera."

"We come from an *unusual* family," Gladys added.

Prudence stood up abruptly and put on her coat. "I'm so glad to have finally met you, Dante Omero Sabato. I hope we meet again." And she left.

"She's working the enigma angle," Gladys said, once she had gone. "In our different ways, Prudence and I are picky about men. But I can tell she likes you." She held out another cigarette for me to light, wrapping her moist fingers around my wrist to steady the flame, her grasp hard and insistent, her gilded eyes determined. "And so do I."

On our way out of the restaurant, I did have the thought that taking Gladys home could ruin my chances with Prudence, who appealed to me more. I also had the sense that not taking Gladys home might have an equally unfavorable outcome. And I might not see either of them again, so what did it matter? Our little constellation had twinkled brightly that evening, but by morning its luminescence could well have dulled for all of us, our desire already seeking light in other parts of the sky.

two

Castiglioncello

I own a villa on the Ligurian Sea just south of the port and seaside resort city of Livorno in a lively little town called Castiglioncello. Across the bay are the fluorescent blue waters and sparkling white sands of Rosignano, where the Solvay chemical plant glistens night and day like Oz. The house was left to me by my Great Aunt Pia from Rome, probably because she felt comfortable that I would comply with her belief that property, like a child, was under no circumstances to be sold.

Aunt Pia was, in fact, my mother's second cousin. My mother admired Aunt Pia greatly while disapproving of her unconventional ways. It took me a long time to learn, however, that it was Pia's unconventional ways that had earned her my mother's reverence. Aunt Pia had always especially liked my mother but found my father unsatisfactory. I was never sure what my aunt disliked about him most: that he worked as a clerk in a bookshop ("books are meant to be written or read, not sold") or that he was Florentine ("if it's not nailed down, they'll try to sell it"). Father, well aware of Pia's antipathy for him, once suggested that she was the unfortunate consequence of a family patriarch's indiscretion with a maid. To avoid scandal, Pia had been carted off as a newborn to Rome, where she was brought up by wealthy but childless relations who lavished her with all the advantages. My father must have been jealous of her fairy-tale life. He would say, "She read a few books, bought herself some art, and now she thinks she's an aristocrat. She ought to move to New York."

I cherished Aunt Pia because she was everything my parents were not and she saw the world in the most wondrous shades of gray. From the first moment we met, and for as long as I knew her, I sensed she understood what I was thinking better than I did myself. And though she could be quite critical of me, she loved me without limits and seemed to have an infinite curiosity about who I was and would be.

My visits to Aunt Pia's villa began in a sad way. In early April, when I was six years old, my mother gave birth to Giovanni Virgilio, a fine, healthy baby boy. I was not allowed into the hospital, so my father held the tiny pink infant up to the window for me to see as I stood in the courtyard with a neighbor who was looking after me. I was initially excited to see that ball of flesh, proud of this new addition to my family whom I would be able to play with and teach and make my own. But as I was staring up at the window, I saw my mother's smiling face join my father's. She kissed the baby and stroked my father's cheek, failing to notice me at all. My father waved once more, but his gesture seemed cursory, even something of a shoo. The three of them, a perfect trinity, faded away, and all I could see was my own small reflection in the window glass. I wished I had never been born and then quickly revised that idea to wishing Giovanni Virgilio had never been born.

Three weeks later my brother was dead. Though my mother blamed the nurses for not keeping his severed umbilical cord clean, I knew better. Soon after Giovanni Virgilio's funeral, my mother and I left for Castiglioncello, invited by Aunt Pia, whose condolences to me included, "Why your mother wanted another child when you are just fine, I will never know." I appreciated her sentiment but wondered if she would be as kind to me if she had known how efficacious my wish making had been. To add to my guilt, that same month Italy joined the war, my father was sent to the front and I lived at Castiglioncello with my mother and my aunt all to myself until 1919.

For most of that time, I lived in terror that my father would be killed and that I would be responsible for yet another death. I would lie awake at night listening to the sea or the wind in the trees while concentrating with all my might on my father's survival. In my mind, I searched for him in a trench or a tank or sleeping in a tent and when I finally found him, I whispered into his ear over and over again that I did not want him to die, that he could not die, that he needed to come home, which he did, eventually, unscathed. I, however, was thoroughly exhausted.

Aunt Pia's villa was perched on a cliff overlooking a cove a mile or two out of town along the twisting via Aurelia. It faced north (away from the Solvay plant) and, from the second floor, looked across a cove to a medieval fortress, one of many along the Etruscan coast built by the Medicis to combat a burgeoning pirate problem. From the top floor, where I now had my bedroom and study, I could see the entire Tuscan archipelago. From a young age, I had spent every June, July, August, and half of September with Aunt Pia and my mother in the villa. Much of the time, when I was small, was passed in the shade of the Aleppo pines towering over Aunt Pia's colorful and fragrant garden crowded with oleander, roses, and bougainvillea. As I grew older, I divided my time between roaming the hills behind the villa and reading in the garden with Aunt Pia. Though I could swim and would go for a dip often enough, I was never at ease with the sea.

Aunt Pia's was the only villa on that small stretch of coast, but she shared her promontory, the rocky beach, and the vertiginously steep stairway down to it with a convent occupied by the order of the Passionisti. The nuns never spoke with us because, as novitiates, they had sworn an oath of silence. The precious few words they did utter were reserved for God. The Passionisti did, however, sing, and their music could bewitch me. At the canonical hours, most especially vespers, their honey-eyed voices would transform into a tantalizing siren's song meant to lure me out to sea. Many mornings just after dawn, and many evenings just before sunset, the nuns, dressed in their bright white habits and rabbit-eared headdresses, would each choose her spot on the beach to pray, meditate, or soak in the sun. Those hours were my hours, too, since my mother feared the heat of the midday sun on my child's skin, but she would never let me go near them. The Passionisti were known to take in wayward, fallen girls, prostitutes, the victims of incest and rape. Every so often, one of the nuns would appear accompanied by a girl with a swollen belly wearing a gray smock, and my mother would whisk me off the beach and write a letter to the Mother Superior. Aunt Pia laughed at my mother and said she was making it very difficult for any woman I might fall in love with someday. I told Aunt Pia I would never love any other woman besides her and my mother so there was nothing to worry about. But I did wonder what those smocked and bloated girls had done to cause my mother such agitation. A few times, a girl would disappear and there would be a search through the town and along the shore. Usually, they were found at the station or in a bar down by the port, but once a body was found by the fishermen. After that, I never saw any of the pregnant girls on the beach again.

As far as I could tell, Aunt Pia had developed her own particular aesthetic approach to living. She conceived of herself as a character in a book, a detail in a painting, and did anything she could, such as living in a place much painted, to cultivate her stratagem. So my aunt had chosen Castiglioncello not so much because it was a pretty spot, but more because it was where, in the nineteenth century, the *Macchiaioli* painters, whose work she collected, had spent large chunks of time translating their impressions of the landscape into iridescent canvasses. At the turn of the century, when Aunt Pia first visited Castiglioncello, the nearest hotel was in Livorno (known as Leghorn to the masses of English who summered there), prompting her to build a villa far from the madding crowd. Eventually, the Hotel Miramare was built in town and became a favorite place of ours for my afternoon tea and Aunt Pia's pink-martini aperitif.

"It is important," she once told me while we sat on the Miramare's terrace watching the handsome and distinguished guests parade by, "to show off." No one there, however, was as effortlessly fashionable or stunningly beautiful as my aunt. She was always the center of attention wherever she went, without ever seeming to call for it. I must have been nine or ten years old and was enthralled by her ability to turn the expected upside down. "The intellectual peers out at the world," she said, "while the exhibitionist peers in at himself. Both activities are fundamental to a rich life."

Over a decade before this exchange, in 1906, my Great Aunt Pia showed off by building her three-story villa in the Liberty style, with undulating wrought–iron balconies and stucco ornament swirling about the facade. The high wooden-beamed ceilings were each painted with a Pompeian motif and the drawing room was decorated with seventeenth-century prints of scenes from the *Odyssey*—*The Land of the Lotus Eaters, Polyphemus and His Flock, Circe and the Hogs,* and so on. The dining room, which I almost never used, was dominated by a three-leaf cherrywood table, and decorating the walls was a series of eighteenth-century French etchings entitled *Vues de Livourne,* given by the Grand Duke of Tuscany to the Prince of Bohemia and, in turn, won by my aunt off a Slovakian businessman in a poker game. She liked to tell me about her art and I was never sure which was more fantastic, the story of how she acquired the work or the story she told me the work depicted.

Aunt Pia's husband had done very well as a shoe manufacturer but had died of a heart attack minutes before the countdown to the new century. As I gathered from my father and mother, Aunt Pia was even more attractive in black, and marriage proposals had not been wanting. But she came to enjoy running her husband's business and didn't want to give it up to be someone's wife again. As for children, Pia disliked them but made an effort with those she happened to be related to, taking a particular interest in me once I let it be known, when I was eight years old, that I intended to be a writer.

"With a name like yours," she had said, "you would do better to become a plumber, but let's see what we can do in spite of it."

At some point, my mother began sending Aunt Pia my stories and poems and she would return them, the grammar and syntax corrected, clichés underlined. That she took me seriously enough to give my juvenile efforts her attention made my heart thump with pride. She believed I was worthy of correction, which meant with work and dedication I might one day be worthy of her. Each black ink mark and squibble, however, which I imagined her dashing off between sips of pink martini or during pauses in clever conversation with a suitor, was a delicate thrust of a knife, wounding me grievously. To comfort myself, I often imagined my own funeral and all those who would mourn, and finally I would envision my large and imposing gravestone made of Monte Altissimo marble with the

―――

inscription: "Here lies the greatest author who ever lived. He never wrote a line."

Every year I couldn't wait for school to finish in June so that I would be once again in Aunt Pia's aura, having our cultured conversations at the Hotel Miramare, and continuing my apprenticeship in the world of genteel erudition. During our many weeks together over the summer, Aunt Pia would read to me from Tasso and Ariosto, Petrarch and Boccaccio, but also from Chaucer and Shakespeare, Donne and Spencer. (She had perfected her English in order to converse more easily with some of her most important shoe customers.) She disapproved of my reluctance to swim and would try to convince me to bathe more often in the sea by telling me, "these waters hold the flesh and spirit of Percy B. Shelley," an argument I did not find persuasive.

In 1931, when I was twenty-two, Aunt Pia herself died. One July morning, she went for a swim (the nuns had seen her) and never came back. My mother who, along with the church, believed suicide the gravest of sins, insisted that Aunt Pia had run off to start another life in South America. True or not, she had recently been to a notary to draft a will stipulating that in case of her death or disappearance, all her property—the villa, her automobile, and her apartment in Rome—was to be given to me. She left the shoe business to another nephew and her money to my mother.

I wasn't in Castiglioncello when Aunt Pia vanished. As soon as I heard the news, I took the next train from Florence and stayed for the rest of the summer, half hoping she might show up one day and dismiss her absence with her disarming insouciance. I didn't mind waiting and as the years went on I continued to wait. Her image was never far from my eye and her voice spoke to me habitually, as if her body hadn't drifted out to sea but had drifted into mine.

Since then the house had become a source of great solace for me. These days, in Rome, when feeling out of sorts, I would find myself thinking—*There's always Castiglioncello. Only a three-hour journey by train. I can be there by lunchtime. Or to see the sunset. Or to have a chat with Ubaldo.* And on this particular morning when I felt things were becoming ominous, I had followed my own advice and fled to Aunt Pia's. I had arrived at the villa only a few hours earlier, a limpid day in early June, and immediately I felt better.

The previous evening, I had attended another of Tullio's cocktail parties, this one in conjunction with the Italian premiere of *The Paleface*, a comedy western starring Bob Hope and Jane Russell, neither of whom had shown up to the screening, much less to the party. As Benny Goodman's "On a Slow Boat to China" played in the background, I was regaling the voluptuous Baroness Ghisolabella with the peculiar death of the eighteenth-century French moralist Nicolas-Sébastien Roch de Chamfort. He had shot himself in the temple but failed to kill himself, the bullet removing his nose and right eye instead. He then took a dull knife and slashed his wrists, throat, and ankles. Still, he lived, and was well on his way to recovery when the inattention of a doctor finally did the trick.

———

"What kind of inattention?" the Baroness asked, and I could tell by the slightest droop in her eyes and the rasp in her voice that the success of my seduction was assured. I was about to tell the Baroness that the doctor had mistakenly given Chamfort an overdose of arsenic when across the room I spied Prudence Godfrey. Our eyes met, but mine flinched away as I quickly hunted the room for Gladys, images of our night together furiously returning—her wrists and ankles lashed tightly with silk rope, one of my hands filled with her hair, yanking her head backward, the other around her soft white neck, my fingertips hard on her throat, her pulse rapid and strong. She had wanted me to go further. To my relief, I could not see Gladys anywhere in the room. I turned back to Prudence, but she was gone. Had I already betrayed her? Like Tristan in possession of a one-way ticket to the fifth circle of hell, part of me ached for the one missing, even while the rest of me made a silent vow to the other.

I extracted myself from the Baroness and went in search of Prudence. When I couldn't find her, Tullio told me that she had left in a hurry. It seemed she was fleeing me. Normally, I found this flattering. It was even something of a professional requirement that I caused people to feel discomfort, fright, surprise or embarrassment. But this was not flattery, this was rejection. I wasn't sure Prudence even knew that I had been with Gladys. I had assumed she did—when I accompanied Gladys home to their place in via Leccosa just after two in the morning, tripping into each other as we walked, a light had been on in the window—but I had no experience with how siblings communicated, and assumptions were mostly wrong.

None of this was actually the problem, though. The problem was my inertia. I had met Prudence weeks ago, recognized in her something challenging, even dangerous, and I had done nothing. When I saw her a second time at Tullio's, my response, after the weakest of pursuits, was to give up, to flee Rome, possibility. But perhaps my instinct had been correct—the danger here was me.

When I arrived at Castiglioncello, a slight chill had sharpened the late afternoon air and, once inside the villa, I contemplated lighting a fire in the fireplace, but did not. Instead I perused some stories that had found their way to me from the University of Iowa by a young woman named Flannery O'Connor. The stories were gravely hilarious and I began to feel better. I decided halfway through the first that I would see about getting them into *La Voce di Aretusa*. I was in the middle of a story called "The Turkey" when I detected a shadowy figure moving through the grove of pines toward the house. I knew it was Ubaldo. He had come from the other side of the train tracks across the via Aurelia, from a cluster of houses lived in by local fishermen, workers at the Solvay plant, and Ubaldo. He owned the only shop within walking distance of the villa, selling everything from ties and pasta to umbrellas and fishing rods. He also had a very decent selection of classic and contemporary novels; essays on history, philosophy, and literature; and comic books. If he didn't have what you were looking for, he would find a way to get it. And if you were hungry he would cook you a meal. During the war, Ubaldo had asked me if he could store his miraculous collection of goods in the villa and since then he had taken it upon himself to look out for the property, not to mention myself. Ubaldo's bond with me, however, predated the war by many years.

He knocked on the front door and I shouted for him to come in. I heard the door open and his footsteps on the stairs up to the library, where he knocked, then gently pushed open the door but remained standing in the hallway.

"I don't want to disturb you," he said. "If you would let me know when you're coming I could prepare the place for you." His accent was Livornese, hard c's, rolling vowels.

"Come in. Come in," I said.

Still, he hesitated.

When I was fourteen, I remembered, it was I, having come up to Ubaldo's place unannounced, who had hesitated. As usual, I and my mother were visiting my aunt during the summer. The sun had set, the night air bringing no relief from the heat. In the presence of my aunt, my mother became nervous and inattentive to me—other than to tell me to sit up straight, or to wash my face, or to smooth my clothes. During dinner, Aunt Pia managed to elongate her favorite subject—my father—from aperitif to coffee. Why had he no ambition? What did my mother see in him? Was he a suitable role model for "the boy"? She suggested to my mother that I come to Rome to live with her so that I could receive a more "worldly" education.

"One must realize," she said, her demitasse raised, her pinky long, "that Florence is a provincial town."

My mother didn't answer right away. She put down her fork and stared out the window, the expression on her face calm and unreadable. I was aching for her to acquiesce to my aunt's request. Rome meant a life full of glamour and ideas where I could discover independence and savoir-faire. But if my mother said I could go, the suspicions I had harbored since my brother's death would be confirmed.

"Dante's moving to Rome is out of the question," my mother said.

"All right," Aunt Pia said, "but you must remember Machiavelli was a Florentine."

"You remember this: Mussolini lives in Rome."

My mother surprised me. She was never anything but obsequious with my great aunt. I could tell Aunt Pia was surprised too. She shrugged her shoulders dismissively but had a pleased look in her eye.

I stood up from the table, left the house, and headed for the train tracks. Once there I lay down like a damsel in a silent film. As the minutes passed, I lost myself among the stars and it occurred to me that if I failed to jump up when I felt the vibrations of the approaching train, all my troubles would be over. When a train didn't come, I arose and saw a light still on in Ubaldo's shop. As I neared, I heard grunting and huffing inside. I hesitated, unsure what was happening. That it was something illicit I was certain. I moved slowly toward the window and peered into the back where Ubaldo usually sat. A large man was standing over Ubaldo pummeling him with his fists and feet. Again, I hesitated. I felt icy sweat trickling down under my arms. Would this man beat me, too? Even kill me? I turned and ran. Seeking help was nowhere in my thoughts. Instead, I reassured myself that no one would ever know I had been there. And when Ubaldo was found dead the following morning I would say nothing. Aroused by my depravity, I ran, my heart pounding, my breath uncatchable. And as I ran I began to feel invincible. So armed, I stopped short, pivoted and ran back just as fast to the door of the shop and screamed Ubaldo's name. The man looked up, his eye caught mine, and my invincibility withered into the conviction that what had failed to happen on the train tracks would now be taken care of.

The man kicked Ubaldo hard one more time, pushed me out of the way, and was swallowed into the night. Ubaldo, who was then in his late thirties, the age I am now, picked himself up off the floor, his face bleeding and swollen, and said to me, "Thank you, Dante. You are a brave man. You saved my life and I will always be indebted to you." He dabbed at the blood on his face with his shirt. "But I need to ask something more of you. This incident must remain between us." He begged, his voice softer now, urgent. "You're not to tell your mother or your aunt or any of your mates." By "mates" I knew he meant his sons and nephews, with whom I regularly cavorted.

Ubaldo and his brother, Ranieri, a fisherman, lived next door to each other and each had four sons, all with names particular to the region. Ubaldo's were Anelito, Congedino, Eteocle, and Risveglio. Rainieri's were Edamo, Iliade, Norge, and Goete. Every summer of my childhood, I fished, swam, threw rocks, and played ball with them. All eight of them fought on one side or the other, or both, during the war. Edamo, Iliade, Norge, and Goete all returned home during the summer of 1945. Ubaldo's four sons perished. Ubaldo's wife, Duella, died of grief, although I suspected she had poisoned herself. A belladonna leaf or bit of the root ingested daily over a short period was known to work. Some time later, after seeing Ingrid Bergman slow-poisoned by her Nazi husband in *Notorious* and Humphrey Bogart doing the same to Barbara Stanwyck in *The Two Mrs. Carrolls*, I had the thought that Ubaldo might have been the culprit. Not a week after Duella's funeral, Corinna, a woman from Rosignano, and her daughter Nerina and Nerina's husband Beppe and their newborn daughter Isola all moved into the house with Ubaldo. Since then, I had been tempted to ask Ubaldo if Corinna was the reason for the wrath of the man who had tried to beat him to death those many years ago, but I never did. I knew Nerina was Ubaldo's daughter—she looked just like him—and the man, father or uncle, had no doubt been defending the family honor. Ubaldo never spoke about anything out of the past and what had once been a house of men became a house of women.

For the rest of that summer of my fourteenth year, having lost Rome to my mother's fears of Fascism, I was miserable and taciturn. My mother attributed it to growing pains, my great aunt to the influence of the Florentine temperament.

"Let us read some Flaubert," she said to me finally one afternoon. "I think you are in need of some tried and true melodrama." So I listened to *Madame Bovary,* a book I did not appreciate in the least, content, however, to sit next to Aunt Pia in the garden, hearing the sound of her steady voice above those of the sparrows, titmice, and woodpeckers, while I tried to distinguish her citrus and palm oil scent from the ones offered in competition by the garden.

"It may seem a dull book to you," she said one afternoon, interrupting herself, though from what part of the story I did not know. "But it sums up the mediocre nature of life quite fairly. Living a life of substance, Dante, means accepting that there is no such thing as fidelity, integrity, or even honesty."

Although I said nothing, this statement of hers repulsed me, and for the first time I understood why my father held Aunt Pia in disfavor. The following day I announced that I would be returning to Florence for the remainder of the summer.

How Aunt Pia knew I was grappling with my sense of moral failure just then I would never know. The question that plagued me for a long while to come was: How could I have not only hesitated, but run away, when I saw a man being beaten to death? As the years went on, I experienced many kinds of hesitation. I hesitated when asked to join the Resistance. I hesitated when a lover in Rome needed to hide from the Nazis in my apartment. I hesitated before pulling a friend from the line of fire after his foot had been blown off. I hesitated when asked to name my anti-Fascist friends to the police. I hesitated when a woman told me the child she was carrying was mine. In time, however, hesitation became a luxury for me, a precious thing, a gem sparkling with my humanity, my shame, my fear, my ambiguity, my instinct for self-preservation. I knew that when hesitation finally abandoned me, I would then do what had to be done.

But just then it was Ubaldo who was hesitating at my door.

"Come in, come in," I repeated, but he made no move.

"Shall I tell Corinna you'll come for lunch tomorrow then?" he said.

"No, Ubaldo, but thank her for me. Not this time. I will try to work."

"I'll send Nerina over with some food."

Nerina often found her way into my bed when I was in Castiglioncello. "That will be fine," I said. "But Ubaldo, do come in. Have a drink. Sit a while."

"If everything is all right, I'll be going home."

"Yes, Ubaldo, everything is all right."

three

Rome

Glory be to God that fish have bones! Prudence is mine, or at least she was for a night, and a chaste one at that, but we did share a bed. Although a serendipitous fish bone was, in the end, the pick that opened the lock to Prudence's affections, not to mention her bedroom, most of the credit must go to Gladys, for it was she who encouraged me in my quest, ultimately heading me to the right place at the right time, even priming me to seize an opportunity. But I should explain.

When I returned to Rome from Castiglioncello, calmed after several days of quiet reading and tender June afternoons with Nerina, I telephoned Gladys. I was not anxious to see her or worried about having offended her. I was getting back in touch with Gladys because I wanted her to lead me to Prudence, who had become, since I last glimpsed her the night she fled from Tullio's, something of an obsession.

I was fond of my obsessions. Some had been lifelong. Some came with intensity and went without a moment's regret. While in Castiglioncello, I repeatedly tried to assure myself Prudence was not the obsession, my fascination with her nothing more than the latest variation of a perennial preoccupation with women and sex. After all, I knew little about Prudence and had barely spoken with her.

I realized that Gladys might not find my motivation for getting in touch with her complimentary. Seducing one woman to get to another was a hackneyed device, yet my desire for Prudence was such that I didn't care. Gladys was too smart to fool, so when she answered the phone I told her straight out, "I'm calling you because I want to see your sister."

"It's about time," she said. "Shall I come over?"

Who could refuse such directness? She possessed a disarming national trait that would lead to her country's world dominance. I reminded her where I lived and hung up the phone. The apartment Aunt Pia left me was on the via Giulia, just north of the Farnese Palace. It was on the top floor and the living room had a checkered view, between buildings and over rooftops, of the Tiber, the Janiculum hill just west of the river, and a slice of the Regina Coeli prison.

I had lived in that apartment for seventeen years—having moved in the autumn after Pia died—and since then hardly a thing had been altered. I never changed the wall colors—ochre, oyster, and Tuscan red—or the wallpaper in the dining room depicting bucolic scenes of English country life. The furniture, the rugs, the curtains were all hers. I had added some books to her library where she also kept her gallery of paintings by Italian impressionists known as the *Macchiaioli*. Aunt Pia was never very far away.

It was early afternoon when Gladys walked in my door for the second time, looking ripe and smelling of plums. Like a bride, she was all in white, from her very wide-brimmed hat to the peek-a-boo shoes. Without a word between us, as soon as the door closed, in a few motions, her linen dress and silk slip were off, revealing not only a lack of undergarments but a breathtaking purple flower of a bruise around her right hip— the kind that could only have been caused by a strong hand. Against my better intentions, I was on her, in her, with no thoughts of stopping until I had left a lasting mark or two of my own. She came many times, and then, with the skill of the adept, let me reach my apex while inside one of her infertile orifices. Afterward, she crossed over to her clothes, found her cigarettes in her bag, lit two using a monogrammed silver lighter, and handed one to me.

"Don't get me wrong," she said, "but you suit me. Of all the men I've known, you seem the least complicated."

Her words made me uneasy. Was this some sort of proposal? I had assumed she understood my purpose, even if little conversation had taken place between us.

"No one," I told her, putting on my robe, "has ever paid me so high a compliment."

She laughed. A rectangle of sunlight from the window framed her lithe body and caught the highlights in her hair. She had no thought to cover herself. Lucky Strike Venus, I thought.

"No need to tease," she said, her tone playful. She gathered up her clothes and headed for the bathroom. "I meant what I said. I find you refreshingly straightforward."

"About Prudence," I began.

"See," she said, closing the bathroom door.

She emerged fully dressed, hair smooth, lips too pink, the plum scent stronger. "Prudence is up north for a few weeks," she said. "They're filming 'on location,'" she smirked. "Everyone wants to be Visconti these days. Lucky for Prudence, at least this director is using actors." Her voice softened. "Until she gets back, I'll just have to do." Then she left.

We saw each other every few days over the next month and our conversations were almost exclusively about Prudence. The Berlin blockade, Tito's break from Russian control, the Korean divide, the Olympics—none of it held any interest for me. All I wanted was to hear Gladys talk about Prudence. She described their childhood in North Dakota—the long cold winters, the cows, the boredom. Their parents were rarely home. Their father was a train conductor out of Fargo and their mother was a high school English teacher and an aspiring concert pianist. When Gladys was fourteen and Prudence fifteen, their mother left for Chicago and never came back. On Prudence's sixteenth birthday, the sisters took a bus to Los Angeles with fifty dollars between them.

"L.A. was chock full of girls like me and Pru, but we were lucky," Gladys said during a lazy afternoon lounging around my apartment. The windows were open, the shades up, the shutters splayed, despite the heat. Gladys found the Italian practice of closing out the hot summer air suffocating. "We got respectable parts in respectable films and were paid something for it. After the war things got worse, you know, 'Rosie the Riveter, Go Home'? Well, they didn't go home, they came west, and the work got harder to come by. Still, that's not why we left L.A." She paused, wanting to give me the impression she was finally going to say something she shouldn't about her sister. "The real reason we left L.A., as Pru told you, was because of a man, but he was really Pru's man, not mine." Meaning that Gladys had had her way with him too. I went to the kitchen to make us coffee.

"She'd been having an affair for almost two years with a swish Hollywood director, who was very married," Gladys said, following me. My robe had fallen off her shoulders and down her back, resting loosely around her hips. Lucky Strike Venus became Venus de Milo. "One day, after two years of his telling her exactly what to do—he even chose the shape of her eyebrows—he pronounced their relationship over." I took Gladys by the hand in mid-sentence and led her over to a small oak breakfast table beneath a window framing the Janiculum. "Look," I said, facing her toward the window and letting the robe fall to the ground. She continued to tell me about her sister. "Everyone knew he left Pru for Jane Russell. How bad could she feel about that?" I licked my finger and made a dark spot with it on the table. I told her to put her chin on the place I had marked. I pressed my palms into the center of her back, her breasts flattening against the wood. "Anyway, he arranged for us to come to Rome, and for her to be in the film with Silvana Mangano." Her hands gripped the sides of the table. She winced once or twice, but her voice never wavered. "Of course, Pru never loved him. She'd be the first to tell you, she's incapable of loving a man." Gladys arched her back into a quiet moan.

I stepped back as she lifted herself up from the table. "She comes back tomorrow," she said, then smiled at me as she left the room. The coffee gurgled on the stove. I picked up the robe and put it on. As was becoming usual with Gladys, I felt trumped, and like a seasoned con artist she had caught me off guard by using the most obvious trump card—in this case, the reality of Prudence.

Gladys, dressed and looking stylish in a navy and white polka-dot dress, tight at the waist with a full skirt, and shiny black pumps with ankle straps, fresh and ready for all the street's eyes to be upon her, stood in the doorway. "I leave Rome the day after tomorrow," she said. "Prudence will be here until she finishes the final shooting at Cinecittà. She'll join me in Capri when they've wrapped. You must come visit us." She kissed me good-bye, leaving behind the waxy taste of fresh lipstick. "Pru hates to cook, so you'll find her at Da Filomena in Piazza Nicosia every evening. As I've already said, she doesn't dislike you."

I waited a few days. I needed to clear the air—and my bed— of Gladys. Still I delayed. I had grown so accustomed to my longing for Prudence I was reluctant to part with it. Then one hot night when I was supposed to be dining with Tullio (I had wanted to ask him if he knew anything about Prudence's notorious affair), I decided to make my way instead over to Piazza Nicosia.

It was the first week of August and Rome was empty, a sea parched of water, a wild boar drained of blood. I walked, knowing that I would be drenched in sweat. Typically, I was more scrupulous about my appearance and cleanliness. It was one of my milder obsessions. Even in prison, I hoarded soap and shaved with a dull blade. But that evening, as I set off in the direction of the Campo de' Fiori, I felt blissfully free of myself.

As I walked, I imagined various scenarios of meeting Prudence in the restaurant—all culminating with her in my arms, followed by a fade to black—but my mind rather quickly abandoned these for the more familiar thoughts of suicide. I had been neglecting them recently, distracted as I was by Gladys's unquenchable desire and the prospect of Prudence. Over the years, I had devised a list of suicide categories. It was something of a whirligig: no clear order. Definitions, examples, whole categories shifted, disappeared, reappeared, reversed each time I recalled them. Both language and suicide were uniquely human, but as a species we had only begun to master the grammar of suicide. On my way to Prudence, this was the version that carouseled around my head:

Suicide for Good Reason: a) You have an incurable and painful disease. b) You are a serial killer or a mass murderer.

Suicide for the Greater Good: You believe that by ending your own life, those left behind will benefit or you will go to a better place, e.g., Kamikaze pilots, Jesus Christ.

Honorable Suicide: a) You believe it is preferable to die by your own hand than by another's, e.g., Samson, the 960 Jews at Masada. b) It's either that or rape, e.g., St. Pelagia.

Dishonorable Suicide: You have committed heinous crimes and can't own up, e.g., Judas, Hitler, Goebbels, etc.

Impatient Suicide: a) You're down and out, i.e., the men on Wall Street during the Great Depression who jumped. b) You have a broken heart, e.g. Romeo, Lupe Velez. c) Life hasn't turned out the way you wanted it to quite yet. d) You can't stand the suspense of not knowing when, where, and how you are going to die, e.g., Robert Burton, author of *Anatomy of Melancholy,* first published in 1621, who correctly prophesied the date of his death by hanging himself when the fateful day rolled around.

Red-Faced Suicide: a) Your dirty laundry is aired in public. b) You are discovered to be a fraud or a sexual deviant. This category could also be called *Ironic Suicide* as a whole sector of society makes a career of such attention.

Revenge Suicide: Killing yourself instead of murdering someone else.

Botched Suicide: A category of special interest to me. I had no fear of death but was terrified of the means of arrival, the actual dying part.

Unintentionally Unbotched Suicide: Dying in suicide attempt with no intention of actually dying. This type is surprisingly frequent and a shame.

> *Too Good to Be True Suicide:* You reach the place you
> have always dreamed of being and it's not at all what you
> expected, in a bad way.
> *Psychotic Suicide:* Everyone thinks you're suffering from
> the sorrows of Young Werther, but actually you're crazy
> as a bedbug and you've heard the order to kill yourself
> over the car radio.
> *Optional Suicide:* Most suicides fall into this category and
> I imagine a time not far off when suicide will be a matter
> of choice, like getting married or having children.

When I reached the Campo de' Fiori, most of the fruit,
flower, and vegetable vendors had closed up and gone home,
though a few stragglers remained. It annoyed me that indulging in suicidal contemplation caused me to feel as if I had committed some crime against humanity. I would hurt no one by
taking my own life—my mother and father were dead and I
had no siblings, no wife or children. Friends would feel sad
but they would not feel at fault. Suicide was a sin, yes, but I
had committed them all already. Murder, adultery, hypocrisy,
betrayal and many more. I hadn't yet killed myself. I just cov-
eted the act as if I were a pretender to the throne and it was the
crown.

I bought a bouquet of red gladiolas for Prudence but I hadn't
made it across the square before I realized my mistake. Gladiolas were so obviously a flower for Gladys in more ways than
alliteration. Their bland scent and blatantly erotic flower—an
assembly line of orifices—proudly eschewed subtlety. I gave

the bouquet to a pretty girl who sat on a bench reading a book by the last of the day's light. She took it from me with one hand while using the other to mark her place on the page. She thanked me quickly and naturally as if a strange man offering her flowers was the most normal thing in the world, then returned to the sentence she had left waiting for her.

I walked on through semi-deserted streets, my armpits damp, my groin itching. I had accomplished little in the past weeks. When I wasn't with Gladys, I had spent my time doubting the wisdom of my affair with her. I never entertained calling it off for very long, however. I did manage to translate another Woolrich story for *Racconta* entitled "Murder Always Gathers Momentum," which I was considering shortening to "Momentum." I had also begun translating O'Connor's "The Turkey" for *La Voce di Aretusa.* Translation was probably the closest I would ever come to intimacy. The way one lived and breathed the words of another's imagination was extreme. You were privileged to know the author's mind on a level few ever would, but you also were intimately exposed to the flaws, the tics, the weaknesses, the unconscious foibles. Although, at times, I found such closeness distressing, mostly I rejoiced in it, especially since a text, like a pet, had restricted reciprocity.

As for my own book, I had been avoiding the question of whether or not to write about the war. I could fathom so little of my own experience, much less anyone else's. I used to regard myself as something of an observer but I no longer trusted my observations. And worse, I had lost interest in the god-like role of looking down on mortals floundering about. In *Harper's Maga-*

zine, Hemingway had said that almost any liar wrote more convincingly about the war than a man who was there. All I could muster was an occasional note to be read after my death. Halfway across Piazza Navona I stopped in front of Bernini's Fountain of the Four Rivers to reassure myself that there was no "after death."

The piazza was packed with young lovers, mothers with children, artists and their easels, jugglers juggling, birds bathing, vendors hawking sweets and ices. I felt as if I had stepped onto the beach in Rimini, not into a city square in August. At any time of year and in all weather Piazza Navona, was a petri dish of relentlessly hopeful life. There must have been just such a place in Dresden. I left the piazza and continued on my way along via della Scrofa—dark, vacant, undeviating.

As I neared Piazza Nicosia and Da Filomena, my pace slowed. Why Prudence? Gladys was perfect for me. She made no demands. She was eager and quick-witted. And her nose for the erotic was even finer than my own. Why was I doing this to her, to Prudence, to me? As much as I wanted to place the blame on my manhood, I knew the reason lay elsewhere. My desire for Prudence, and my headlong race into a situation that would lead to no good, had to do with me as a poet. Prudence, like writing, frightened me, and fear could inspire courage.

I plunged into the restaurant and was greeted by hysteria. Several waiters were running to and fro while others gathered around a table ministering to a woman in distress. One was patting her back, another urging her to eat bread. The woman, of course, was Prudence and she was holding her throat, her eyes wide and vitreous. A large woman I assumed was Filomena came out of the kitchen and ordered Prudence to open her mouth as wide as she could. Filomena held up a candle and peered into the dark cavern.

"Take her to San Giacomo degli Incurabili," she told a waiter. "She needs the pincers. Hurry, before it swells."

I moved closer. "I'll take her," I said. "She's a friend."

Prudence whispered to me, "I have a fish bone stuck in my throat."

"Don't talk," I said, and loved how it felt to tell her what to do.

I left money and gathered her things—a leather satchel and a copy of *Nightjar,* my most recent collection of poems. As I slipped the thin volume into her bag, our eyes met and she blushed before looking away. Needless to say, with that little interlude, my ardor reached fever pitch. We briskly walked arm in arm to the hospital only a few blocks away. With her other hand she continued to hold her throat. On the hospital steps, she whispered, "I'm so embarrassed."

"Let's hope that's all you are," I said, without thinking.

During our walk, I had been imagining her death by asphyxiation—her face turning red, then violet, then a deep blue, as I held her in my arms, and how upset I would be. I actually wasn't at all worried. The little I knew about fish bones was that if you were going to die it happened very quickly. She tightened her grip on my arm. Once inside the hospital, I told the reception nurse who I was, that my companion needed immediate attention, and to see if Dr. Lippi was available. Livio, whom we used to call hydra-head because of his corkscrew curls, appeared in a matter of minutes.

"Ah, Dante," he said, "you're always getting women into trouble."

He took us into a room, sat Prudence in a chair, and took an instrument resembling a prehistoric insect from a drawer. He lit a Bunsen burner and held the instrument over it for a minute or two. He then pulled a light over Prudence's head and told his patient to open her mouth and stick out her tongue. She obeyed. Her docility made my legs tremble.

"My goodness," he said, "that was quite a fish you were eating." He got a piece of gauze from the drawer and gave it to me. I felt a shiver of delight. "Hold her tongue," he said.

My first contact with Prudence's tongue, quivering between my thumb and forefinger, was transcendent—to be so swiftly engaged with her in this unlikely manner was beyond my wildest dreams. For Prudence the ordeal was visibly unpleasant. I watched the color of her eyes deepen as Livio plunged the silver tool into her mouth. She coughed and spewed, was admonished and told to stay still. I squeezed her tongue harder between my fingers so as not to lose hold of it as she reflexively tried to pull it back into her mouth. I could barely look at her eyes, wet and full of panic like those of a calf being branded. The look of those terrified eyes caused the grip of my obsession to tighten.

As he worked his tool deep in her throat, Livio asked her, "So who will it be, Dewey or Truman?" Not expecting an answer, he went on, "They all predict Dewey, but I bet you Truman wins. They say he reads poetry. Perhaps he's even read yours, Dante."

———

Finally, Livio proudly held up a two-inch white bone for us to see.

"What a souvenir," he said, handing the bone to Prudence.

I stopped Livio's arm and said to Prudence, "May I?"

"Always the devil," Livio said, and put the bone in my hand, neither of us waiting for a response from Prudence. I then formally introduced Prudence to Livio, who invited us to his house for dinner the following week. "I promise not to serve fish," he said.

We left the hospital and walked slowly back toward Prudence's apartment. She was silent and humbled, the way one is after death teases you. Her hair was slightly mussed, her green linen dress wrinkled. A slight breeze rose now and again but the thick, swirling air only added to the heat's discomfort. Even so, Prudence walked with her arms wrapped around her body as if she felt a chill. We arrived at the emperor's decrepit tomb in the Piazza Augusto Imperatore. The night was still, and the sound of our footsteps loud on the stone pavement. We then heard clear theatrical voices coming from the other side of the mausoleum. As we rounded a corner, we came upon a large crowd, some sitting on blankets, newspapers, cushions, or chairs, some in or on top of cars, many smoking, eating, kissing, others sleeping, nearly everyone staring at a large freestanding screen.

"Oh, look," Prudence said, pointing to a gigantesque young woman in a nightgown, lying on a bed, bathed in fear, as the telephone rang and rang, each ring louder and more menacing than the last. "It's Ruby," Prudence said, indicating Barbara Stanwyck. "This must be the Litvak picture she made with Lancaster." She surveyed the crowd, then turned back to me. She whispered, "Thanks for tonight, but if you don't mind I'd really like to see this. You needn't stay. I can get home by myself with no trouble." Not waiting for an answer, she tip-toed off to a free spot on the pavement and sat down on her leather bag. I followed. There was nothing else I could have done. I squeezed myself between her and a woman whose lap was heavy with sleeping children.

Burt Lancaster was on the screen. "Look at those eyes," Prudence whispered to me, as if she had never considered for a second that I might leave. "Who wouldn't tremble beneath them?"

I wasn't watching his eyes. I was looking at hers, still fearful but now innocent, like those of a child, glad to be distracted by another of life's wonders. As for Burt, I was grateful that for the moment his eyes belonged to an image and not a man. The plot was not complicated—a woman is stalked and terrorized for no reason. I spent most of the picture captive to Prudence's smell. Again, I could discern nothing specific—nuts, citrus maybe—then I heard clapping and everything went dark. I could see nothing but tiny points of light—red from cigarettes, white from stars. Prudence had vanished. When my eyes ad-justed, she was still there, next to me.

"Ruby," she said, pointing to the screen, "is nothing partic-ular to look at." She spoke more to herself than to me. "But she gives you the sense that she has nothing to hide, that she wants you to see it all, the strength, the talent, as well as every de-fect and failing." Prudence stood up and smoothed her dress, strands of her hair still out of place. "While I have made an art of hiding. Here I am in Italy, darting in and out of the shadows of others."

I said nothing. Despite the angles, Prudence, like most of us, was afraid to be seen. Roosevelt demonstrated that he understood the mechanics of fear when he said, "Let me assert my firm belief that the only thing we have to fear is fear itself." But fear, as the Fascists knew well, was humanity's lifeline. Fear was God. The twentieth century put fear into mass production. Fear kept us all from running amuck. Fear itself had long ago conquered the world.

We walked down the via di Ripetta in a stream of chatting, smoking Romans who seemed to possess the glee of those who had narrowly escaped some tragedy. When we came to the door of Prudence's building, she said, "I should warn you my idea of sex is Claudette Colbert's in *It Happened One Night*. I like talking to men and having them near, I enjoy the aura of sex, but I don't like to be actually touched."

"Never?" I asked.

"Rarely, and then I don't like it much."

"I like sex quite a bit," I said.

"Is that a fact?" she said.

I blushed. How odd that I would find myself blushing at my penchant for sex. I wasn't sure if that had ever happened to me before. My Prudence had already begun to lead me to new places, new sensations. That night I lay next to her waiting until she fell asleep, then watched her breathe for an hour or so until my own breath fell in with the cadence of hers and I, too, finally drifted off and slept soundly until morning.

---

four

Capri

"No man is an island," wrote John Donne. Had he but visited Capri in September he might have amended that to "Ah, to be an island." Vermilion sunsets, Homeric views from Ischia to Vesuvius, limestone cliffs, the insidious face of Monte Solaro, tintinnabulation from Baroque bell towers, sand-white cottages surrounded by high rose-trellised walls suggesting the gardens they concealed, all this while sipping yellow Capri wine on a terrace high above the emerald sea. I was mentally composing this guidebook description of my destination as I rode the rinky-dink ferry across the Bay of Naples. In fact, the morning sky was overcast, the water olive-green, the air thick with humidity and the odor of salted diesel.

My fellow passengers were mostly islanders, so I was treated to a generous dollop of Caprisian gossip. Graham Greene had just bought a house for a song in the island's other town of Anacapri as a getaway for himself and his married American lover. Greene was writing the screenplay for *South Wind,* a novel by Norman Douglas, the island's ailing literary guru, and relations between the two men had become strained. The writer Curzio Malaparte, forever fickle and contrary in his politics, author of the damning and derisive *Kaputt,* the best piece of writing about the war yet to be published, had returned to his self-built bunker-style villa to work on a new book apparently excoriating the Allied liberation. Island regular, American beauty, and four-time divorcee Mona Harrison Williams was to be photographed the following week by Cecil Beaton. One of the Krupp family—German industrialists, Nazi sympathizers, and owners of a large villa in Capri Town—had just been sentenced in Nuremberg to twelve years in prison for war crimes. Axel Munthe, the Swedish doctor and bestselling author of the Capri-featured memoir *The Story of San Michele,* was dying in his villa at the foot of Mount Barbarossa. For Caprisians, if you didn't have some association with the island, you didn't exist.

Envy combined with *schadenfreude* made time pass quickly and the ferry pulled up to the dock in the marina. The sun came out from behind the clouds and the air went from wet washcloth to rayon. My visit to Capri was singular in purpose. I had made the journey from Rome to give Prudence a present. It was to be a surprise. I knew she and Gladys had taken a room in Capri Town and it was never hard to find someone on an island. From the ferry landing at the Marina Grande, I took the funicular directly to the *piazzetta* where I asked the barman at the Gran Caffè if he knew of the sisters and could tell me where they were staying.

"Ah," he said, smelling the tips of his fingers. "I know just who you mean. They're staying at the Danish widow's *pensione.*"

He hollered to a boy who led me through a maze of paths and stairs. When I finally arrived at the *pensione* out of breath, a tall blonde in her sixties informed me that the "American girls" were gone for the day and she had no idea which island excursion they had chosen.

"I do know that occasionally they take their afternoon tea at the Hotel Quisisana if you want to try there later on," she said.

I thanked her and left a note inviting Prudence and Gladys to join me that evening for dinner at Da Gemma, a restaurant known for its belletristic clientele. I decided to fill the time until then by walking out to the Villa Jovis, the ruins of a Roman imperial villa built atop sheer escarpments of limestone for the Emperor Tiberius. In the many times I had been to Capri, I had never visited the villa despite the allure of the Tiberian Leap, a cliff four hundred meters high from which Tiberius, a paranoid recluse with inspired sexual appetites, forced those he disliked, or liked too much, to jump.

I asked the Danish widow to point me in the direction of the path to the Roman ruins. The air had become hot and I kept my pace slow. Jumping to my death appealed to me, but I feared there was too much time for regret as one fell. Nevertheless, I did not intend to die that day. I very much wanted to give my present to Prudence. Still, because I was not planning to die did not mean I wouldn't. It is often said about a suicide that he could not possibly have taken his own life because he had made all sorts of plans for the upcoming weeks. "His calendar was full," the living point out. "He just bought a house in the country," the survivors claim. "Why agree to go to a dinner party in three weeks time or invest in real estate if you're planning to die?" A suicide, however, obsessively plans his death with the same meticulousness and intensity he uses to make plans to stave off his suicide. In the end, it comes down to which plan triumphs.

The path continued steadily, but not steeply, upwards, sometimes shaded by umbrella pines or flanked by cypress and crowded by ferns, creepers, acanthus, agapanthus. The wildlife I spotted was hardly wild: cats, dogs, a donkey, goats, gulls, lizards. The sounds were of the expected kind: the buzz of a bee, the wind's whistle, a dog's bark, the distant chug of a boat. I saw not a human soul, however, as I made my way up Mount Tiberio.

After the summer, the island had begun to reflower—azaleas, geraniums, cyclamen, jasmine, the lethal belladonna lilies. Poison was the preferred means of self-inflicted death for lovers, warriors, and poets. In my *Impatient Suicide* category belonged Thomas Chatterton, the seventeen-year-old English poet and darling of Keats and Coleridge, who allegedly poisoned himself after being accused of plagiarism. What youthful earnestness! If Chatterton had let himself live just a little while longer, he would have discovered that all writers are plagiarists. We are scavengers, vultures, rats that steal and live off the words, sentiments, experiences of others. A writer sneaks, slinks, insinuates himself into life solely to gather material: his mission to build that filthy nest known as the imagination. The imagination was a sewer, having the advantage that the stench was only metaphoric.

What had brought me to Capri was the antithesis of stench—perfume. Having, over the past weeks, explored the smell of Prudence's hair and skin and neck, I found her scent to be elusive and changeable. When she left Rome after my having spent every possible minute with her—waiting for her until all hours, calling her incessantly, plotting her every movement so that I might capture them all—I was bereft. Prudence had not asked me, as Gladys had, to come to Capri. She simply announced one day that her work on the film was finished and that she was going on holiday, not bothering to tell me where. Although I had discovered prodigious new ways of humiliating myself with Prudence, I wouldn't ask her if I might come along. To distract myself from missing her, I worked from morning until late at night for the two weeks following her departure. During that time, I fretted: Had I let her get away? Would she be gone forever? And was it for the best? That a woman might pervade my life so entirely was unnerving, yet my preoccupation with her had much in common with my attachment to suicide. I wondered if two such preoccupations were tenable.

Then one day as I stood outside a perfume shop on a small street just off the Corso Vittorio Emanuele, I knew I must see her. I stepped into the shop, not sure why or what I wanted. Prudence did not wear perfume. It would have to be a scent that appealed to her in such a way that she would be compelled to wear it—and when she wore it I too would penetrate her skin. What I hoped to achieve belonged to the realm of al-chemy.

The shop's mirrored walls were layered with glass shelves, on top of which sat bottles, big and small, clear, colored, and opaque, boxed and not, their shapes pear, square, and cylindrical. The salesgirl—eyes dark, hair black, buxom—looked up briefly from her magazine. She finished the paragraph she was reading, licked her finger, folded down the top corner of the page, then set the magazine down.

"May I help you?" she said, without looking at me.

"I hope so," I said. "I am looking for a scent for someone who never wears perfume and quite possibly doesn't even like it," I explained. "It must please her as much as it does me. You see, I like perfume on a woman, but not consistently. I need this to be a perfume I will always like. It would be a failure," I continued, "if I bought a perfume that soon became intolerable." I hesitated, then added, "Perhaps what I am looking for does not exist."

"Please sir," she said, looking directly at me, her black eyes finally taking me in. "We will find what you are looking for. If you will be patient and assist me, I assure you we will be able to reach our goal."

We spent the next half hour or so smelling together. She would dab scent onto a small strip of paper, we would both breathe it in, and she would describe it to me.

"This one," she would say, softly waving the paper underneath my nose, "has notes of oriental spices, blackberry, and fig."

I would shake my head and comment. "Too exotic."

"Here you have lavender and vanilla with minor notes of orris and oak moss."

"Too woodsy," I declared.

"You are uncommonly discerning," she said. "And know well what you don't want."

"What is your name?" I asked.

"Letizia," she answered.

Apparently, she was not interested in mine.

"Ah," she said inhaling. "This is special. Mimosa, jasmine, Parma violet, just slightly soured with tonka bean."

"Young but not youthful," I said, entranced with each new scent but discouraged by not finding the one for Prudence.

Somewhere along our aromatic journey, Letizia, almost in a whisper, said, "Perfume is like opera—if it's successful the subtlety is found in exaggeration."

Our eyes met. My hand lingered over hers as I helped to close rejected bottles.

"I think I've got it," she said, brushing against my arm with her ample bottom as she moved around the counter. "Musk rose, iris, and frankincense."

"Too Mary Magdalene, not enough Virgin Mary," I said, drawing a finger across her collarbone and eliciting a raised eyebrow.

"Tangerine blossom, lime, tuberose, and, oh my, a stroke of genius here—tobacco." She was about to wave the paper under my nose when she stopped herself. "No," she said, jealously closing her fist around a triangular lapis-lazuli bottle. "Not this way. Go outside, take a little walk, breathe fresh air, then come back and I will have it ready."

I willingly did as she said, and as I walked around the block I convinced myself that whatever happened it was all for Prudence. When I returned the lights were off and Letizia was waiting just inside the door. Once I was in, she threw the bolt behind me, took me by the hand, and led me into a cramped storeroom at the back of the shop. In the pitch of the room, I could just make out her wrist extended toward me. I cupped the back of her hand in my palm, my fingers wrapped around hers. She lifted her arm toward my face and I pressed my nose and lips against the pillow of flesh beneath her thumb.

"Inhale deeply," she said.

I did and was transported.

"The true scent of a perfume is revealed by the pulses in the neck, below the ears," she whispered, guiding my hand in the darkness to these places. I greedily followed, first with my nose, then with my mouth, biting her tender earlobe so that she gasped, tracing with my tongue the hard curlicues of her ear until I plunged in as far as I could go. She flinched, her neck craning away from me, but I held her head firmly. Our hands still clasped, I brought her wrist back up to my face, inhaled again, taking her fingers into my mouth and sucking. I then moved her moist hand down inside her shirt to her breast where together our fingers brushed back and forth over her large nipple until finally I clasped it between my thumb and forefinger and pinched until she cried out. I guided her hand

---

farther down, now encountering a respectable resistance from her, to the hem of her skirt, up the inside of her stockinged thigh, over the stay, beneath the silken material of her panties, where again, our fingers together wriggled and pinched and stroked until she let out a wail before falling to her knees. I brought our hands to her mouth and this time placed my fingers inside. She sucked on them, like a girl with a lollipop, while I readied myself. I then removed my hand from her mouth and, as I had done earlier with my tongue in her ear, pushed myself deep inside.

Afterwards, Letizia handed me a black velvet box with ivory ribbon ties. I gave her a considerable sum for it and left. I now took the box from my pocket, lifted it to my face, and inhaled. It was unlikely I would ever see Letizia again, and as I arrived at the remains of Tiberius's imperial villa and found myself alone among the piles of crumbling brick, I bemoaned the fact that I only had one life.

I made my way through the rubble to the northern end of the complex where I would find the famous "leap." I had never believed in monogamy. Human beings were too multifarious to have their needs quenched by a single person. Yet I had the idea that Prudence might be someone from whom I could extract all that I would ever need, and relish the project of doing so. Why, then, did I indulge myself with Letizia, not to mention Gladys or Nerina? I knew that I did not deserve Prudence. But beyond this, I knew that the deeper our hold on each other became, the more vigorous the urge would be to destroy her, in so far as she was a part of me.

———

As I came upon the precipice, I heard myself gasp. Even forewarned by literature, the terse and eternal fall into the sea elicited in me a vertiginous terror. Standing on the brink of that breathtaking drop, I felt dizzy. I wasn't sure if my light headedness was coming from the temptation to jump or from the voice I heard in my head while standing on the edge of this particular abyss. The voice was young Werther's and he said this:

Alas, that I ever knew her! I should say to myself: You are a fool to search for something that cannot be found on this earth. But she was mine, I felt her heart, her great soul, in whose presence I seemed to be more than I really was because I was all that I could be.

I was becoming concerned about the romantic syrup that seemed to be coursing through my veins when it hit me that I had neglected to bring Gladys a present! How could I possibly give Prudence my gift? The scene I had imagined—a table near Da Gemma's enormous fireplace, lit to nip the autumn chill, where we would drink light-red wine from Anacapri with our dinner of cuttlefish stew—quickly disintegrated. I moved closer to the edge of the cliff. I glanced down without thinking and the differentiation in perspective caused me to lose my footing. I fell and slipped about five feet along an initial incline where I came to rest for a moment before my body continued to slowly slide toward the point of no return. Small rocks loosened by my mad scramble to get back to a level spot were pushed to their long, silent descent.

Queerly shaped boulders emerged from the rock face like a leper's festering boils. I was scared, but not out of my wits. It was not my fate to die by accident.

I grabbed with one hand a jutting rock and to my relief found it solid and unmovable. With my other hand, I grabbed a precarious root and managed to bring my slide to a stop while advising myself to not, under any circumstances, look down. For some time, I stayed there splayed against the rock face as if in a lover's embrace—hard but not hurtful—and though my body remained unmoving, I felt the receding and repulsing of flesh and stone. I had this thought: Suicide is a romantic act.

I inched my way back up to safety, and after defiantly peering one last time over the infamous cliff, I set off toward town. During my little incident, I had arrived at the solution to my problem. I would buy Gladys some token or other in one of the town's shops. She was easy to please and Capri had once been notorious for its luxurious selection of goods. Something had to be left over that would do. As I rushed along the path, I surprised three cats—one black, two calico—lazily basking on a rock like seals. They reluctantly lifted their heads to see who might bother them. I ran on, worried about what item to get for Gladys. I remembered the old story about the sheik and his harem—if he gave one wife a sapphire, all the other wives would have to receive the same gem or life for the sheik would be made prickly by the thorns of envy. It would have to be perfume. I would not be able to take the time or care I had dedicated to Prudence. I would simply buy the first bottle I could lay my hands on and that would be that.

But as I neared town, I knew I never should have come to Capri. I retrieved my note from the Danish widow. I gave her, the barman, and the boy a few lire to keep my antic quiet. I then departed on the next ferry back to Naples.

five

Venice

My old friend Elio asked me to do him a favor and take his manuscript to "Papa" in Venice. Since October, Hemingway had been in the north of Italy with his fourth wife, Mary, and had graciously agreed to write a preface for the American edition of Elio's novel, *Name and Tears.* The meeting was to be at Harry's Bar on an evening in early December. I tried to convince Prudence and Gladys, who had been to the "pearl of the Adriatic" several times, to come with me by telling them they would meet Ernest Hemingway.

Gladys said, "Whether you like his work or not, one should never meet the author."

Prudence said, "Venice must be beautiful in December. With any luck it will snow."

The Hemingways had a suite at the Gritti Palace Hotel, but Elio told me that Papa had been staying alone at the Locanda Cipriani, an inn on the island of Torcello, so he could get some writing done. "There's speculation about another woman," Elio had said, "but when isn't there? It's just as likely he's spending his days hunting with the Locanda's gardener."

Our train originated in Rome's brand new Termini Station but was, in post-Fascist fashion, late. We waited as pigeons swooped overhead and long black railroad cars glided up and down the tracks. Prudence and Gladys, wearing white cashmere coats with white rabbit collars, hats, and muffs, looked as if they'd just walked off the set of *Anna Karenina*. Gladys's hair was cut short and dyed platinum for a picture she had just finished shooting. It was known as the "Rita look," alluding to Rita Hayworth in her femme fatale role in Orson Welles's *The Lady from Shanghai*. Prudence's hair was still light brown and that morning smelled of soap and mint.

When the train finally arrived, we found our first-class compartment, which we would have to ourselves as far as Florence. Prudence took a seat by the window and Gladys sat opposite her. I slid next to Prudence. Since the sisters' return from Capri in September, Prudence and I had become what the tabloids labeled "an item." Gladys was "the younger sister who often accompanies the couple on their outings." The notice went on, "Neither girl is a great beauty, but they are both talented and apparently possessed of enough intelligence and wit to satisfy our national treasure, Dante Omero Sabato." Another paper had remarked: "If only Sabato had a younger brother for Gladys, but such sublime symmetry is too much to ask. For the moment, he'll just have to do for both."

I had made it clear to Prudence and Gladys—separately, of course—that I was taken with them, indeed obsessed, but that I was not to be counted on in any permanent way.

Prudence's response was: "I have yet to meet anyone in life, literature, or religion who could be trusted in a permanent way. You are too romantic, Dante, and it worries me."

Gladys's response was: "I have no desire to become your mother. Whether I do or not is entirely up to you."

So, to use a variant of an expression I have never fully understood, I was having my cake and eating it, too. I was more or less chastely sleeping with Prudence every night I could persuade her to let me, while Gladys and I compulsively sought our sexual limits in order to exceed them. In spite of myself, it seemed I had found an attachment, albeit tripartite, that I could envision lasting for some time. Was I dreaming? Yes, and for a brief while my contentment was such that I believed anything was possible.

How did it happen that Gladys *gladly* engaged in sex and Prudence *prudently, prudishly* did not? Gladys liked having sex in the same way she ate her meals, with a hearty appetite, eager to try anything, delighted by new combinations of tastes. She would finish one repast only to be greedy for the next. I would see her across a room and in her glance would be the understanding that at the earliest convenience we would find a bed, a closet, the back seat of a car, a bathroom, a darkened doorway. For Prudence, the mere thought of sex flustered and exhausted her. She was beyond cajoling, requiring new heights of finesse and indirection on my part, and even then she was like a kitten hesitantly lapping at a bowl of milk, spooked by the slightest sound or movement, scurrying off to starve herself until she mustered the nerve to taste the milk again.

Gladys once told me it was because of their father that Prudence avoided sex. "I'm convinced she enjoys it more than I do," Gladys said. "That's why she won't do it. She likes it too much."

"I don't understand," I responded, wanting very much to understand.

"Let's just say she was my father's special little friend," Gladys said. "When he came and got her from our room at night, I used to ask myself, why her and not me? What is wrong with me? And then when we got to L.A., almost every girl we met had a story about being fondled or fucked by someone in her family—father, uncle, brother."

In much the way Gladys had a knack for sex, she had a knack for truth-telling.

Prudence and I made love for the first time after a rigorous but finely executed campaign I launched the day she returned from Capri. When she finally yielded to my punctilious onslaught, she kept her silk gown on, allowing me to pull it up only as far as her hips. The softness of her naked thighs on mine, her small silk-veiled breasts touching my chest, her arms rigid as though they were bound, made me come as quickly as a boy. She barely exhaled at my murmured apology as I worked my way down to the hem of her nightdress and slowly coaxed her into a soundless frenzy, holding her fists in mine all the while. I then fell into a dreamless sleep.

The next day, when asked by the reporter Teodora Bora Bora if there was anything to the rumor that Prudence Godfrey and I were romantically involved, I was so proud of my achievement I let it be known that Prudence was mine. If I had thought that such public avowal would gain me easier access to her loins, I was gravely mistaken. Still, I had no regrets and Prudence seemed indifferent to her new semi-official status as my consort. Gladys, on the other hand, was excited by it and loved to play with fire by passing herself off as Prudence whenever we were careless enough to be spotted during one of our clandestine encounters. About a month ago when she became a blonde, however, the risk of our being discovered rose considerably, so I avoided meeting her unless I felt certain that we would not be seen. I had the suspicion that this latest precaution of mine did not sit well with her.

The train to Venice finally began its slow crawl out of Rome, accompanied by squeaks, grinds, wheezes, and whistles, an orchestra warming up for the performance to come. I extracted from my briefcase my copy of *The Snows of Kilimanjaro*, which I had brought along to have signed by the author.

Pointing to the book, Gladys said, "They say he likes to dress up in women's clothing and has a thing for women who look like boys."

"All writers who are any good are perverts," Prudence remarked. "And Hemingway can be very good. The last story in that collection has the perfect ambiguous ending: Did the wife murder her husband? Or did he commit suicide?"

I wasn't at all sure what Prudence was getting at. So far I had done nothing extreme with Prudence, unless she was hinting at my involvement with Gladys. I could have told her right then how I would love to give her a good spanking, how it would please me to take a sharp knife to her clothing and shred it until it fell off. I could have told her how I wanted to feed her like a baby before furiously fucking her. The usual stuff—things that Gladys, of course, already knew something about. I could have explained to Prudence that given time and concentration I might easily become a fully functioning pervert. I would dress up in women's clothing, follow random women through the streets, hide in a ladies room, and so on. Curious sexual thoughts often filled my minutes, hours, and days. If I were not easily distracted from these preoccupations by writing—my greatest perversity—I might never get my work done at all. But Prudence knew none of this, unless Gladys had told her. Once I had asked Gladys if Prudence was aware of our sexual liaison.

"Most likely," she had answered. "She knows the way mother and I knew what was going on between her and father. But Prudence never mentioned it and we never asked. Sometimes not mentioning things suits everyone involved for different reasons. Our mother just up and left one day, but that might have had nothing to do with Prudence and Father, or, if it did, perhaps our mother kept her mouth shut so she could feel justified in leaving. Who knows?"

The train lurched into a faster speed, and as we hastened toward our destination I thought of a line from Melville's *Pierre*: "Love is built upon secrets, as lovely Venice upon invisible and incorruptible piles in the sea." But Melville had it wrong. Nothing was incorruptible, and for some time now Venice had been sinking into the sea.

I said, "I have my doubts as to whether all good writers are perverts, and further doubts as to the quality of my own writing, but I do confess to being something of a pervert. I don't sew girls' undergarments into my hat, but I'm not beyond such things."

Gladys masked a titter with a cough, and out my window, as if on cue, I saw the knickers of Rome's periphery hanging on clotheslines. I did hanker after Prudence's panties but she never left them anywhere I might happen upon them, denying me the opportunity to squirrel a pair away. Often Gladys didn't bother to wear undergarments. When she did, she left them strewn about and wouldn't have noticed if they went missing, which was a good part of the draw. But both these women, in their unique ways, were taking me to new erotic heights: Prudence, a thorny creature, whose trust I had to earn through delicacy; and Gladys, who trusted I would go with her as far as she wanted to go, and beyond.

"I remember that Hemingway story," Gladys announced. "'The Short Happy Life of Francis Macomber.' It's about how evil women are, how hunted poor men are. And doesn't Macomber ask the white hunter not to tell anyone about how he bolted when faced with a wounded and charging lion? Another male writer nervous about losing his juice. It's all a big yawn if you ask me."

"Hemingway once beat up Wallace Stevens," I said. "Stevens was vacationing in Key West. Hemingway irked him somehow and Stevens challenged him to a boxing match. Stevens wound up with a black eye and a bruised cheek. He asked Hemingway to keep the affair quiet."

"Apocryphal," Gladys said, with a bit of a sneer. "And anyway Stevens is twenty years older than Hemingway, so if it's true it's pathetic. One thing for sure, though," she said with relish, "I bet you Papa is a monster in bed."

She pulled a cigarette from her silver case and waited for me to light it. The compartment soon filled with the sweet cloying smell. I had a sinking feeling that Gladys would find a way to test her theory.

"Do you suppose, Dante," she said, blowing her smoke in my direction, "that there are more synonyms in English or Italian for 'vagina'? We have pussy, cunt, beaver, mound of Venus . . ."

The train was moving at a steady clip, cityscapes giving way to landscapes.

"Sparrow, fig, puppy dog," I offered, with restraint.

A waiter from the dining car stood at our compartment door. He cleared his throat, then informed us that our seating for lunch would be at half past one, soon after we left Florence. He cleared his throat again and left, but not before he and Gladys had given each other the once-over.

"Hemingway does write rather well about war," Prudence said, opening Thomas Hardy's *The Return of the Native* to somewhere midway through the book.

Like a splinter—or a bullet—deep in the flesh and festering, I felt the pain of envy for other writers.

"Hemingway's stories don't hold a candle to the one in here by Shirley Jackson," Gladys said, pulling a copy of *The New Yorker* out of her bag. "Hemingway believes that if he tries hard enough he'll figure out why we do the things we do. Jackson knows she never will."

We all read quietly, until we glimpsed Florence's ginger-bread Duomo. After we waited for some time in the magisterial Santa Maria Novella railway station, an American couple tumbled into our compartment.

"Sorry to disturb you all," said a tall man with a mop of wavy honey-blond hair, wearing a full-length beaver coat. "This is first class isn't it?" He seemed to be almost singing his words—so unlike the flat staccato of the Godfreys' accents. "I do believe," he went on, "that the seats by the window are the ones we paid for, if you wouldn't mind terribly."

Gladys winked at him. "We were just keeping them warm for you," she said.

"Well, God bless America!" the man said. "Y'all are from home." His gaze landed upon me as if I were a water buffalo in a herd of gazelles.

Gladys said, "Yes. And this is Dante Omero Sabato, Italy's most famous poet."

"Dante," the man repeated, taking off his fur. "Even *I've* heard of you."

Beneath his coat he wore an expensive shiny new suit sold to him by a Florentine tailor who must have enjoyed his steak with extra pleasure last night. The man's doll-like wife was prettier than my companions but had the erotic appeal of chamomile tea. I did like her scent: honeysuckle, starched cotton.

"Oh, no, darling," she said, her voice too high. "He couldn't be *that* Dante." She looked around for reassurance. "Right?" She asked no one in particular.

"I bet you two are on your honeymoon," Gladys said.

The woman's face lit up. The man looked genuinely surprised. "How did you know?"

"Just a hunch," Gladys said.

The Kewpie wife removed her mink coat and hat and pushed her curls back from her cute, shiny face. She was a blonde, but unlike Gladys would have the pubic hair to match.

"I've seen you in the pictures," she said to Prudence.

"Yes, you have," Prudence said warmly. As they spoke, Gladys's eyes kept drifting over to the husband.

"I can't remember which picture," the woman said apologetically, "there are so many of them these days."

Her husband was staring back at Gladys, beguiled.

"Not to worry," Prudence said. "I can't remember the titles myself most of the time."

The train began to pull out of Santa Maria Novella and after settling into our new seats, we learned that Walter and Betsy Pope were indeed on their honeymoon and hailed all the way from Charlottesville, North Carolina. On their Grand Tour, they had come first to Italy ("I just adore Henry James," Betsy said). They would visit Switzerland, France, Belgium, and Holland, before sailing home from England. They were avoiding Germany and Austria "for obvious reasons," Walter said. Looking at me with disapproval, he added, "I would have skipped Italy too, but Betsy wouldn't come unless we visited Florence and Venice. She likes the art and the buildings. Luckily, I like the food and the women."

He playfully squeezed his wife's middle.

"Such talk," Betsy said, giggling. She squeezed him back. "He's incorrigible."

The chatter went on until the steward came and announced lunch. Prudence and I and Betsy all rose to go. Gladys said she wasn't hungry and would take a nap. Walter said he wanted to go over the itinerary for a minute and would catch up with us. He kissed his wife on the nose and told her to keep his pasta warm. We hadn't made it to the end of the car before I heard the compartment door locking and the curtains being drawn. I did not know if Prudence or Betsy was aware of what was happening, or if they cared. Self-deception was far and away humanity's most perfected art. But I was overcome by a lover's jealousy, a sentiment not previously a significant part of my emotional repertoire, although that seemed to be changing rapidly.

During lunch, to which Walter showed up just as the dessert was being served, all I could do was wonder what I was missing—did he have her pressed up against the window or hanging from the luggage rack? Was she on his lap, or he in hers? Was he using his belt? Was she using the stiletto heel of her shoe? When we returned to the compartment, Gladys was asleep in Walter's seat by the window. I picked up *The New Yorker* and began to read "The Lottery." Prudence and Betsy talked about the Botticellis in the Uffizi ("His models are so pudgy," Betsy observed) and the sated Walter joined Gladys in a postcoital nap.

I read: *The morning of June 27th was clear and sunny, with the fresh warmth of a full-summer day; the flowers were blossoming profusely and the grass was richly green.* I knew I was about to be devastated. When I finished the story, I almost immediately fell asleep. I had never read anything like it. Our lust for ritualized violence was ancient, our consciousness of what that meant barely born. I awoke suddenly as we were arriving in Venice. I had a metallic taste in my mouth, like blood. I remembered a German soldier bound to a chair, blindfolded, and gagged. He was covered with knife wounds and he pleaded with me not to kill him. I asked him politely to answer my question. He shook his head, crying, "I don't know. Please, believe me, I would tell you if I did. I want to live." Certain he couldn't tell me what I needed to know, I put the knife point just below his left ear, punctured the skin so the tip disappeared into flesh, and pulled the blade across his neck.

I looked down at *The New Yorker* on my lap, then handed it back to Gladys, having already forgotten the story.

Naturally, the Popes were staying at the Gritti Palace Hotel. Gladys, Prudence, and I were staying at La Calcina, Ruskin's former residence on the Giudecca Canal, which had been turned into a *pensione*. ("You do know Ruskin was impotent," Gladys said, making clear her opinion of my choice of lodging.) At the train station, we boarded a *vaporetto* while the Popes motored off in a private water taxi. As they were leaving, Walter shouted out to us, "How about y'all joining us for dinner tomorrow night at Harry's Bar?" We smiled, waved, and nodded agreement as their boat sped off, although seeing them again was the last thing I wanted to do. I was seething. I didn't mind what Gladys got up to when I wasn't around, it was only fair, but flaunting her forays in front of me was unbearable. I became intent on reclaiming her, fucking his smell off her, bruising the places he had touched.

The boat ride was wet and cold as we slipped along the full length of the eel-shaped Grand Canal, under the marble arch of the Rialto Bridge, past the balconied facades of Palazzos Grimani, Grassi, and Pisani, and out into St. Mark's Canal where the gray fog wrapped itself around Palladio's San Giorgio Maggiore like a winding sheet. Prudence took my hand in hers as Gladys leaned back and nuzzled her breast into my other side. She was not looking for forgiveness, she was looking for me. Enveloped by the two of them, my fury subsided. Gondolas, those vessels Thomas Mann had described as floating coffins, passed silently next to us.

Prudence whispered in my ear, "No one ever drowns in the canals of Venice."

She knew me too well, too fast, my Prudence. She had become my translator, a dangerous job. At times she seemed de-

---

termined to save me, and I let her try, not because I hoped she would, but because her resolve on my behalf was too sweet to deny.

The boat left us at the Zattere, a broad quayside along Venice's southern flank facing the island of the Giudecca. A late sun had emerged and in the citrine light, we walked along the promenade to our hotel. The lobby of La Calcina was cramped and unimpressive but led on to a breakfast veranda facing the splendid pink Church of the Rendentore on the Giudecca. We registered with a tall Venetian woman who had no eyebrows. Gladys and Prudence shared a room and I had my own. "Scandal is a commodity not to be wasted needlessly," Gladys explained.

Gladys and Prudence went to their room to have a bath before dinner, and I, after dropping my bag in my room, headed for the bar. I had made for myself something of a rule—if Prudence was within a mile radius, I would not indulge myself with Gladys. Rules, however, were fragile things, and when I heard Gladys asking at the desk where she might buy cigarettes, I followed her. She didn't get far before I was pulling her down a cat-piss-redolent alley that never saw daylight. When a suitable doorway presented itself, I pushed her into it. One hand closed around her throat, while the other was fast up her skirt. With a couple of strong tugs, I ripped her panties off and put them in my pocket. She sputtered and tried to pull my hands off her neck. I shoved her against the wall and she desisted. When I had finished, I said, "You've had a busy day." I left her there, coughing, momentarily subdued. But Gladys was expert at quick recoveries.

Back in my room, I wondered if I had gone too far with Gladys, but I needn't have worried. When we met up later to go out to eat, she was affable, even solicitous toward me. We took a stroll along the Zattere, a favorite place of Ezra Pound, and I thought of his first collection of poems, *A Lume Spento*, which he had published in Venice, and which contained the poem "La Fraisne," about a man who becomes so mad from lovesickness that he takes a tree in the forest as his bride. Gladys was right—it was best not to know the author. Why had I agreed to come see Hemingway? Whatever happened, it would be a disillusionment. We made our way past Venice's Ospedale degli Incurabili, which I pointed out to Prudence. "I still have that fishbone, you know," I said.

"What fishbone?" Gladys asked, and as Prudence told her the story I again wondered about what these two sisters did and did not tell each other.

"And you kept the bone, Dante?" Gladys said, having some fun. "You are so *outré*."

When we had walked as far as the salt warehouses, we turned inland and found a wine bar where we filled ourselves with *cichetti*, little sandwiches made with crab, shrimp, grilled zucchini and eggplant. On our way to the bridge in front of the Accademia galleries connecting the districts of Dorsoduro and San Marco, we passed by the Campo San Vio, and the Palazzo Venier dai Leoni. Evening had turned to night by the time we reached the Accademia. The air was crisp, the earlier humidity gone, and there were few people wandering about. In the middle of the wooden bridge, we stopped to admire the ducat-shaped moon, its twin reflecting up at us from the wavering waters of the Grand Canal.

"In *The Return of the Native*," Prudence said, "Hardy describes a heathcropper afflicted by an old superstition, that if a male is born on a night with no moon he will never find love and will suffer such bouts of melancholy that he is likely to die by his own hand."

"'No moon, no man,'" I said.

"You know the expression?" she asked.

"I know Hardy," I said, "who knew Leopardi, both of whom despaired even of the moon, but unlike me, they had a moon to despair of."

"It seems we need to find you a moon," Prudence said.

"Here," said Gladys, scooping the moon out of the canal and handing it to me. "Look no farther."

"Why, thank you," I said, taking it from her and swallowing it. "I am the happiest man alive."

I linked arms with both of them and we walked on past the Fenice Theater and into St. Mark's Square, where we took a table at the Caffè Florian in the moonlit shadow of the church's five gray domes. We ate *Giandiuotto* ice cream and then moved on to *grappa*. We talked until we heard the midnight chimes. As we walked slowly home, my elation wore off as I realized I would be spending the night alone. In the lobby of the hotel, we parted ways. I lay on the bed in my room without turning on the light.

Perhaps I was the happiest man alive, but I knew I would be an even happier dead man. Like Hardy's heathcropper, I did not know how to be with another person in this world. If I could renounce Gladys and make my way with Prudence, I might have had a chance, but my desire for oblivion was such that I began to consider how I might purge the cold, inconstant moon from my body. There was a soft knock on my door. I knew it was Gladys and that yet again I had been granted a reprieve.

"C'mon upstairs," she whispered, "quick and quiet." She scurried off and I followed directly behind her.

What might have been a drab room was rendered cheerful by a chrysanthemum chandelier, its glass petals striped with candy colors, its leaves a leprechaun green. Prudence sat at the dressing table brushing her hair. The way she handled her tresses so deliberately, the soft pats and touches of her fingers to the silken threads, making sure each was in place, aroused me. I loved to watch her do the most menial things, such as dress or eat. She did them with extraordinary care, as if she were afraid of being punished were she to err in any way.

Gladys, languishing on the double bed, placed her hand beside her. "Lie here a while," she said.

Prudence stretched her body along the other side of me. Both women were wearing pale yellow satin pajamas. A sleeve from one, a pant leg from another brushed against my skin.

"Happiness tonight knows no bounds," I said, with all my heart.

"Tomorrow, I think I shall ask Hemingway if he would put on a dress for me," Gladys said.

———

She meant no harm really, but I became enraged. "I'm sure that's not all you'll get him to do to you," I said, shattering what we had exquisitely begun to spin out in that room in La Calcina. My words made Gladys roll away from me and shut her eyes. The three of us lay there listening to the lapping sounds of water and the whine of cats beyond the windows. My reprieve had been brief, happiness far too uncomfortable a pursuit, no matter how skewed the form. After a while, I rose to leave. As I departed, I saw in Prudence's eyes her distress that she hadn't been able to save the moment somehow. I began to whisper something to her, anything to show her how foolish I felt, but she put a finger to her lips. I quietly shut the door.

I stayed in bed the next day. I left a note for Prudence and Gladys to meet me at Harry's Bar that evening, where they turned up right on time but where, as it turned out, Hemingway never showed. Instead, Mary Welsh came into the bar to make her husband's excuses and to fetch Elio's manuscript. I had read that she often introduced herself as "the short happy wife of Mr. McPapa," but not that night. She was, in fact, short and stocky, with blue eyes and cropped curly brown hair, much like a boy. She assured us that Papa would receive the manuscript when she next saw him.

"He's very fast when he actually writes," she said.

I breathed in her scent—rose, lemon, and thyme—and I knew it was one she'd worn long before Hemingway and would wear long after he'd moved on. She tried to take her leave, but Prudence said, "Please, sit," in a manner even Mrs. McPapa wasn't able to refuse.

"So where is the Great Man?" Gladys asked, helping Mary relieve herself of her sealskin coat.

Before Mary could answer, the Popes breezed in, Walter bedecked in his beaver, Betsy with a silver fox wrapped around her shoulders. They rushed up to us like spoiled children, eager to recount their smallest accomplishment. Gladys barely looked up, and instead started a quiet conversation with Mrs. Hemingway beneath the din. Searching for my cigarettes, my fingers landed upon Gladys's panties still in my pocket.

"We just about emptied out all of Murano this afternoon—we'll be giving chandeliers as Christmas presents for years," Walter said. I did another round of introductions before we moved upstairs, where a jazz band from New Orleans played quietly in the corner. Gladys had linked her arm in Mary's.

"And don't forget the miles of lace we bought from all those adorable little girls in Burano," Betsy added.

"They are adorable," Mary said, "but horribly mistreated, poor things."

Walter insisted on buying everyone Tizianos—a Harry's Bar specialty of grapefruit juice and champagne tinted pink with grenadine. While Walter was talking to the waiter, Betsy leaned in toward us and whispered, "I prefer the Giorgione." We all, even Mary, nodded in agreement, although I, for one, had no idea what a Giorgione consisted of. Betsy was a person you agreed with for her sake.

Walter nodded toward the band and said, "The Italians seem to love their music and all, but during our entire stay I don't think I've seen more than a handful of negroes walking down the street. It's so different from home."

Prudence said, "I have to say the only negroes I've seen are American soldiers stationed here."

Gladys said, "Don't get me started on the soldiers."

"But colored people are everywhere in the paintings," Betsy said, "especially here in Venice."

As the token Italian, all eyes turned to me for an explanation.

"We're profoundly racist," I said.

Betsy giggled. "Don't be silly, Italians love everybody."

"Mary was going to tell us of her husband's whereabouts," Prudence said.

"I'm not sure where he is, really," Mary said, unable to disguise her pride. "He went mallard shooting in one of the lagoons with Count Kechler yesterday and I had expected him home last night."

Into Gladys's ear, I said, "So much for your chance to sleep with a man in a dress."

"Duck hunting in a lagoon with a Count," Walter said, lathering us with his awe. "How very glam."

Gladys whispered back, "You do forget what a busy girl I am."

Walter repeatedly tried to catch Gladys's eye, but Gladys's eyes were fixed on the boyish Mary.

"He called this morning," Mary continued, "to say the shooting party had decided to go on to Latisana and to send you," she turned to me, "his sincerest apologies. He's simply not a man to turn down the opportunity to shoot a gun. And then, of course, you know Papa," she laughed, "where there's a Count, there's bound to be a Countess."

The edge in her voice told me that Mary and I had some things in common, things that I might not have recognized in myself even a day ago.

"You know how to shoot a gun, don't you, Dante?" Gladys said.

For the first time that evening, Prudence gave her sister a quizzical glance. I had seen her use it before, and at first I had thought it meant that Gladys was genuinely confusing her, but finally I understood that it meant: *You're going too far.*

"I'm better with a knife," I said.

"Never read Hemingway," Walter confessed. "But I've heard of him, just like I'd heard of our famous friend Dante here."

"I'll tell you what Papa says about you," Mary said, offering me a consolation prize. "He says you've earned your place in the ring."

I was flattered, of course, but Papa hadn't bothered to show up for this particular fight. He had chosen a gun over me. I'd read that when Hemingway was still a boy his father had killed himself by putting a gun to his head. I had thought seriously about that method during the war but decided it was both too messy and too unreliable.

"We learned from our gondolier," Betsy said, still bubbling, "that Venice was recaptured from the Germans by a whole fleet of gondolas."

We drank our way through Harry's art gallery—Tintoretto, Veronese, Carpaccio, Canaletto, Tiepolo, Guardi, Longhi—

and ate great portions of fish soup and lasagna. When we made our way out of Harry's Bar on to the Calle Vallaresso, Betsy begged Walter to go on a midnight gondola ride. Walter was trying to get out of it when Gladys spoke to him directly for the first time that evening. "Go on, Walter. It's your honeymoon."

Mary invited Gladys, Prudence, and me back to Gritti Palace Hotel for a nightcap, but Prudence demurred, pleading fatigue.

"You two run along back to Ruskinland, then," Gladys said, "and we single girls will see how much trouble we can get into."

As she kissed me goodnight, I slipped the panties into her hand. "You would do well to wear them," I said.

She whispered, "I doubt another pervert of your caliber exists, but if I get the chance to find out, I'll let you know."

Prudence and I headed off. I was grateful to her for getting me away from Gladys. I would have gone to the Gritti, not because I wanted to continue the evening with Mary, but because I wanted to keep an eye on Gladys, an oxymoronic proposition. That night at Harry's Bar she had upped the ante yet again, but I wasn't sure if she was motivated by my rough behavior in the alley, by angry words in her bedroom at the *pensione*, or simply by the sport of it.

Prudence and I wandered back toward La Calcina, but when we crossed the Ponte dell'Accademia, Prudence said, "Let's not go home just yet." By the light of the moon, given anemic assistance by flickering street lamps, we made our way down close alleys and over the dark, quivering canals, not speaking much, until we came to Campo San Barnaba. It was a large square with a church at one end, a canal at the other.

Patrician mansions and gothic palaces faced each other across the *campo* like foot soldiers in an ancient war. A great elevated cistern rose at the center of the square. We sat on the steps encircling its base.

"I'm sorry about Hemingway," Prudence said. "You must be disappointed."

"How could I be disappointed about anything when I have you?" I asked, pulling her to me and kissing her. I had been afraid she would ask me what was happening with Gladys, but instead, like a diviner, she had gone straight to the heart of the matter.

"Don't patronize me, Dante, listen to me. It doesn't mean anything that he didn't turn up, just as it wouldn't have meant anything if he had turned up. You're so dead sure that no one loves you, you have to prove it to yourself incessantly."

We sat there for a while, my stomach a pit of love for her and fear for her.

"You should have children," Prudence said.

"It would be irresponsible of me," I answered. I wasn't sure what I meant by this since I was not exactly a pillar of responsibility. I had the vague idea that I meant it would be unfair to the mother, whom I would never marry, and to the child, who would suffer from being a bastard.

"Irresponsible? You mean to have a child and then die?" She asked.

"Yes," I said. "Having a child would be irresponsible because such an event might delay or interfere with my suicide and I would be resentful."

———

"A child might help you get over yourself," she said.

"And what about the child?" I asked.

"A child would love you unconditionally."

"That's not what I meant," I said.

"I know," she said, "but it's true all the same. Damage repeats itself through time, but so does love. If you go ahead and commit suicide, which plenty of people with children do, the damage will be greater, but so will the love."

I said, "My wounds—the ones I nurse day in and day out, and now you nurse for me too—they are nothing compared to yours."

"Mine?" she said.

I kissed her on the nose.

"Look," Prudence said, sticking out her tongue where a single white flake landed and vanished. "It's snowing."

Oh, to be that flake, I thought.

Back at the *pensione*, when she turned to go to her room I took her hand and pulled her toward mine. She didn't resist. That night I made love to her as if it were the eve of my execution—taking no precautions and wanting the night to never end. How many children in the world, I wondered later, had been conceived as the result of men having this same fantasy?

The next morning, Mary sent a valet from the Gritti Palace to collect Gladys's things. He brought a note from Gladys saying she had been invited to go with Mary to join the shooting party, which had moved on to Baron Franchetti's estate in Latisana, and that she'd see us back in Rome in a few days.

1949

six

Castiglioncello

This morning, as the sun rose, the nuns were singing on the beach. Later, while I was having my coffee, I heard on the radio that the communists had declared victory in China and for the first time in recorded history it snowed in Los Angeles. There was no telephone in the house and I hadn't spoken to anyone in Rome for some time. I had told Prudence I was coming here to write—my Torcello, I called it. But really I was here because I did not want to be alive. Over the years, I had been more or less successful at finding reasons to dawdle—a political matter, another book, a love affair—but those things no longer seemed compelling.

And I found my onanism depressing. I was unable to take more than a passing interest in the fate of others, unless, of course, it could be useful to my work. Everything in life had a way of repeating itself, so I knew where this threesome with Prudence and Gladys was headed. I would have liked to spare them the torment that loomed close by, and I was filled with an uneasy sorrow for what the future held, but I would do nothing to change it. When I did finally commit suicide, there would be no purpose to it. I would do it thoughtlessly, a spasm of will at the end of just another day.

These histrionics had inspired me to begin a novel, so the excuse I gave Prudence for coming to Castiglioncello was not a complete lie. The writing wasn't going too badly. I had stopped around midday to give my nerves and fingers a rest. The January sun was warm, the air salty. I sat in a chair by an open window in the drawing room and read *Four Quartets*. In just a stanza, Eliot gave me an antidote to the eternal question: Why bother? He was so impossibly good that he made all effort seem worthy.

Since my arrival in Castiglioncello, Ubaldo's daughter Nerina had visited me almost every day after lunch, and when I heard the knock at the door indicating her arrival the clock said it was already half past two. I hadn't risen from my chair since noon. I hadn't eaten, nor did I feel hungry. I was pleased, as I liked to fornicate on an empty stomach and Nerina's schedule hadn't allowed for that lately. I let her in and followed her to the bedroom, where she began taking off her clothes—a navy wool cardigan that pulled nicely across her ample breasts and a navy wool skirt, taut and smooth over her roller-coaster hips and buttocks. She undressed slowly and carefully, placing each item of clothing neatly on the bedroom chair before she slid naked between my sheets.

Sex with Nerina was bland, the way I imagined countless married couples had sex. Perhaps Nerina's love-making with her husband was so unorthodox that she was happy to find someone who simply climbed on top, sank deeply into her many warm folds, and was soon done. For me, our automatic love-making was extraordinary. That afternoon, once I had rolled off her and her head lay in the crook of my arm, her soft black curls strewn across my chest, our limbs entwined, I was moved to ask her, "Why do you come to me?"

After a short silence, she said, "I will tell you. It was because of a bond like ours that I came to be born. I feel very safe being with Beppe and having you whenever the possibility arises." Nerina's explanation fit neatly into my hall-of-mirrors view of the world—Ubaldo had an affair with Nerina's mother (the reason for the beating he took and I witnessed that night long ago in his shop) and so Nerina does the same, as will her offspring and so on.

"And you like me," she said, "because I remind you of her."

We both knew she meant Germana. Early in our relationship, I inadvertently had called her by Germana's name. Nerina had wanted to know who she was, so I told her what I could. When I thought of Germana, the first thing that came to mind was the extraordinary color of her aureoles—a bright purplish red, somewhere between pomegranate and plum. They were the size of communion wafers and capped two rotund mounds of flesh as soft and sweet and flushed as newly ripe peaches. "Tell me about her, Dante," Nerina asked me on occasion, and

I would immediately think of Germana's breasts but would be unable to search any further for her through my beehive-like memory. It wasn't Nerina's looks or shape or voice or manner that threw me into a place where fantasy bested memory. She smelled like Germana. Nerina's skin gave off the faintest odor of white lupine. Nerina raised herself onto her elbows, her breasts dangling against my skin. "I love being her for you," she said, then slid her tongue over my lips and into my mouth as I remembered Germana.

~~~

Germana came from Cuneo, a small city in the North. Her father, Gregorio, was born into a noble family. In a classic case of Oedipal rebellion, when he was nineteen he had married Mirta, a girl from the local whorehouse. Gregorio's father had introduced him to her when initiating his son into the world of manhood. After Gregorio's marriage, his family cut him off completely. The young couple immediately had four children, of whom Germana was the first. They lived a good enough life—Gregorio made a fair living as a schoolteacher and private tutor for the rich. When Germana was fourteen, Gregorio died from a heart attack. The years immediately following the tragedy were difficult, but Mirta, with Germana's help, eventually managed to get enough work ironing, sewing, and tutoring small children to make a living for the family. When things stabilized, Germana, encouraged by her mother and sister and two younger brothers, had gone to the University of Rome to fulfill her father's dream for her—that she earn a university degree.

In pursuit of an education, I had gone to Rome in the same year. It wasn't a university degree I was after, however. I had already earned my degree from the University of Florence in literature and philosophy, my thesis a translation of Herman Melville's *Moby Dick,* for which I received the highest honors. My ambition was to become an international man of letters and the place for me to begin my training was Rome. London and New York, naturally, would follow. My own Five-Year Plan was to translate into Italian as many classic English and American novels as possible. Luckily for me, in a country intent on promoting "Italianness," our literary culture promoted anything but. Most of the literature published was in translation. Every so often the government would issue a statement calling for publishers to stem the flow of translations, but to little effect. Since the publication of *A Farewell to Arms,* portraying Italy's defeat at Caporetto in the Great War, Hemingway's novels had been banned, although I translated a few of his stories for journals with no problem. But there weren't many other examples of censorship, yet.

It was the autumn of 1932 and I was twenty-three years old. My first chapbook had been published to some critical acclaim and my second would be out before the end of the year. Several of my poems and a short story would soon be appearing in various literary journals and I had an idea for a novel. In Rome, Mussolini's grand boulevard, the Road of the Imperial Fora, extending between the Victor Emmanuel Monument and the Colosseum, was nearly finished. It was an impressive piece of road. It did not say "make way for me;" it commanded, "I am the Way." Italy's triumphant performance in the summer Olympics, held in Los Angeles at the height of the Great Depression, was a double coup for Mussolini and Fascism. The German government had fallen and the Nazis were becoming alarmingly popular. Rin Tin Tin had died in Hollywood.

The timing of Aunt Pia's death could not have been more perfect. When I finished my degree, I longed to go to Rome, but money was tight and the idea of my cohabiting with my aunt did not sit well with my father. It smacked to him of charity and he suffered from pride, especially when it came to Aunt Pia. In order for him to let her give me anything, she had to die—and that she did. My best friend, Vanni—his family lived in the apartment just above ours in Florence—came with me to live in Aunt Pia's apartment. He would share the expenses and had hopes of finding a job in the film industry.

In all ways but blood, Vanni was my brother—his name Giovanni, the same as my dead brother. But we looked nothing alike. He was very thin and had a tubercular mien. He was a head shorter than I and had dark blue eyes. His nose and chin were sharp but not pointy. What little hair he had was light and silken. We both considered ourselves better looking than the other. I believed I had the edge because of my full head of hair, but women always seemed to notice him first. I envied Vanni his ease in the world and how sure he was of what he wanted from life—to work in the movie business, get married, and have lots of kids. His great passion was the cinema and mine literature, so we often worked on screenplays together. He, too, loved all things American and our taste in literature merged perfectly in the detective story, the more hard-boiled the better. As teenagers in Florence, we had spent most of our afternoons either at the cinema (the vast majority of the films were foreign, many made in Hollywood) or at the American Bookshop in Piazza San Marco, reading issues of *McClure's*, *Dime Detective*, *Thrilling Mystery*, and *Breezy Stories*. Books by writers such as Hammett, Woolrich, and Cain were translated and distributed in Italy before the ink was dry on the American editions—and we then read them with equal speed.

Vanni and I believed that moving to Rome would put us closer to intellectual and sexual freedom, which in our minds meant America. We were, on first impression, sorely disappointed. Aunt Pia's apartment was on the via Giulia, a little pocket of the Renaissance amid an architectural layering of the ages. We had left Florence desperate to get away from just this sort of quiet, tastefully genteel, fifteenth-century time-freeze. Soon enough, though, we discovered that all we had to do was cross the Ponte Sisto to Trastevere, where we found artists, writers, and revolutionaries spending their days smoking Nazionali and drinking jugs of bitter red wine. Or we could wander in the other direction to the Campo de' Fiori where, under the bemused gaze of Giordano Bruno, everything imaginable was being hawked—apples, artichokes, kumquats, curry, passage on the next ship out of Ostia to New York or New Zealand, and women of all ages and races. I already had half a decade's worth of experience with women—mostly older and mostly married, and all Florentine. I had, however, never been with a foreigner or a whore, so a rapid sampling began. Vanni joined me now and again but his sexual appetites were less egregious than mine.

Compared to stately Florence, cacophony filled our days. At first, Vanni and I were rendered deaf and dumb by the noise—Romans howling at each other like the inmates of an insane asylum, church bells clanging, workers pounding their tools, opera singers belting out that evening's arias, but above all the wailing of car horns. The excessive number of cars in the city all tooting their horns was such a problem that Mussolini had decided to address it by razing a few thousand dwellings, a chunk of the forum, and three churches to lay down the Road of the Imperial Fora. He then called for Romans to buy more cars. If the problem continued and no one could move through the streets, he reasoned, the motorists would have to stop blowing their horns and organize themselves. The Duce sincerely believed that if he dug deep enough into the Italian character he would find Germans.

Vanni began by looking for a job at the Cines Production Complex, SAFIR studio, and in all the branch offices of the major American studios, but was finally hired by Stella Films, a small, local production company. He was initially hired to read scripts but started off as a boy Friday around the studio— fetching coffee, assisting the set designer, helping the continuity person, searching the city for props, and at the end of the day some script doctoring. He did well and was soon promoted to production assistant.

I embarked on my translation project, beginning with James Joyce's *Ulysses,* a challenge that some of Italy's best translators had turned away from. But I had a self-destructive bent, and I was very young. I spent long hours between sentences staring out my window at a sliver of the Tiber, trying to figure out how to render into my own language what seemed impossible to understand in any language. Finally, when I couldn't bear to inspect one more inch of imaginary Dublin, out I would go to climb the Janiculum. I stood where Livy, Ovid, and Pliny had stood and I gazed upon, more or less, what they had—the whole of Rome. But what gave me even greater euphoria was to dip my hand in the cool waters of the Fountain of the Acqua Paola, to run my fingers along the twisted crevices of Tasso's Oak, knowing that Henry Wadsworth Longfellow, Nathaniel Hawthorne, Herman Melville, Thomas Hardy, Mark Twain, James Fenimore Cooper, Charles Dickens, George Eliot, Lord Byron, Percy Shelley, and Henry James had been there before me.

One particularly mild October afternoon, Vanni came home from work to announce that we had been invited to a Tullio Merlini soirée. Tullio Merlini fancied himself the Gertrude Stein of celluloid, his apartment Rome's 27 rue de Fleurus, the meeting ground of would-be directors, novelists, cinematographers and poets. Film was the century's gold and the rush was on. Despite hard times, the production companies, actors' agencies, prop houses, wardrobe and set designers, and businesses that specialized in catering for film crews were cropping up like mushrooms after a heavy rain. Tullio was involved in the industry's development, though no one knew exactly to what end or extent. He was friendly with everyone in the business, a ubiquitous presence at all the studios, then, as now, something of a facilitator. (Soon after we met, he arranged for me to write a monthly film review for *Cinema*.) We figured he was helping his father, a high-ranking administrator at the brand new Ministry for Press and Propaganda. The cinema was an important propaganda tool for the government and they wanted to encourage its expansion while keeping strong control of the medium. In 1937, the Fascists would open the sprawling Cinecittà studios, which would become the most advanced production facilities in Europe. At first, Tullio would frequently let drop the names of powerful politicians, producers, directors, and actors. He claimed Ezra Pound was a great friend of his father, who had arranged for Pound's nighttime radio broadcasts. But we didn't pay much attention to his boasts, and in a short amount of time he stopped making them.

Tullio lived by himself in a large apartment in a building owned by his family just off the via del Corso. When we entered Tullio's that autumn evening, the first thing we saw were the spinning reels of a movie projector. On a large wall across the room, Stan and Ollie were silently chasing a piano tumbling down a long flight of stairs. Paul Robeson's "Got the South in My Soul" played softly in the background. On another wall hung a large framed poster of Mussolini, his expression goofy and belligerent, that of a child who knew that the best toy would always be beyond his reach. Although I found Mussolini and his coterie to be charmless thugs with a flair for mass manipulation, I didn't hold Tullio's patriotism against him. Posters of the Duce and other Fascist paraphernalia were in just about every shop, office building, school, restaurant, and home in the country. During the twenty years of Mussolini's reign, at some point or other all of us had marched in a Fascist parade, participated in a Fascist youth organization event, mouthed the words to the Fascist anthem "Giovinezza," worn the black shirt.

Since my parents were Socialists, I was drawn to what they had rejected and for a time read D'Annunzio and worshiped the Futurists. I did an about-face and became virulently anti-Fascist when the opposition leader Matteotti was assassinated, but my fervor soon waned. One afternoon at the Hotel Miramare during the summer just after his murder, Aunt Pia said to me, "Politics are practiced by the unimaginative. I wouldn't recommend it."

If Vanni and I as teenagers had any other allegiance than to the American Bookshop, it was, briefly, to the Giubbe Rosse, the German-owned caffè in the lackluster Piazza Vittorio Emanuele in the heart of Florence. The up-market beer hall with waiters wearing flaming-red dinner jackets and white aprons had been home to Florence's avant-garde since some time before the Great War. When Marinetti published his Manifesto in 1909, the year I was born, the Giubbe Rosse intellectuals publicly ripped it up, infuriating the Milanese artists, who immediately made their way south to the bar in Piazza Vittorio Emanuele and started a brawl. The next day, in a singular act of contrition, the Florentines admitted their mistake and embraced Marinetti's Manifesto and Futurism, until the movement all but died as the First World War began. My and Vanni's flirtation with literary Fascism began in the 1920s and included memorizing the Manifesto's opening lines with far greater passion and precision than we had memorized the first stanzas of the *Inferno* in school:

> We want to celebrate love of danger, of unflagging energy, and of courage. We want to promote heading in aggressive new directions, feverish sleeplessness, running, deathly leaps, slaps, and blows. We want to destroy museums, libraries, all types of academies, and combat moralism. We are launching our devastatingly violent and inflammatory manifesto, with which we intend to found the Futuristic Movement in Italy in order to free this country from the fetid cancer of its professors, archaeologists, leaders, and elders.

By the time we were old enough to hang out in the Giubbe Rosse's mirrored rooms, the Futurists were long gone and a new generation of the radically literate had taken over. The habitués included Montale, Saba, Gadda, and it was here I first met Elio Vittorini. As Vanni and I played chess and drank beer, we joined in their conversations about being an autonomous literary society immune to political compromise and moralizing. It all sounded well-meaning, but even to our young ears their words were empty. Soon Vanni and I were back at the

American Bookshop and I was well on my way to becoming my own country.

Under Mussolini's *l'enfant terrible* gaze, Tullio made a great show of how excited he was that Vanni and I had come to his salon. Tullio was tall and thin with fair skin and features so delicate he might have been sculpted by Bernini. He looked no older than eighteen but his manner put him nearer twenty-eight. His chocolate eyes flashed from beneath the long curled eyelashes of a girl. His dark ringlets were in perfect disorder. He draped his lanky body on furniture or people or even the floor as if he were modeling for a painter or posing before the camera's eye. When he spoke, he always touched his interlocutor, lightly brushing an arm, hair, hand, back, waist. He rarely touched me, which I was both grateful for and wondered about. Tullio's effeminate nature led to one assumption: he was, as Hammett would put it, a fairy.

On some basic level, we were probably all bisexual, but culture kept us from having sex with both men and women. The closest I ever came to having sex with another man was with Vanni, and though I would have liked to experiment more, the farthest we got was to masturbate next to each other a few times when we were in high school and he was sleeping over at my family's apartment or I at his.

Tullio grabbed a bottle of champagne and three glasses and we drank while he scanned the room, giving us a quip or two about each guest. "I won't bother to introduce you as most aren't worth your time," he said intimately. I assumed he said this to everyone, but I found it a novel method for avoiding introductions.

"Here, however," Tullio said, grabbing the arm of a striking girl with short ginger hair, gray eyes, and lovely breasts, "is someone you two will want to know." It took me and Vanni less than a second to fall hopelessly in love with her.

"But you said there was no one here I would want to meet," Germana objected to Tullio in her limpid northern accent. She even smelled of alpine honey. Tullio put his arms around her and whispered something into her ear before slipping away. We soon found out that beyond her alluring appearance, Germana possessed superior intelligence, abundant charm, and an unorthodox sophistication. But really we three were drawn together that evening not because of any particular personality trait but because we immediately recognized one another as outsiders. None of us wanted to be Roman, but we wanted Rome to become ours.

Falling in love with Germana included falling in love with Rome. As Germana later pointed out, *Amor* is Roma spelled backward. Although our Rome surely included moonlit walks in the Forum discussing Daisy Miller's ineluctable fate, the Rome we fell in love with was the illusion its polygenetic architecture gave us of being free from time or convention. In Rome we felt connected to humanity but in no way beholden to any particular expectation it might have of us. We were gloriously anonymous yet by no means isolated. And Rome's peculiar and unrelenting beauty pushed us ever deeper into the intensity of experience we assumed would lead to great achievement.

In other words, we were tourists. We visited the Baths of Carcalla, strolled in the Pincian Gardens, let the *granita* ice melt on our tongues at the Caffé Greco, and gorged ourselves on pizza in the *osterie* of Trastevere. Rome was an inside-out place where we gazed through our cigarette smoke toward an invisible horizon, like a hazy day at the seaside where sea and sky merge.

We were among the last to leave Tullio's party that night, though we had spoken to no one else, our triumvirate having encompassed the entire universe. We persuaded Germana to let us walk her back to the convent where she was staying near the Piazza di Spagna, but once out on the street Germana confessed to us that it was too late for her to return home; the door would be locked until daylight. The nuns would send her packing if she were to ring the bell at that late hour. She would just have to hope that her roommates would cover for her. We immediately offered her a bed in our apartment, but she claimed she wasn't tired and as it was such a pleasant and unusually warm evening she would rather wander about the city until the sun came up. The sky was moonless and full of stars. We walked and talked without paying any attention to where we were going.

Like us, Germana was passionate about the cinema, her favorite directors Eisenstein, Ozu, René Clair, though she also went crazy for any movie starring Clark Gable. We chatted away, Vanni visibly entranced, I making Herculean efforts to remain aloof, Germana falling in love with us both, wishing we were one person, yet enthralled that we were not. The three of us stopped short, our breath quickened. Before us lay a massive, cavernous and craggy structure, so high the stars seemed to be falling into it. We had, in our impassioned delirium, stumbled upon the Colosseum and found our way into the very center of the vast amphitheater. The three of us lay down, Germana in the middle, first at arm's length, then closer until we were pressed up against each other like sardines in a tin. We watched the dawn, like a Roman crowd, creep through the arches and fill in every inch of space, anxiously awaiting the spectacle of death in the afternoon. We heard the howls of wild beasts, the prayers of Christian martyrs, the din of gladiators' swords. We had all read Byron and Goethe, Hawthorne and Poe, but, like new love, it didn't matter what had come before or how many people had lived the exact same experience; for us it was the first time, unique and incredible. Why, we wanted to cry, didn't anyone tell us about this?

Not long after, Vanni found Germana a job at his studio as an extra doing non-speaking walk-on parts and crowd scenes. Soon they were having sex. I could tell by the way Vanni touched her. His hand would rest gently and easily on her shoulder or his fingers would clutch her elbow with a possessive hold. Initially, I told myself that I had no time for such alliances with women, that my intellectual and artistic development had to take precedence, that a woman would get in the way of my ambition. I never could convince myself this was true, but such thoughts added salt to my wound.

After work, the three of us would often meet at the Caffè Greco, and Germana and Vanni would entertain me with stories from the set. Their favorite source was Vanni's boss, an assistant director named Silvio Busoni who loved to give them lectures. "Today's seminar," Vanni began, "took place in a prop room full of classical busts, women's and men's wigs, and racks of fur coats." There was something about the way he said "fur coats" that let me imagine what Vanni and Germana were doing together in the prop room in the first place, how they must have been surprised by Silvio, and how he had known what they were up to, his lecture a way of masking his own envy and embarrassment.

Germana's giggle was sweetly sinister. She went on: "Silvio sat us down among all that hair and said: 'Kids, I'm going to tell you this once only. In America, time is money, in Italy time is wasted, therefore in Italy we waste money. Here inside these walls of this studio you must think that you are in America, where time is money and money is never wasted. This means that when I ask you to do something, not only do you do it fast—next time you beat me to the punch. A few days from now, if I have to open my mouth and waste muscle movement and breath to ask you for something, you are not doing your job and will be sacked. Is that clear?'" Germana and Vanni dissolved in breathless laughter. I felt sorry for Silvio.

"We nodded our heads vigorously," Vanni said, taking the story over from Germana as if they were in a relay race. "Silvio said, 'You, the actors, technicians, sound men, the cameramen, set designers, the prop men, all of you are essential to my craft, to my art. If I were a carpenter, you would be my hammers, my nails, my saws. If I were a painter, you would be my paint-brushes, my canvasses, my oils. If I were a writer, you would be my words, my rhymes, my themes. If I were a musician, you would be my notes, my tones, my melodies . . .'"

"If I were a whore," I interrupted, "you would be my dildos, my whips, my butter."

"Butter?" Germana asked.

I invited Germana to come live with us in Aunt Pia's apartment. The rent was free, I argued, and she could have her own room. She hesitated because I think she knew exactly what it would mean, but she was too young and too inquisitive to resist, and within days of her moving in I was having sex with her, too. One evening, when Vanni and I were home alone, he said to me, "If there's something between you and Germana, don't ever let me find out." Germana wanted desperately to tell Vanni about us and to see if the three of us could be together openly, so I told her what Vanni had said to me. After that, Germana and I were careful not to take any risks or leave any clues. Seeing her alone was not simple and devising opportunities to meet her on the sly became my sole preoccupation. Gone were my forays up the Janiculum or to the Campo de' Fiori. In the end, I probably only made love to Germana a score of times—each time believing in that youthful way that I had arrived at a never-before-reached state of rapture. But the thrill of her wasn't as huge as the thrill of betraying the person I was closest to in the world. Many poets have uttered the dark truth: to love someone was to betray him. Love without betrayal did not exist. This idea was at the heart of every story.

I wondered why I never told Gladys or Prudence about Vanni and Germana. Was I afraid of revealing my "true self"? Or was I protecting a time in my life when I still believed in the idea of a "true self"? Perhaps I was afraid that if I opened up my past to interpretation, I would taint and change it. I wanted to preserve who I was then from who I am now.

After Germana and I had sex, I would do a strange thing. I would wait for her to fall asleep and then masturbate while lying next to her. I hadn't done this with any other woman before or since. I had considered masturbating while lying next to Prudence, but only because we hadn't had sex and my desire was acute. I usually coped by either masturbating before I saw Prudence or after she was gone. With Germana, the issue wasn't lack of desire. She was indefatigable. If I had leaned over and touched her, she would have woken up fully aroused and ready to satisfy both of us. But that was not what I sought. By masturbating next to her while she slept, I was proving my undying loyalty to my only true love: myself. And warding off the obvious questions: Did she love him more than she loved me? Could he please her better than I could? Questions I emphatically wanted to avoid.

For two exuberant years, Germana and Vanni and I explored the topography of our concupiscence. When Germana learned she was pregnant, she told me first. One evening, while I watched as she orchestrated a silly argument with Vanni that sent him out the door, slamming it behind him, I became elated with the prospect of having Germana to myself. As soon as he had left, I was by her side nibbling on her ear and unbuttoning her shirt, when she placed her hands firmly on mine and said: "I'm pregnant. He doesn't know."

I hesitated. My face must have revealed my crushing disappointment. I said, "When he learns of it, I am sure he will be happy. He'll make a good father."

Her eyes revealed neither hurt nor anger, just disdain. She left the apartment and I never saw her again. Her casket was closed because her body had been smashed by the bus she had stepped in front of on the Road of the Imperial Fora. Was it suicide? No one ever considered it. A tragic accident was the verdict. I came to the conclusion, after many years of trying not to think about Germana's death, that it didn't matter whether it had been random or planned. The result was the same.

Soon after her death, I joined a Communist group in Rome and spent most of my nights plotting to overthrow Mussolini in basements that smelled of mold and doubled as breeding grounds for cockroaches. We wrote pamphlets and distributed them at factories and in working-class neighborhoods. I took particular pleasure in harassing Ezra Pound when he gave lectures on the economic and cultural benefits of Fascism. We mounted our own version of the "Exhibition of the Fascist Revolution" and called it "The End of Civilization on Display for the Curious Viewer." The display consisted of six canvasses painted entirely black. By day, I continued to translate—*The House of the Seven Gables, The Sound and the Fury, Dark Laughter*—and the publisher Corbaccio agreed to include them in the "Writers from All Over the World" series. In September, 1935, I was arrested for subversive activity and after a short stay across the river in the Regina Coeli prison, I was sent to a detention facility in Basilicata. I was released in October, 1938 on an amnesty for a handful of political prisoners.

Vanni never got over Germana's death. And the fact that she had been nearly five months pregnant—something he learned at the morgue—made it worse for him. After her funeral, Vanni moved back to Florence. He joined the Resistance early on in the war and became one of Lanciotto Ballerini's band. He burned to death in a barn during the battle at Valibona on the 3rd of January, 1944.

My second climax of the afternoon was accompanied by a rapid knock on the door. I looked into Nerina's dark eyes and saw, briefly, the excitement of getting caught. I knew so little about her and I would probably never do anything about it. Neither of us moved from the bed. Finally, we heard Ubaldo's voice, insistent, but only loud enough to make himself heard.

"Dante, are you at home?"

I rose from the bed, grabbed my robe, and went downstairs to open the front door.

"I am sorry to disturb you," Ubaldo said. Flushed and breathing heavily, his eyes carefully reached mine. "But an American woman just off the train from Rome was asking where you live. She is on her way here now."

He was quiet a moment.

"I thought," he continued, "you would like to know."

"Thank you, Ubaldo," I said.

As I closed the door, Nerina appeared fully clothed. "I'll be on my way then," she said. My hand still on the doorknob, I opened it for her and as she passed I grabbed her hand lightly, then let go. I shut the door and turned my attention to Prudence's impending visit. It was not easy to be pursued. When Ubaldo told me that Prudence was on her way, my heart both sank and leaped at once. The sensation was that of a child playing hide and seek, both terrified of being found and desperate to be discovered.

I went back into the bedroom to quickly wash and dress. I had gotten in too deep with Prudence and now she felt she had permission to seek me out and invade my privacy. I reminded myself that she had been the one to bring up the obnoxious subject of a child. I began to rehearse all the arguments a man makes to himself when he perceives that a woman has become too needy—*I can never give her what she wants. The greater our involvement, the more she will dominate my life.* I looked at myself in the mirror as I was brushing my teeth and became annoyed at having fallen into this tedious mindset, especially with Prudence, with whom nothing ever felt routine. I was bringing myself around to feeling excitement at the prospect of her arrival and soon found myself intrigued by the spontaneity of her visit. I heard a knock at the front door. I wiped soap off my chin with a towel. I looked again into the mirror, my face perfectly inscrutable.

Gladys stood on my doorstep, the Rita look gone, her hair brunette with fiery tints that burned brightly in the afternoon sun. I hadn't seen much of her since Venice, but I had heard something about her sexual escapades with Hemingway & Co. I was momentarily overwhelmed by conflicting emotions: disappointment that she was not Prudence, euphoria that she was not Prudence, delectation at the prospect of sex with Gladys, rage that she had offered herself freely to others while keeping herself from me.

"I woke up this morning feeling a particular kind of horny," she said, her painted lips curling with sweet mischief. Dropping her Chinchilla at the door so that all she wore were her hat, gloves, and shoes, she said, "I'm in search of a long slow fuck with all the trimmings." She paused, then sniffed the air. "But something tells me you've already had one of those today."

"Not exactly," I said.

She caressed my cheek with her black leather glove. "I like it when you're spent. More for me."

I pulled her inside and shut the door. "Don't move," I said. I undid my belt buckle and slid the leather strap from my trousers. I reinserted the strap through the buckle and drew it through until I had made a noose. I placed it over her head and tightened it around her neck. The strap in my hand, I dragged her halfway up the stairs, sat her down on the stone steps and gave her the end of the belt.

"Hold that," I said. "And keep it firm."

She did as she was told while I went to the bedroom, took the gold brocade ties from the curtains, and selected a necktie from the closet. When I returned, her eyes were watering but she was sitting quietly, holding the belt taut. I took the belt strap back from her and turned her around, tying her hands behind her with the curtain cord, the tassels resting over her rump like a tail. I then bound her ankles and gagged her with the silk necktie. I led her slowly up to the landing. She struggled, making her way up the jagged slope on her knees and shoulders, her usually pert breasts dangling and swaying. Now and again she let out a strange grunt. When she made it to the top, her fine white skin was scratched and bruised.

I said, "Tell me what you are."

Speaking what sounded almost like gibberish through the necktie in her mouth, she said, "I'm your dirty little slut."

I stroked her head, kissed her brow.

She said, "Show me your knife, Dante."

I used a trick or two I learned from my own interrogation at the Regina Coeli prison and from interrogations I had conducted myself toward the end of the war. But I didn't hold the war responsible for my erotic proclivities. It was much more likely that my, our, erotic proclivities were responsible for war. What I did to Gladys, what the Germans did to the Jews, what the Italians did to the Ethiopians, what the Turks did to the Armenians, what the Soviets did indiscriminately, the serpent forever biting its tail, could be summed up by a child's simple demand: Look at me.

In the evening, after we had tended to her wounds—the chafing burns on her wrists and ankles, the cuts and scratches, the welts around her throat—Gladys put on a violet dress she had brought in her handbag and wrapped a black chiffon scarf about her neck.

"Let's go to Dino Duranti's," she said.

We drove in Aunt Pia's old Lancia DiLambda to the big yellow and white wedding-cake house wedged between a bend in the Aurelia and a sheer cliff. The late January sun sat low on the horizon, casting an unnatural orange light over the opal sea. In its glow, Gladys's complexion became as electric as her mood. Her hair was a bit tousled, her eyes moist and bright, her cheeks flushed pink—details, as Gladys knew well, that could make a girl beautiful.

Dino Duranti's house was actually owned by Doris Duranti, the diva of the "white telephones," 1930s parlor comedies so-called because of the opulent living room settings featuring the status symbol of the white telephone. Dori fled to South America after the war with her lover Corrado Pavolini, former head of the Ministry of Popular Culture. Neither Dori nor Corrado was a bad person. Ignorance, indifference, even collusion often became heinous only in retrospect. At the time, shrugged shoulders and getting on was the norm. Dori's nephew Dino, a composer of film scores, was carrying on her tradition of opening the house to actors, directors, musicians, painters, poets, anyone in the arts who, passing through Livorno, needed a fix of worldliness. Once upon a time, on any given evening at Dori's you might have found Alessandro Blasetti, Alida Valli, Massimo Bontempelli, Clara Calamai, Vittorio De Sica, and, my favorite simply because of her name, Emma Gramatica. That evening, I didn't recognize many faces and felt old.

As soon as Gladys mentioned Dino, I understood that the purpose of her visit to me was not purely salacious. Gladys was on a mission and I was the beard. I tried to determine her mark from a corner of a large glassed-in cantilevered terrace that extended over the sea. Gladys and an actor of recent success were engaged in an animated conversation that included a fair amount of surreptitious fondling. Over Mel Tormé, I couldn't hear a thing they were saying to each other. In the end, Gladys left the party with a young blond man whom I thought I recognized but couldn't place. I only caught a glimpse of him sitting in the driver's seat of a new silver-bronze Alfa Romeo 2500. Before she climbed into the car, she kissed me passionately on the lips, whispered "Hope you liked the present, Pops," then stuck her tongue deep into my ear. She then added, "Papa's bad but you're better."

While I watched them speed off down the Aurelia, I contemplated the various meanings of her epithet. The most obvious was the Hemingway correlation, but I also remembered what Gladys must have known: she had paid her visit to me on my fortieth birthday. Such a lapse of memory was not only a sign of age but, worse, it indicated a fear of aging. And it happened to be a decade marker, the midway point, the beginning of the end. Only once before had I paid attention to the number of years I had accumulated and that was when I turned thirty-three, the age Christ died, the age when Byron declared in his diary, "In twelve minutes I shall have completed thirty and three years of age!!!—and I go to my bed with a heaviness of heart at having lived so long, and to so little purpose."

Age was something the owner of the years could never understand very well, much in the same way he could never comprehend the appearance of his own face. It was easy to understand the characteristics of a specific age in another person—angry at sixteen, conceited at twenty-two, magnanimous at thirty, obstinate at sixty. But with oneself it was nearly impossible. When I was younger, I never thought about getting old because I was sure I'd be dead by thirty. The recent signs of physical decay— lines, like scars, slashed across my forehead, my hair thinning, my skin porous as sandstone, the fact that I could no longer piss like a racehorse—reminded me that I was relentlessly alive. I'd probably live until I was ninety-nine still plagued with Camus's "one truly serious philosophical problem," waking each morning with Hamlet's six staccato words on my lips, spending each day devising the means to do myself in, and in the evening castigating myself for not having pulled it off yet again. "Being able to remain on that dizzying crest—that is integrity and the rest is subterfuge," Camus wrote of the suicidal man. How I was drawn to subterfuge!

I left Dino's and drove home, taking the curves too fast. I loved the thought of driving off a cliff into the sea. I relished the incongruity of being encased in metal while becoming, for a second, lighter than air. The tires squealed like a baby and I was alerted to yet another way of interpreting "Pops": Prudence was pregnant and I was to be a father! Ever since our reckless night in Venice, the possibility had been fermenting at the back of my mind.

That night, I lay for hours nauseated by fears of paternity but grateful to Gladys for having led me back, once again, and in her particular manner, to Prudence. As dawn approached, I decided that if I had to endure being responsible for another life, who but Prudence would I do that with? I fell asleep warmed by the thought that my adoration for Prudence might replicate itself. On the train to Rome, I was jubilant, my thoughts pinballing among the chiming bumpers of new life, no life, and status quo.

seven

Rome

"Prudence," I said, reaching across the table at Da Filomena and running two fingers down her silken cheek, "is there something I should know?"

"Many things," she said. "For example, I don't like mushrooms, I'm an atheist, and I have a part in a new picture."

It was not like Prudence to be coy. "When I last saw you," I said, "you brought up the subject of a child . . ."

"Oh," she laughed, "I'm sorry about that, Dante. Sometimes I can be so presumptuous."

"So then you're not . . ."

"Not what, Dante?"

"Gladys seemed to indicate . . ."

"Gladys?"

"I thought you might be pregnant," I said finally.

She blushed and looked down at her hands. In almost a whisper, she said, "No. Better not. I wouldn't make much of a mother."

"Well, there you are," I said, as the niche I had hollowed out in my soul for our child sealed over, "it seems we are in the same boat, at least on that score."

Soon Prudence and I were back where we had left off—I seeking her out at every opportunity and she basking in my attention. Our evenings together often culminated in dinner at Da Filomena and the occasional party at Tullio's. My work continued to go well. In a surprising development, Prudence began to read what I had written at the end of each day and without ever saying very much, conveyed her appreciation for what I had done. Prudence and Gladys rarely spoke to me about my work, probably because whenever they brought it up I immediately changed the subject. Writers often babbled on about their work to anyone who would listen. My own tight-lipped policy functioned as a countermeasure for the same affliction. Since my work occupied nearly my every thought, I found it a relief to pretend I was thinking about something else. I imagined Prudence had read my every word and that Gladys had read not one, but the opposite could have been true. Gladys, in the meantime, had gone AWOL. Prudence said she was filming on location somewhere in the Veneto, which to me meant she was back running with the great American bull. I wondered if she'd ever gotten him to wear that dress. I was even glad, though I knew it would be temporary, to have a break from Gladys and all that she evoked in me.

While I was ensconced at Castiglioncello, Prudence had won a small part in a picture directed by a young and very ambitious filmmaker named Rocco Pompei. He had refused to film at Cinecittà, the massive state-run film studio, since MGM had taken it over to shoot *Quo Vadis,* calling it "Hollywood on the Tiber." He also claimed he was furious that there were still over seven hundred refugees (since 1944 the studios had been used as a refugee camp) living in abandoned sound stages, using scraps of furniture from sets, wearing ragged costumes, and being exploited as extras. But many speculated that his decision to locate his own production company in a group of warehouses near Piazza della Radio was probably a publicity stunt—a way to keep the press focused on him and his films. Whatever Pompei's talents as an artist, Tullio had once quipped, Rocco had a natural ability to keep himself at the center of attention. Tullio had said the same of me, and I found it distasteful, as the truth has a way of being.

One morning I accompanied Prudence to the set. On our way we stopped off for a cappuccino in a caffè in the Piazza Santa Maria in Trastevere. The cold and drizzle kept us from sitting outside. Despite the nasty March climate, the air held the insinuation of spring, leading to a vision of Prudence and me at an outdoor table with the sun in our laps and the scent of oleander, hibiscus, and lemon entertaining our noses. What I actually smelled was coffee and wet wool.

Prudence wore a pin-checked sorrel suit, the jacket unfastened, the skirt narrow. She was flipping through the latest issue of *Cinema* containing my review of *Gun Crazy* as well as my predictions for the winners of the upcoming Academy Awards. "I should like to be famous just for a little while. Do you like being famous?" Prudence asked.

———

I listened to the small sounds of spoons clinking against cups and saucers, the shuffle of feet, the scraping of chairs, the steaming of milk, the swish of the door opening and closing again. I remembered Aunt Pia telling me at the Hotel Miramare how it was essential to "show off." It occurred to me that Malebolge, Dante's amphitheater-shaped eighth circle of hell, where the flatterers are buried up to their necks in human excrement, was fast becoming prime real estate.

I said, "Rilke described fame as the quintessence of all the misunderstandings that collect about a name."

She gave me an indulgent look and recited, "'There's not a thing on earth that I can name, So foolish, and so false, as common fame.' But to have all those people love and want you even if you know it's false, must be exhilarating."

"When I was younger," I said, "I shuddered at the fate of Emily Dickinson or Herman Melville—of any number of writers whose real talent wasn't recognized until after their deaths. I had once believed that those who toiled with their words day in and day out with no hope for public recognition were self-indulgent fools. My hunger for fame was so great that I hounded my professors with poems and short stories until one of them secured publication for me in a small journal just so I would leave him alone. Armed with this early success—barely eighteen and published—which I announced to all and sundry, I spun a myth of wunderkind around myself. When this did not seem enough, I went further. I wrote letters of recommendation, reviews, blurbs for myself, signing them with invented names of critics and academics from around the world. Journals accepted my work thereafter not on its merit but because they were afraid if they didn't publish they would miss out on the phenomenon—me. If I were turned down, I would pursue the editor and make him articulate precisely why I had been rejected, then redraft my story—again and again if necessary—until he published it."

The light inside the bar turned from gray to lavender. Prudence was staring at me, her eyes excited. I went on, "But a writer's fame and an actor's fame are incomparable. A writer's audience is so much smaller. Fame for an actor is useful. Fame for a writer almost ensures the destruction of his talent. If fame comes at all for a writer, it should come posthumously."

"What good is that?" she said.

"I assure you," I said, "that whatever fame I have has been a burden to my work and not a boon. I suffer a greater crisis of confidence from success than I do from failure."

"Perhaps you're right," she said, "but isn't it a bit easy for you to say now? We will never know how you might have got on as an artist if you hadn't had the least bit of public encouragement."

Outside, the drizzle had become a downpour and several people came in off the street in an effort to stay dry. From behind the bar a large man with a bulbous nose called out, "We are not in Bethlehem and this is not a manger. We are in Rome and this is a bar. If you stay, you buy a drink."

I looked over at the barman, who shook his head at the growing crowd by the door and muttered loudly, "Wretches."

I realized that no one was going to have to die to go to Dante's shithole. We were already there.

After breakfast, Prudence and I took a cab to the studio, a series of hangar-like buildings along a couple of blocks. We were half an hour earlier than call time. None of the other actors had arrived yet, but the crew and staff were there. Prudence's dressing room was the size of a closet. She said she was just happy she didn't have to share it. Pushed up against the wall was a skinny chintz-covered chaise lounge with a scroll headrest, which we had to squeeze by sideways. I was immediately reminded of Letizia, the perfume salesgirl, and our brief encounter in the small backroom of her shop. Sex in tight spaces gave me a special frisson. For example, at a party, choosing among a bedroom, a bathroom, or a closet, I always selected the closet. The word *paradise,* after all, came from the Persian for a walled enclosure. It seemed that women tended to prefer a child's bedroom or a bathroom, but I prized having sex among the coats and shoes and hats, or in a pantry with the pungent mixture of food smells, or tangled up with brooms and mops while immersed in the strong odor of bottled cleaners. Almost no one would join me in the cleaning closet except the maid. In fact, when surveying a party for a potential playmate, I investigated the maid first. Maids were terribly obliging, often good-natured, presented no obvious complications (no husband, no other lover, no expectations for the future), and the next time I came across them, they were always glad to see me. All this to say that the size of Prudence's dressing room made me very keen to take her right then before her day of filming started. Our eyes met in the mirror as she was removing her hatpins.

"C'mon," she said. "I'll show you the set."

At times, especially in the beginning, I had caught myself confusing Gladys and Prudence, they resembled each other so closely. The sound of their voices was identical and they shared a delectable edge to their vernacular. Earlier in our dalliance, at a moment such as this, I might have cupped my hand on Prudence's breast or over the cheek of her buttock only to realize, as I observed her blush and retreat, that I had mistaken her for Gladys. My disorientation would unsettle me more than her rejection. Prudence and Gladys were by now distinct, and if Prudence had acquiesced in that moment to my will, the surprise could have rendered me limp.

We entered a sound stage where cameras and lights and microphones hovered over and around a large sitting room with an impressively realistic view of the Sabine hills. Windowpanes were broken and patched with wood. The floor was strewn with rubble, the walls pockmarked with holes. Furniture was broken, the upholstery ripped, and pieces of smashed china littered the floor.

"We're shooting in here today," Prudence said. "It's the final scene, when the sisters are reunited after the war in the family villa. Last week we did the scenes from early in the war, when the house was still intact. It took the set people nearly a week of work to wreck the place so perfectly."

———

Prudence played the Fascist younger sister of Isa Miranda, a spy for the Resistance, whose intelligence-gathering leads to the Allied forces' successful invasion of Sicily. Much of Italy's post-war picture-making was devoted to this sort of thing—trying to ameliorate the staggering damage Mussolini wrought upon the image of the Italian, not only in the hearts and minds of the rest of the world, but in ourselves. That Gladys and Prudence had become swept up in this effort, even if inadvertently, moved me deeply.

"Gladys and I always seem to be playing roles in which we are betraying someone or are being betrayed. Her new script is about a woman who seduces her sister's lover, then kills him."

We heard a door close loudly. "'If there is no betrayal, there is no story.' I'm sure I read that in one of your poems, Mr. Sabato." Striding toward us was Rocco Pompei, handsome, tall, with wispy blond hair and clear blue eyes. He wore brown suede shoes, tan gabardine slacks, and a bright yellow cashmere jacket. Dressed in a gray flannel suit and white turtleneck, I was a pigeon next to a peacock. I recognized him as the man Gladys had driven off with in the Alfa Romeo from Dino Duranti's party.

"She's so professional," he said, placing his body between me and Prudence, his back to her. "Always ready to work. Never forgets a line."

Prudence said, "It's a job."

"How rude of me," he said, taking a step backward so that he was now facing both of us. "We haven't met. I'm Rocco Pompei."

"Dante Sabato," I said, and we shook hands.

"Of course I know who you are," he said. "Prudence is a very lucky girl to have such an illustrious man for her very own."

"The luck is all mine," I said.

"Luck had nothing to do with it," Prudence said.

I remembered our first meeting at Tullio's, her ten-minute challenge to Gladys.

"Well, then, Prudence, congratulations." Turning to me, he said, "I am a great admirer of yours. Your poems are so visual, who needs the cinema? And I've read every review you've ever written. I can't say I agree with you often but your reviews are marvelously arrogant. What will it be for April's issue? *Christ in Concrete*? *East Side, West Side*? That Barbara Stanwyck's no looker but she's sure fuckable."

"Fuckable or unfuckable," Prudence said, "Stanwyck deserves to win Best Actress for *Sorry, Wrong Number*."

"Tut, tut. She isn't usually so naive," Rocco said. "Imagine using the word 'deserves' in this context. But that explains why you," he said to me, "chose Stanwyck for Best Actress—to please your pussycat. You must know she can't win. No one likes her, and, besides, Jane Wyman is the obvious choice. A deaf-mute girl is untouchable and therefore the one we all want to fuck. She'll win." Rocco lit a cigarette. For the first time since our exchange began, I thought there might just be some iota to like about Pompei. Prudence, of course, had given me no prior indication of what a prick this man could be.

Prudence said, "With that logic Olivia de Havilland should win for *The Snake Pit*."

———

Rocco sneered. "Crazy women you fuck for free. No one will admit to stooping that low. Hamlet doesn't bother with Ophelia once she's a nutcase—although I'm sure Olivier bothered with Jean Simmons when Vivien wasn't looking. No, I promise, Best Actress will be the untouchable."

"I've got to go to makeup and hair," Prudence said. I started to go with her.

Pompei said, "Stay with me, Dante, if I may call you that, while I plan out the morning's shots."

"I won't be long," Prudence said.

As soon as Prudence was gone, Rocco said, "We haven't slept together, in case you were wondering. It's not that I wouldn't. I've done her sister. Personally, I don't get the appeal." He was on the set now, thumbs together, forefingers toward heaven, making a frame. "Tullio said you were smitten," he added, shaking his head. "I just don't get it. Now, if you were doing both at the same time . . ." Rocco was repulsive but I could not object because so was I. His eye landed somewhere and he swore. He stamped out his cigarette and lit another. "This is all wrong. These windows are supposed to be French doors. We shot the whole first scene with them as windows but the sisters are supposed to exit through French doors in the closing shot." He hollered for someone named Gino.

I lit a cigarette. Rocco said, "When the crew starts to come in, I'm afraid you'll have to put that out." He stamped his own underfoot. "Only I am allowed to smoke on set. Otherwise, the smoke would be overwhelming and cloud the shot."

———

Gino showed up and Rocco yelled at him in a continuous stream interwoven with expletives about the doors, the cost, how they would have to shoot the whole first scene over again. During Rocco's diatribe, members of the cast and crew came timidly onto the set. Gino, in the fearful patter of a servant who was used to being beaten, told Pompei that it all could be fixed in the editing room. Rocco demanded to see the early rushes again immediately. He screamed that he didn't have time for this sort of imbecilic error that could cause his personal rack and ruin. He told Gino to tell the cast and crew that shooting would be delayed for at least a couple of hours while they sorted out the problem.

"And call Isa and tell her to get her ass down here. She's probably still in bed." He lowered his voice, but not so low that I couldn't hear. "That's what I get for sleeping with the help." The voice went up again. "By the time she gets down here we'll be ready to roll. And get the Vaseline. These doorknobs and brass lamps are glinting like flashbulbs. Do I have to do everything myself?" He lit another cigarette.

Rocco Pompei was a pompous ass, but I found myself feeling almost grateful to him. For a moment, while he prattled on, it was as if time had reversed and I was with Germana and Vanni while Silvio was giving one of his lectures, but this time I was included. We were all each other's tricks of the mind and Prudence was one more trick of mine. I knew that for Prudence and Gladys, too, Rocco and I and countless other men were tricks, stand-ins for their father, the man Prudence wanted to love, the man Gladys wanted to fuck.

—

Prudence walked in—costume, makeup, hair all done. "Give her the good news, Dante," Rocco said, then told her himself. "Shooting delayed two hours. Go on, get out of here." As we turned to go, Rocco quickly came over to us. He said, "You'll have to excuse the eccentric director act. The crew want it, need it, it's part of why they work for me. If I didn't do it, they'd be disappointed, wouldn't give everything they've got to me. I hope I didn't offend." He grabbed my hand and shook it. "Nice to have met you, Dante," he said. "Prudence, do me a favor and watch the hair. You've got two hours."

Prudence said, "Let's go to Testaccio. I've never been to the Protestant Cemetery. It's just across the river from here."

She grabbed her coat and hat from her dressing room and we headed toward the Ponte dell'Industria. The rain had stopped and the sun was battling its way through an army of dark clouds. *Amber* was a word frequently used to describe the color of the Tiber. *Cow-piss* worked just as well. As we crossed the river, a strong gust blew Prudence's hat off her head and up over the water. It hovered there for some time like a flying saucer before sailing down onto the dark yellow brew. We walked along some train tracks toward the cemetery. Prudence pulled her hair back and tied it up with a piece of colored string. The wind, still strong, caused strands of her hair to escape and leap about her face like ribbons around a Maypole. Above us loomed the Pyramid of Caius Cestius, a stunning monument to mediocrity. Caius Cestius was a minor Roman bureaucrat, but his tomb had managed to remain throughout the ages in an excellent state of preservation, its mere duration something to celebrate. A great dead writer or artist passes through periods in which it is fashionable to love him or hate him. During the dark periods there is considerable risk that his work will be removed from memory for all time. But mediocrity suffers no such fate because it raises no such passions. It endures. I had a very good chance, therefore, at the immortality shared by Caius, my compatriot in banality.

From an obscure street lined with warehouses and car garages, we entered the cemetery through a portal marked RESURRECTURIS. My first English cemetery had been the one in the center of Piazzale Donatello in Florence, where I kissed girls while leaning on the grave of Beatrice Shakespeare, a descendent of the bard, or while stretched across one of the Trollope tombs. I had also been to the English Cemetery in Rome many times before in order to worship at the graves of Shelley and Keats and pay tribute to the old heretic Gramsci, who died in prison the year I got out. Each time I visited I was surprised by how aesthetic death could be. Shelley himself had written of that graveyard: "It might make one in love with death, to think that one should be buried in so sweet a place." And Oscar Wilde had declared it "the holiest place in Rome." The gravestones, elaborate and varied, were arranged with the care of a prized menagerie. The grounds were perfectly manicured: the cypresses tall and proud, the grass combed, the violets a flourish of color. I wondered again how many in that graveyard had killed themselves—their sin neatly hushed and forgotten.

The graveyard was suitably silent except for the occasional toot from a train horn or the chirp of a sparrow. We wandered a while through the graves, passing an enormous angel draped over a tombstone and a monument with a bilingual explanation of how a woman lost both her daughter and husband in separate tragedies. We read names aloud—Thomas Jupe, Philippa Lemon, Thomas Twichen, Flora McDuffy, Tyrone Pile, Stephen Upright, and Emma Hatch—summoning them and their stories back from the dead.

We stopped in front of Keats's grave. Prudence read the inscription aloud:

THIS GRAVE
CONTAINS ALL THAT WAS MORTAL
OF A
YOUNG ENGLISH POET
WHO,
ON HIS DEATH BED
IN THE BITTERNESS OF HIS HEART,
at the malicious power of his enemies,
desired
these words to be engraved on his Tombstone
"HERE LIES ONE
WHOSE NAME WAS WRIT IN WATER"
FEB 24 1821

Next to Keats's grave was that of his companion, the painter Joseph Severn. The shape, size, and color of their tombstones matched—on Keats's the relief of a pen and paper, on Severn's a palette—and, fitting to a devoted companion, on Severn's grave was Keats's name, but the opposite was not true. I wanted Prudence always by my side, and like Keats with Severn, my name etched upon her grave. The inequality of it mattered not at all to me. Desire excluded democracy. I considered pulling Prudence into the shadow of a mausoleum and making love to her. I had done so with other women brought here at the conclusion of my standard seduction tour of literary Rome, but, naturally, Prudence showed no interest in joining my graveyard collection.

We headed over to the newer part of the cemetery near the ancient Aurelian wall, where Shelley lay. I read his inscription—three lines from *The Tempest*—which was briefer than Keats's and more tragic in its hopefulness.

Nothing of him that doth fade,
But doth suffer a sea-change
Into something rich and strange

"Would you ever like to return to America?" Prudence asked.

"Return?" I asked.

"Yes, go back and visit sometime with me."

"I've never been," I said. I remembered Germana, Vanni and myself making plans to sail to New York, buy an old Model T Roadster and drive across the country to Los Angeles.

"All those translations and you have never set foot in America? In your reviews, you are always pointing out geographical inconsistencies and anachronisms. I was sure you had been. You must come with me then."

"I am afraid," I said, pushing a wisp of hair out of her eyes and enjoying the futility of my gesture, "if we go to America, you might not come back."

She smiled and said, "It's possible."

We walked silently for a while among the graves.

"I did almost go once," I said, "with Tullio."

⁓

When I was released from the crumbling castle that was my prison in October, 1938, Tullio was waiting for me outside the gates. It was a bright warm day and he was a welcome sight. I immediately forgot the suspicion I harbored that Tullio had given the police the address of the cat- and cockroach-infested basement in Trastevere, home of the anti-Fascist poster and pamphlet press. The evening of the raid Tullio had insisted that we meet but I changed my mind at the last minute and went back to that hovel of well-meaning rebels, where I was not permitted to wallow in anything bourgeois, including personal tragedy. I was sure now, though, that it was Tullio who had managed to obtain my discharge.

My three years of exile in the southern region of Basilicata had been uneventful and relatively comfortable. I had been able to work. I translated and wrote at a steady pace, having been permitted paper and pen for a few hours twice a week. I was well-fed, had a large room, and was allowed to wash once a week and to keep my head and beard shaven to avoid lice. I had no access to newspapers or the radio, a silly deprivation since the press was controlled by Mussolini. Still, news from the outside world filtered in. The day after I arrived in early October, 1935, I learned of the war with Ethiopia. A chorus of church bells and sirens sang throughout the day. The guards said that we had been forced to retaliate after being viciously attacked. When, some time later, I was told by Carmelo, one of the guards, that the Ethiopians were unanimously hailing us for bringing justice and the virtues of western civilization to their country, I gave my best effort at a guffaw.

I was permitted as many novels and books of poetry as I liked—most of them sent by my father—since works of the imagination were not yet perceived by the authorities as a threat. The fact that most of the books I received were in English caused minimal concern. In 1935, we were still formally on good terms with the British. The chief warden barely glanced at Huxley's *Brave New World,* but *The Autobiography of Alice B. Toklas* was initially forbidden. I explained that the book was about a rich American lesbian who liked European art.

"Stein is a Jewish name," the warden observed.

"It is also a common German name, like Rossi or Bianchi here," I countered.

Mussolini had been sending out mixed messages regarding ethnicity and race. He ridiculed the concept of pure races and had denied that a "Jewish problem" existed in Italy. Yet by the end of my stay in Basilicata, Mussolini had published his anti-Jewish, anti-Arab, and anti-African "Manifesto of Racial

Scientists," had instituted a discrimination policy against employing Jews, and had outlawed Jewish teachers in the schools. Shortly before I was released, he denied all Italian Jews their civil rights, and the worst had yet to come. In the end, the chief warden let me have Stein's book.

After the Italian army began fighting in Spain against the republicans, a guard taunted me saying I would never get out of prison now that my anti-Fascist colleagues had joined the fight against Franco. "Mussolini calls this treason," he said. "All Italian prisoners captured in Spain are to be shot dead." The guards clearly loved the Duce for having made their country a significant player in the world theater, but it was apparent from furtive remarks that none of them liked Hitler, and—after he annexed Austria—even less so.

But these scraps of news comprised very little of my life during those three years. I never learned the identity of any of my fellow prisoners. I don't think we were more than twenty, since the castle was small and each person was kept alone. We ate in our rooms and were given fifteen minutes each day outside in an enclosed courtyard. My room looked onto the courtyard, so I could see who was out there, but I didn't recognize anyone. No one appeared to be ill-treated, just bored or sad or crazy. I worked on my translations in the morning, on my novels in the afternoon, and on my poetry in the evening, memorizing what I would write down when granted pen and paper. Carmelo brought me my meals, which were feasts compared to the thin soup and stale crusts I'd had while at the Regina Coeli, where the only protein had been an occasional worm.

Eventually he began to linger in my room and we would talk. Most subjects were off-limits—current events, family, and, of course, politics were out. He asked about my work, although he really wasn't interested in literature. He couldn't understand why I would bother translating a novel from one language into another—the whole enterprise being a double exercise in uselessness. I didn't think he was wrong. I told him the minute art started to become useful it was no longer art. It could teach and preach and have a strong point of view. It could try to persuade and change minds. But when that became its goal it was nothing but propaganda.

Carmelo said, "I'd rather go to the pictures."

Carmelo, it turned out, was addicted to the cinema. He hesitated at first to tell me about the movies he went to see because he was afraid the chief warden wouldn't approve, since films were forbidden to the prisoners, but he was even more concerned that I might find it cruel to be told about all the wonders I was missing. I assured him that I enjoyed hearing a plot recounted, a character sketched, or a room, a city, a landscape depicted.

"My words," he would bemoan, "are miserable and can't begin to give you the magnificence of the pictures."

I had to reassure Carmelo that I was content with his descriptions, that his words became lively images in my head.

Horror films and thrillers were Carmelo's preferred genres. He told me in detail the plots of *The Bride of Frankenstein, The Werewolf of London, The Invisible Man, The Lady Vanishes, The Pearls of the Crown, The Man Who Knew Too Much, The Crime of Monsieur Lange, Crack-up, The 39 Steps, The Informer,* and *Pépé le Moko.* He would see an adventure film now and again, such as *Mutiny on the Bounty, Scipio the African,* and *The Adventures of Robin Hood.* He avoided war movies but saw *The Grand Illusion.* He hated musicals but watched *Top Hat.* Occasionally, he would see a melodrama or love story and once gave me a vibrant portrait of Bette Davis in *Jezebel.* He went to *Becky Sharp,* he said, just to see the new trichrome technicolor, and to *Snow White and the Seven Dwarfs* to find out what all the fuss was surrounding this Walt Disney fellow. He didn't like comedies but laughed all the way through *A Night at the Opera.* All government employees were invited to special screenings of Leni Riefenstahl's *Triumph of the Will* and *Olympia,* both of which he liked, even though he said they had no real plot. And as the term *miscegenation* began to roll off tongues like soccer balls rolling off Italian feet, Carmelo saw Guido Brignone's *Under the Southern Cross,* a propaganda film about an Italian man who has a sexual liaison with a mixed-race African woman. He didn't comment much on the film but told me that such a relationship had become a criminal offense.

At first, I felt I could stay in that dank room in a dilapidated castle in the south for the rest of my life. I felt I belonged there. The fact that I was a political prisoner was ironic, as I was apolitical. More than apolitical, I was amoral. I would fight for a cause I thought just only if I happened to muster the energy for it, knowing that change occurring today would likely be undone tomorrow. I might, at times, have held strong convictions but I knew those convictions could be entirely misguided. I was an armchair action man who would get up out of his chair once in a while to save the universe. Nothing was more diverting in life than having a little fun with fate, and nothing was more appalling than watching fate take its course. But perhaps *fate* was just another word for *character*. If a child was drowning, there were those who would choose to dive in, risking death; there were those who would choose not to dive in and live with the consequences, and there were those who wouldn't notice the drowning child in the first place. I fit into the latter category, but every so often I might catch a glimpse of the child and act. This is how I wound up in prison in Basilicata.

One result of being there was that my suicide fantasies all but disappeared. I would sometimes think about hanging myself with shoelaces or ripped-up sheets, but the Fascists had done so much hanging that I found it difficult to consider with any real enthusiasm. By the third year, penance had worn off as a means of tolerating my circumstances and I began to feel a growing urgency. I needed to leave those walls, that place. I needed to be free again, if only to die. As Freud had written, "Life loses interest when the highest stake in the game of living, life itself, may not be risked." It was at this late stage of my incarceration that I had my only seriously unpleasant moment with Carmelo.

One day after he brought me lunch and before I had even finished, he asked, for the first time, if I might like a cup of coffee. I looked at him. He had brown eyes, a square chin, lips so thin they seemed non-existent. He was in his thirties, overweight, and bathed less than I did. I imagined he didn't have much success with women but had been engaged for a decade to a skinny, pimply girl, the extent of their sex life tongueless goodnight kisses. He was surely a master masturbator. From the look in his eye that day, I saw that he was terribly anxious. I declined his offer, explaining that I had grown unaccustomed to coffee but appreciated his asking.

He said slowly, and in a deeper voice than usual, "They want the names of your anti-Fascist friends. If I get them, they will promote me and release you."

I hesitated. I was desperate. When I left the Regina Coeli for Basilicata, written on my papers under the heading *Term of Incarceration* was the word *Unknown*. I needed to know. I was not amenable to a stint as the Count of Monte Cristo. So when Carmelo asked me to betray my comrades, I hesitated. I figured that those who had worked with me at the press were probably already in jail or safely in hiding. I would be risking little, securing for myself everything. I took a deep breath. I looked again at Carmelo. He was sweating and his eyes were pleading and full of pain.

"I told them," he said, "that you had refused. I said that you swore on your mother's honor that if I asked again you would hang yourself."

We were quiet for a time and then he told me the plot of Josef von Sternberg's *The Devil Is a Woman,* starring Marlene Dietrich.

By my last year in prison, I had the suspicion that Carmelo was going farther afield to find cinemas playing a broader range of movies than those offered locally. When I was back in the outside world, I learned that the government had banned the importation of most American films early in 1938 in order to boost the Italian film industry. Pictures already in circulation were in high demand and more difficult to find, particularly in remote areas. Whenever I saw one of the films Carmelo had described to me while I was in prison I became confused, feeling as though I had already seen another, better version of the picture.

One afternoon, without warning, I was summoned into the chief warden's office. A limited amnesty had been declared and I was free to go. Evidently, it behooved him to give me some parting words of advice. He told me Fascism was an inevitability and if I tried to fight it I would only find myself back in prison.

"I assure you it won't be so snug a turn the next time," he said. As I turned to go, he warned, "Things have changed out there."

I left the building in a rhapsodic daze. Tullio, looking like an angel from a hardboiled heaven, was leaning against a divine driving machine, the smoke from his cigarette rising in a halo over his head.

"It's the latest Figoni and Falaschi Roadster." He spoke to me as if I were his kid brother being picked up after a couple of weeks away on summer holiday, not a man who had been in solitary confinement for three years. "They only made ten of them," he said, as I stood in awe before the car industry's interpretation of a diva. "I've nicknamed her 'The Big Cunt,'" he winked.

She was all voluptuous curves, her white wheels entirely enclosed, her headlights integrated into the fenders. She had a split windshield. Her roof folded like a geisha's fan, disappearing entirely into her interior. She wore black with silver chrome trim that accentuated her rounded shape.

"This baby," said Tullio, "was sculpted by the fingers of the wind."

I stood there understanding for the first time what it meant to want to fuck a machine. I then glimpsed my withered self in her shine. I hadn't cared about my bony body or my shaven head until I saw it caught in the Big Cunt's glow. As we drove off, I looked back at my castle, where a group of guards—including Carmelo—had gathered at a window to stare at the car, their eyes full of lust. I could tell by Carmelo's expression that he was happy for me and proud to have been my jailer.

Tullio said, "Let's go to America."

The Big Cunt's top was down and Tullio's hand swept across a landscape populated by peasants and the downtrodden. "Why should they be the only ones who get to go?" he asked. "The Americans will get the wrong idea about us."

We spent the night at the Villa Cimbrone, in Ravello, where Tullio's family had a suite of rooms. We ate dinner on a terrace overlooking the Amalfi coast and the gulf of Salerno with a small group of glamorous types including, off in a corner, Greta Garbo and the composer Leopold Stokowsky, who were obviously in the throes of a new love affair. Even Tullio left them alone. Given my appearance, I was glad he was not in the mood to socialize. Perhaps it was because of my appearance he contained his usual gregariousness. The next day we drove on, stopping in Naples for a pizza.

"They say," Tullio exhorted, "that the best pizza in all of Italy is in New York. In less than ten days' time, we could be standing in the shadow of the Empire State Building."

Back in Rome, I fell into a deep depression, getting out of bed only to go visit my parents in Florence for a couple of days. Suicide seemed too ambitious a thought. One could have explained my condition as the result of my incarceration, or as a delayed reaction to the emptiness left by Germana's and Vanni's absence, or as a reflection of the larger geo-political angst—most of those I knew were in prison, in exile, or in denial. Last I heard, Gadda was hiding in an attic in Florence and Moravia had fled to Anacapri. Many were out of work and unable to leave the country. No one trusted anyone else. I was a pariah to all who knew where I had been for the last three years and why. And the gears of war were nearing full throttle. But none of these considerations, separately or together, quite explained why I couldn't get out of bed. My paralysis came from an all-consuming fear that if I did get out of bed something fatal would happen to me. A brick would fall on my head, lightning would strike me down, I'd be diagnosed with a deadly disease, a speeding car would smash into me. I stayed in bed to stay alive until the threat had passed and I would once again be able to kill myself.

Tullio came to visit me every day. He tried to get me interested in work. He'd taken the translations I had finished while in prison (*The Autobiography of Alice B. Toklas, Moll Flanders,*

Of Mice and Men, and *Double Indemnity),* two collections of
poems and a novel, and sent them off to Astolfo Falsetta, who
owned a small and prestigious publishing house in Milan. Falsetta had categorically declined to publish everything I had
sent him before, but this time he had accepted the lot, despite
the fact that the publication of translations had recently been
curtailed by the government. With the birth of the Ministry
of Popular Culture, censorship, author blacklisting, and book
banning were pursued with greater zeal. Falsetta had told Tullio that my novel and the Steinbeck might have to wait but
that he didn't think he'd have trouble with the poetry. I asked
why Falsetta had changed his mind about my work and Tullio
said the publisher's only comment had been, "The boy should
go to prison more often."

With the regularity of a cuckoo clock, Tullio would chime,
"Let's go to America, Dante. Let's get on the *Queen Mary* and
sail for New York. We'll take The Big Cunt with us," he offered.
"Even America will be impressed with her."

Tullio would bring me English newspapers. Every so often
I looked at the social pages. A baronet had married a Ziegfeld
girl. A peer had been arrested for embezzlement. A rare flower
had been stolen from Kew Gardens. A young duchess, thrown
from her horse during a fox hunt in Kent, had broken her collarbone, pelvis, and several ribs. One day I saw a photograph of
two young men, and a short notice announcing W. H. Auden
and Christopher Isherwood's departure for China. They both
looked so nonchalant, Isherwood with a sly schoolboy grin,
Auden, smoking a cigarette, his face betraying exhaustion at all

the fools he had already suffered in his short life. It was Auden who finally got me out of bed. If Auden could muster it to go to China, I could drag myself out of bed to go to America.

Tullio, I decided, was an ideal traveling companion for me, beginning with the fact that I didn't trust him. He was beautiful and charming and could surprise me with his intelligence. He made thumbnail assessments of our friends and acquaintances that would put a psychoanalyst to shame. He seemed to comprehend the underlying motivations of any social interaction and he used this knowledge to keep many beholden to him. Almost no one said no to Tullio, including myself, as he continued to wage his campaign for our voyage to New York. He assured me his father had fixed things with the government, that I'd been given a clean slate and would have no trouble traveling.

"Mussolini himself was arrested many times for subversive activity," Tullio said. "It's a rite of passage for all great men."

When I brought up the issue of money, knowing grand sums would not be forthcoming from Falsetta, Tullio said he would get the money from his father and if I felt it necessary to pay him back I could do so over time. He had an answer for every objection, and underlying all protests I truthfully had just one: Tullio was exhausting to be with. He talked incessantly and it was tiring to be continually separating out from his discourse the seeds he was planting about this person or that subject he would exploit in some ingenious way in the future. When Tullio announced he had booked first-class passage for the two of us on the *Queen Mary* out of Southampton in mid-November, I dismissed all my reservations and my spirits immediately lifted. Tullio told me that he had secured us transit visas through France so we could go to London a week before sailing. We would spend a few days seeing the sights and brushing up our British accents—Americans went crazy for a British accent, he said. We would then spend a month in New York before heading for our ultimate destination: Hollywood. I was happy to be a bar of soap sliding around Tullio's palms.

I went to Florence to tell my parents about the trip. The situation in Europe was highly unstable and it was no time to be gallivanting, they said, especially given where I had been for the last three years. I think they were more concerned about my going to London than to the United States, since Mussolini was making it clear that he held Britain increasingly in contempt. In the Italian newspapers, England was painted as a Dickensian world of poverty and decadence without art or literature or scholarship. The English were described as xenophobic, materialistic, and intellectually inferior, not to mention their lack of virility. Given their weak nature, the citizens of the British Isles, it was declared, would surely succumb to Communism. My parents begged me, if I insisted on this plan, to seek passage on an Italian liner such as the *Rex* or the *Augustus,* since Italian submarines had been torpedoing neutral ships suspected of carrying supplies to the Spanish Republicans. I had, in fact, suggested to Tullio that we take the *Rex* from Genoa as it would be cheaper and easier, but he had said that he didn't want to arrive in New York on what was perceived to be an immigrant ship, despite her numerous and spacious decks for games and sunbathing with swimming pools and even lido-like beaches. Arriving in New York on a British ship, he said, cut a far better image.

To arrive on an airship would have been the grandest of all, Tullio claimed, telling me how he had dreamed of showing up in America on the Graf Zeppelin. But the media hysteria that had accompanied the Hindenburg disaster had put an end to luxury passenger airship travel. I was in Basilicata at the time but had since seen the photographs and film footage of the great ellipse balloon burning across the sky like a comet, passengers leaping from the fireball into midair.

"A total of thirteen people died in the disaster," Tullio commented. "The *Titanic* sank, killing 1,513 people, but since nobody saw it happen ocean liners reign on. The word is to a picture as an arrow is to a megaton bomb. Dante, my friend, you are in the wrong business."

I assured my parents we'd be in London only for a few days before sailing. My father did not look well, his skin as gray as his hair. He told me that if there was nothing he could do to keep me from going then he was glad for me, that going to America had always been a dream of his. I had never thought of my father as a man who had dreams, and I suddenly felt hideously betrayed. I had grown up hearing how the world beyond our city was a sorrowful place without culture or custom. Florence meant the pinnacle of achievement in all realms of life—art, architecture, finance, silver, clay, bronze, marble, landscape, food, beauty—we did it best. Most Florentines never ventured beyond the city limits. The rivalry with other Tuscan towns such as Siena, Pisa, Lucca or Arezzo made it sacrilege to set foot in those places, and Rome was considered so barbaric it might as well have been Alexandria or Auckland. This geographic and cultural snobbery was the purported reason why I went to Rome and why I felt suffocated in my hometown. But if I were forced to find the real reason that I rejected my birthplace, I would lay the blame at the feet of my father. Although I appreciated his confession of a desire for a more adventurous life, it only served to confirm my sense that he withheld everything of himself from me.

My mother told me to pay no attention to my father, that he wasn't feeling well and pleaded with me to go close up Aunt Pia's apartment in Rome and then to return home to Florence until things settled down.

"Since Vanni came home, he's doing well enough," my mother said.

My father shot her a glance that said not to bring the subject up. He had written to me in Basilicata about Vanni, who had moved back to Florence after Germana's death. Vanni's parents had asked my father to find their son a job as a clerk in the bookshop where my father worked, which he did, but even being surrounded by books all day had not relieved Vanni's sadness. In his letter, my father wrote that he understood my capacity to help was limited, given where I was, but would I write to Vanni and try to encourage him to go out with some nice girls. "God knows," my father wrote, "I know what it is like to lose someone beloved. You feel as if you have died too. But one must carry on, at least superficially, for the sake of others. His poor mother and father are distraught."

I hoped my father might be alluding to a secret lover of his own who had died tragically, but I knew he was referring to the loss of my infant brother Giovanni. I had written my father back saying that I could do nothing for Vanni, that we had fallen out and were not in communication, although it was not entirely true. Nothing had ever verbally transpired between me and Vanni that might be construed as a falling-out. We simply hadn't spoken to each other. But if I had had any inkling of contacting Vanni, my father's letter extinguished it. I would neither be agent for nor recipient of anyone else's "superficial" attention, which is what I had suffered my entire life from my parents.

As I was leaving Florence, my father said, "If you go to America, then, like Toscanini, stay until all of this has blown over." I heard in his plea a desire to be free of me once and for all. Besides, I was not fleeing my country or the grim situation facing Europe, I was going on an extended holiday. It did occur to me, through the haze of anger toward my father, that this visit might be the last I would see of him.

A few days later, Tullio and I and our trunks were on a sleeper to London. We had left the Big Cunt behind but Tullio had replaced her with a Pathé Baby, his intention being to document our trip on film. After settling in at Brown's Hotel, in Mayfair, Tullio and I and the Baby toured the sites—Leicester Square, Covent Garden, Bloomsbury, Fleet Street, Soho, Hampstead Heath, and, on my insistence, a trip around the corner from our hotel to Curzon Street to meet Heywood Hill, who had sent me in Rome and even in Basilicata many books from his bookshop. He was a gentle, nervous man who seemed to be in possession of a thousand secrets. He bade me bon voyage with five books—*Brighton Rock, Rebecca, Mrs. Pettigrew Lives for a Day, I'm a Stranger Here Myself, Captain Horatio Hornblower*—one for each day of our crossing.

On our excursions about town, because of the Baby, we were often surrounded by a small crowd of onlookers. In that crowd, I saw the same face many times—it was a tired face, sunken in by a combination of alcohol and punches. We had expected to be followed and would probably have been disappointed if we hadn't been, but I did wonder if Tullio might have other uses for the camera. Of course, Tullio wanted me to wonder just such a thing. It enhanced his aura of mystique. We all had ways of hiding in plain sight. I was drawn to those who did it best.

The fact that we were Italians did not make us particularly welcome in Britain—there was some talk of the Italian army attacking the British in Egypt—but we weren't snubbed, either. Mussolini was riding a wave of begrudging popularity after his supposed peacemaking efforts at Munich, and he had made repeated overtures to the British with his "pacts of friendship." In Britain, Mussolini was seen as a ridiculous egomaniac who was, like a child with a loaded gun, potentially quite dangerous. And his infatuation with Hitler was disturbing. Tullio and I spoke English well enough to confuse anyone as to our origins, but Tullio's dark beauty often gave us away. He might have been

Spanish, but, given the civil war, not many Spaniards were traveling.

London was abuzz with news of Orson Welles's radio broadcast in America of H. G. Wells's *War of the Worlds*. Worries about the real war brewing in Europe were put aside for a while to laugh at the gullible and innocent Americans ("a virginal quality," Gertrude Stein had called it) who had been panic-stricken believing they had been invaded by aliens from Mars.

Five days into our stay in London, two days before we were to set sail on the *Queen Mary* for New York, I received a telegram from my mother saying that my father had died of heart failure the previous night. I took the next train home, leaving behind Tullio and the Baby and my chance to see the great America. I felt only somewhat rueful. The excursion had always seemed ill-timed to me, although for Tullio it turned out to be perfectly timed. After the funeral, I went back to Rome. Six months later we were at war, Hitler's Germany our ally. Tullio had sailed to New York and made his way to Los Angeles, where he worked as an apprentice for Louis B. Mayer. Tullio's mother, it turned out, was Jewish.

eight

The Aeolians

Last night, Prudence farted while we made love. I have often done it myself and have heard and smelled the farts of many women during sex. It's just that with Prudence, sex was such a delicate matter. Everything about it seemed to vex her. And yet I had taken what Gladys once told me about Prudence very much to heart. It was Gladys's conviction that when Prudence had sex she enjoyed it more than Gladys and me combined. Initially, I found this theory hard to believe but I had witnessed proof of its plausibility. When Prudence gave in to herself and to me, her pleasure was boundless, and if I weren't awestruck by her transformation, I might have been jealous of the ecstatic heights she was able to achieve.

Our first night on a yacht taking us to the Aeolian Islands was one such night. Gladys had been on location there for a couple of weeks already, costarring in a film with Anna Magnani. We were tucked away in bed after a trying day at sea and Prudence was undulating in synchronization to her second orgasm when the snappy gurgle of trapped air rang out like machine-gun fire. Prudence's pink cheeks turned crimson and her body became rigid. I was frozen with indecision, not knowing whether to ignore her most delicious fart or to somehow take notice of the gaseous egress.

With Prudence, I reasoned, it was better to approach the subject directly. She liked to think of herself as someone who faced the world head on, rarely became embarrassed, and had little to hide. My paralysis set in because Prudence's image of herself, which I adored, had little to do with reality. Prudence's personality was riddled with subterfuge, and what made it so attractive was that she didn't seem to be aware of how deceived she was by herself. If, for example, she could manage not to acknowledge my relationship with Gladys, how could I possibly acknowledge her fart?

The yacht in which this bedroom drama unfolded belonged to Tullio. He had bought it from the French actress Rita La Roy who, in a second career, peddled yachts. During the war, all private seagoing vessels had been commandeered first by the Italian navy and later by the Americans. According to Tullio, who heard it from La Roy, the luxury boats were being auctioned off for a pittance all over Europe because no one knew what else to do with them. La Roy, glad to abandon Hollywood, saw an opportunity.

I disliked boats and tried never to go out in one. Along with the villa in Castiglioncello, Aunt Pia had left me a small sailboat and a dinghy, but I never used either. They sat in a corner of the garden, a pair of squirrels having made a love nest in the dingy from pieces of the sailboat's sail. I suffered from seasickness. Worse was my sea phobia, which was much like my fear of heights. I had an almost irresistible compulsion to throw myself among the sea's silky caresses.

Tullio's boat, *La Speranza*, was a miniature Versailles set afloat. More precisely, it was a seventy-five-foot ketch-rigged Burma-teak gentleman's motorsailer. Above deck, sails unfurled, it was majestic. Below deck, it sparkled. Polished brass sconces, flush-mounted and fitted with faux candles, illuminated the way past five sumptuous staterooms. Hand-carved moldings adorned the walls in the dining room, salon, and library. Three full bathrooms promised I could be sick in perfect privacy. Despite the posh comfort and sheer size of *La Speranza*, while below I felt I had been buried alive. While above, it was as if I had been jettisoned into gravityless space, to float in eternal nothingness, my stomach forever in upheaval.

At first the view had helped, but for most of the day we were looking at the monotonous trinity of sea, horizon, sky for 360 degrees. I considered every cloud a blessing. After translating *Moby Dick* in my youth, I could envision sailing around "the watery parts of the world" myself. Now that I was spending time on the water, try as I might I had yet to know what Ishmael claimed everyone knew—that meditation and water were wedded. Possibly because I was accustomed to spending long stretches alone, meditation was an activity I deplored, even when physically fit, leading as it did to the contemplation of uncomfortable questions such as: Would I be able to give Gladys up if Prudence asked? No, for me panic remained water's bride. My one consolation was that having sex in our berth was much like having sex in a coffin, something I had always wanted to try.

Fausto, *La Speranza*'s captain, had a big barrel chest, a dimpled chin, and curly brown hair. Pino, her first mate, was slight and delicate, with pale skin and coal black hair. His cloudy green eyes were difficult to look into for very long. Tullio had found his seamen near the docks in Naples, in a seedy bar where sailors were known to congregate. Fausto and Pino had been in the navy together during the war. After accepting the job, they had flipped a coin to determine who would be captain. It was reminiscent of the scene in *The Lady from Shanghai*, when Everett Sloane goes to a sailors' hiring hall and attempts to employ Orson Welles as the boatswain on his yacht. It occurred to me that it was just as likely that Tullio had picked Fausto and Pino from among the extras who hung around Cinecittà day in and day out hoping for work. From wherever they hailed, Prudence and I were at their mercy.

We had left Civitavecchia the day before—a warm morning in late June, the sun blazing by nine o'clock, the sea flat as a mirror, our sails quiet. For a moment, I imagined myself Jay Gatsby in my white linen suit, blue canvas shoes, dark glasses, and straw fedora, but my nausea demanded I remember myself. Once underway, Prudence and I sat in two deck chairs—I with my eyes closed squeezing her hand as if I were on a roller coaster, she returning my grasp with one hand while in the other she held Malcolm Lowry's *Under the Volcano*. I had also given her E. V. Rieu's translation of the *Odyssey*, which arrived in the mail from Heywood Hill the week before. I was reading the manuscript of my new novel one last time before handing it over to my publisher, Astolfo Falsetta.

Falsetta had come to Rome on a rainy day in late April "to see how I was getting along." Since I had known him, never had Astolfo concerned himself with how an author was "getting along." Max Perkins he was not. He cared nothing for his writers' creative process. He never did any editing or made verbal suggestions for improving the text. When you gave a manuscript to Astolfo, he would touch it only to read it. When he had finished, he offered little in the way of praise or criticism. Instead, he simply informed you that he had read the book and that it would be shipped to bookstores on a certain date. After the book was published, he never encouraged his writers to write another book. He was glad to receive the next but had no expectations. So when I found him on my doorstep, having journeyed from Milan to ask how I was "getting along," I became anxious. Since he began publishing my work in 1938, I had met him four or five times. In physical appearance he was unchanged—a short, thin man with a salt-and-pepper mustache underneath an aquiline nose. His eyes were small, yellowish, and reptilian. No matter how much I studied his face I could never tell what he was thinking.

"Come in," I said. It was before lunch and I was still in my pajamas.

"I won't stay long," he said, coming into the apartment. He carried no umbrella and didn't wear a hat. He was soaked, rain dripping from the tip of his sharp nose. I offered him a bathrobe, which he refused, but he did make use of a tea towel I gave him. I took him into the library, where he admired my aunt's collection of paintings. I told him it would take me no time to make us coffee.

"I don't drink coffee," he said.

"An aperitif before lunch then?" I asked.

"I don't drink alcohol," he said.

"I'm sure if I'd known these things about you," I said, "I would never have allowed you to publish my work."

He didn't smile. "Tullio tells me you're almost finished with the new book."

"The court spy is never to be trusted," I said.

"I will need a finished manuscript by August. I must publish by December to be eligible for the prizes. Even then it will be tight."

I relaxed. "Prizes are like democracy," I said. "They promote the mediocre. Worse, they tell bad writers they are good and good writers they are bad. They are the antithesis of what they claim to be. They are discouraging. Chamomile tea, perhaps?"

He ignored my offer. "They sell books."

I pulled open the shutters in the living room to a wall of gray. "When I win a prize," I told him, "I swear on my mother's grave I will never write another word. Inevitably, I do so knowing I am betraying her."

"I hardly need to tell you that a writer betrays everyone sooner or later, his mother first and foremost. The better the writer, the sooner it happens. I need your manuscript by the first of August," he said, and left.

Like doctors and priests, a publisher had something of god in him and was not easily defied. Since our meeting, I had done what I could to meet his deadline, which included bringing the manuscript on my yachting holiday.

Lunch on *La Speranza* consisted of prosciutto, pecorino, tomatoes, olive paste, and a bottle of *falanghina*. I nibbled on bread and cheese, hoping it might improve my general state. While we were eating, Pino said, "The Aeolian Islands are an odd destination. Not much there except volcanoes and a prison or two. And the Tyrrhenian sea is known for rough water and sudden squalls."

I stopped trying to eat and closed my eyes.

Fausto said, "Don't listen to him. We were stationed on Sicily. Those islands are paradise on earth. You almost expect to see Adam and Eve frolicking in a cove."

"Not for long," I said.

To me the Aeolian Islands were a place of Homeric invention. I was never completely convinced that they existed—and in some senses they didn't. Fausto had told me that three of the seven were uninhabitable—Alicudi, Filicudi, and Vulcano—and Panarea did not have electricity. The others had tiny populations surviving on the bare minimum. The advent of two feature films—*Vulcano* and *Stromboli*—now being shot on these islands would change things forever. Our destination, Lipari, was where most of *Vulcano*, the film Gladys was in, would be made. The picture's eponymous island lay southeast of Lipari but was deemed too inhospitable a location, without plumbing or electricity, its atmosphere saturated with a sulfur stench. Only a few key scenes would actually take place there. Originally, we had meant to go to Lipari by train and ferry. That boat ride would have been mercifully short. But when Prudence mentioned our journey to Tullio, he had insisted we take *La Speranza.*

"It's a pity I can't come with you," Tullio had said. "You'll be sailing into the most ferocious battle since Zeus and Hera fought over Io."

He was referring to the saga Anna Magnani, Roberto Rossellini, and Ingrid Bergman had been playing out in every tabloid worldwide. The curtain rose on this extravaganza when Ingrid Bergman saw Roberto Rossellini's *Open City* and sent him a telegram calling his film brilliant and hinting that she wanted to work with him. Rossellini, lover of his leading lady Anna Magnani, responded immediately to the communiqué and arranged to meet with Ingrid alone in Paris. Rossellini returned to Rome from Paris and continued working on a feature idea with his cousin Renzo Avanzo, owner of Panaria Film, a small production company known for its documentaries about the Aeolian Islands. Rossellini had appreciated the visual potential of the raw and violent landscape of the "undiscovered" islands, home to Vulcan, the smith God, and Aeolus, the God of the winds, and had begun to write a Magnani vehicle with Renzo.

Next Rossellini visited Bergman and her husband at their Beverly Hills home. Once back in Rome, he cut all ties with both Magnani and Avanzo. *Variety* soon reported that Rossellini would direct a picture, bankrolled by Howard Hughes, set on a volcanic island. The title of the picture: *Stromboli, Land of God.* Magnani lost no time in joining up with the co-jilted Avanzo, who quickly came up with his own script, entitled *Vulcano* and pitched as "a story of passion and blood culminating in an underwater duel." The climax, in fact, had Magnani, ex-prostitute returned home in shame, avenging her sister (Gladys) by severing the air hose of the island's Lothario as he dove for sponges. Magnani watched as sharks devoured his body, then tossed herself into the crater of Vulcano's volcano.

Avanzo's wife Uberta Visconti, Luchino Visconti's sister, got David O. Selznick involved in the project. Selznick brought in the German American William Dieterle to direct, and loaned Rossano Brazzi, currently under contract to him in Hollywood, to play the male lead. Dieterle hired Erskine Caldwell to translate Avanzo's script into English. Even though Anna Magnani would play the female lead if it was the last thing she did on this earth, the new script was circulated in Hollywood to create buzz. Hedy Lamarr, Joan Crawford, Gene Tierney, and Greta Garbo, who was considering coming out of retirement, were all offered the lead. *Variety* quoted Garbo as saying, "Great script, but I refuse to end my career by killing a man in so inelegant a fashion."

After a few days of shooting non-location scenes at Cinecittà, Dieterle had had enough of Anna the Terrible's stomping off the set, screaming at underlings, and so on. Not about to allow that kind of prima donna behavior on his set, Dieterle told Magnani he might replace her. Myrna Loy, who had been living in Italy for some months, was much mentioned in the press as the potential substitute. Fueled as Magnani was by the desire for retribution, she became docile as a lamb, announcing to the press that *Vulcano* would be a classic—as great as *Amore* or *Paisà*—and promising the performance of her life. Magnani and the money brokers now behind the film, were determined that *Vulcano* would be in the cinemas before *Stromboli,* come hell or high water. Both film crews had already colonized their respective islands and were racing neck and neck to finish first. Some even wondered if all these antics were a carefully planned publicity stunt for both movies. Whatever the case, the fray had thrown Gladys into the limelight and her stock rose considerably.

Prudence explained to Fausto and Pino as they ate lunch the story of the rival pictures and Gladys's involvement. "Gladys got the part at the last minute. Geraldine Brooks had been cast but she got pregnant and pulled out."

Pino touched my hand and said, "Closing your eyes makes the nausea worse. Focus on the horizon and think about apples."

I followed his instructions. Both Fausto and Pino had heard about the fracas already, the topic more talked about than the Soviets lifting the Berlin blockade or the FBI's Communist finger-pointing. The stormy affair had even eclipsed the deaths of the entire Turin soccer team in a plane crash. Everything about the story was topsy-turvy, which is what made it so popular. Ingrid Bergman, the beloved innocent of the screen, was now perceived by Americans as a whore, and Anna Magnani, the cinema's leading sexual predator, was now an innocent victim. The American public felt vindicated in their belief that Italians were uncontrollably lecherous, and the Italian public felt vindicated in their perception of Americans as puritan prudes. I didn't pay much attention to what Prudence was saying as I tried to maintain my focus on that most perilous of fruits. It seemed to be working, but every once in a while, when my imagination began to falter, Pino would lean over and whisper in my ear, "Apple."

If I were superstitious, I might have hesitated to sail into this triple triangle of amorous woe (Rossellini's threesome, *Vulcano*'s threesome, my own threesome) unfolding among remote volcanic islands. Surely, a symbologist would have deciphered doom. But, as literary philosophers from Homer to Freud have shown, the triangle is the most alluring shape in nature. My relationship with Prudence continued to blossom like some indefatigable flower and I discovered new corners of her mind and body almost daily. As pleasant and peaceful as this was, I found myself yearning for the disruption of Gladys and our prurient forays. It felt as though the joy and tranquility I experienced with Prudence was predicated on my continued maelstrom with Gladys.

Despite Pino's apples, I retired early that evening, leaving Prudence and *La Speranza*'s crew to enjoy Pino's *tagliatelle* with *ragu*. I had wanted to escape the dread of being on a boat with the help of sleep or sex. While I waited for Prudence, I looked over my manuscript, but that hardly turned out to be a remedy for dread. Prudence finally came below and I persuaded her to indulge me in the sweet distraction of love-making. A glorious crescendo had brought us to the threshold of Shangri-la when Prudence had succumbed to that conspicuous escape of her own. She rolled off me and jumped from the bed as if she had discovered it was full of toads.

"I didn't fart," she said, "if that's what you're thinking. I was clearing my throat. It's suffocating down here. Let's go up on deck."

Her sincerity was stunning in that she said only what she had already convinced herself to be the absolute truth. If it hadn't been for the smell, I would have believed her. I worshiped this kind of thing about Prudence. Everything between us rested on instability, and this gave me great comfort. I did wish I had been more deft and had somehow gently brought the fart into our reality, if only in order to continue making love. The last thing I wanted was to be back up on deck.

Risking it all, I ventured, "But you did, Prudence, and it had the fragrance of a unicorn's breath." I pulled her back onto the bed.

"Dante, I promise you, I don't do that sort of thing." She pulled free of me and began putting on her clothes. In the starlight streaming through the portal, she might have been Artemis.

"Darling, even American girls fart." I stood up to get my own clothes and banged my head on the ceiling, eliciting no sympathy. She finished dressing with professional speed and precision, as if she were between perilously close stage calls. She left the berth without a glance in my direction. I stayed below, wondering if it were better to inhale the lingering breath of a self-deceived unicorn or to go above and face the vastness of the universe.

Tullio had sent a case of Courvoisier to the boat before we left, and, when I arrived on deck, Prudence, Fausto, and Pino were sitting around outside the pilot house making their way through a second bottle. The sea was calm, the air warm, the sky a piece of dark paper randomly pricked with a pin and held up to a brilliant light.

Fausto said, "At night, the only thing for seasickness is to look straight up and think of bananas."

Prudence laughed her chimes-in-winter laugh. I didn't mind that I was the object of her mirth.

"Apples," Fausto sneered. "What a load of dung. This will cure what ails you." He poured me a glass of brandy. "Drink this."

I took the glass from him and sipped.

"No," he said, "like this." He upended his glass. I did the same. He immediately refilled it and said, "Again." I would have done just about anything he told me to do.

Pino said, "Do look up."

We all stared at a moonless sky.

"The brightest star you see," Pino said, "to the right and down, almost orange in color, is Arcturus, in Herdsman. Straight up, blue, is Vega, in the constellation Lyre and the first star to appear at nightfall. Over there you can see the Milky Way, the galaxy we are on the edge of, which gives a man something to think about."

"And the reddish star over there?" Prudence asked, pointing low.

"Antares, in Scorpion. See the tail, the claws? If you look hard enough you can see Cat's Eyes in the tail. Serpent Holder is standing right on top of Scorpion. He has the head of the serpent in his left hand, the tail in his right. Do you see it?"

"Yes, I see it," Prudence said.

I did exactly what I wasn't supposed to do and closed my eyes to listen to the words.

"Vega, Deneb, and Altair form the Summer Triangle, a navigator's landmark," Fausto said. "You can see Eagle and Swan winging it toward each other in the brightest part of the Milky Way. Farther up is Cassiopeia and next to her is Andromeda."

Pino said, "Spica is over there, bluish, the Virgin's arse. You can see her lying there, waiting for the inevitable."

"We've had plenty of time to contemplate this sky," Fausto said.

"Tullio says you were in the navy," Prudence said.

"*Giulio Cesare* was our ship. The Supermarina told us to fight with the Germans against the British and we did," Fausto said.

I detected a sliver of defensiveness in his voice, which surprised me. Since the liberation of Italy from the Germans and the capture and execution of Mussolini in the spring of 1945, the Italian collective unconscious had moved fast toward the conclusion that, since we were all guilty for our role in the war, none of us was guilty, that we had, in the end, recognized our evil ways and taken the path of justice. In Catholic parlance, we had confessed and been forgiven. But Fausto was talking to an American, even if she was a woman.

"The Brits had our codes," Pino said. "They knew how many ships, how many cruisers, and how many destroyers we had. They knew everything. The battles of Punto Stilo, Taranto, Matapan, Sirte—we were always at a disadvantage. Nothing ever went our way. Not even the weather."

"We were lucky," Fausto said.

"He means the two of us," Pino said. "In December of 1940, we had been transferred to the torpedo boat *Vega,* but at the last minute we were reassigned to a cruiser division in Sicily. The *Vega* was sunk in January. Two survivors. A year later we were fighting the Germans."

Fausto said, "When you realize that you've been fighting on the wrong side of a war, it's like having a night of ecstasy then waking up the next morning to see that the woman lying next to you in the bed is your mother."

"Where were you during the war, Dante?" Prudence asked.

"I laid low," I said, "feeling much as I do now, nauseated and drunk."

"Think bananas," Fausto said.

⁓

War is made up of a million little scandals. My job for the Action Party was to organize them. We assassinated soldiers at random and bombed their cars, bars, brothels, and homes. We moved in their direction like mosquitoes in search of warm blood. At first the violence caused me a fair amount of disgust, but it was not long before I took to it. I was already familiar with the exhilaration of ending a life and the emotional detachment that brought the sensation of supreme control. I had killed off many characters both kindly and viciously. These fictional deaths exacted their toll, but I knew the deaths were necessary to the integrity of the work, and it was not long before I was enjoying the planning and executing of my creations. The size of the leap from killing the imaginary to killing the real was for me more puddle than canyon. And the benefits of killing real people included an intensification of the physical sensations I had previously simulated while sitting at my desk. The magic key that had opened this Pandora's box was the fact that I was killing bad people for a good cause.

My bellicose heroics, however, came late in the game and in spite of myself. For as long as I could, I had remained a stone in a stream, the war rushing over me. After the Duce's declaration of war from the big balcony of the Palazzo Venezia in the spring of 1940, I knew it was only a matter of time before OVRA, Mussolini's secret force of political police, would come knocking at my door. The word *OVRA* instilled fear and trembling in the hearts and minds of everyone and was uttered only at a whisper in darkened doorways and secured basements. It was a meaningless word, made up by Mussolini to do just what it did, and I gave him credit for his dexterity at onomatopoeia.

Many anti-fascists I knew had already been thrown back into prison, exiled to concentration camps in the south, or placed under house arrest. Jews, unable to work and certain the German influence on Mussolini would just get worse, left for South America, the United States, and Israel. Others moved to friends' villas in the country. The rest made do. Journalists wrote under pseudonyms or worked for radio and film, writing dialogue anonymously. Small business owners transferred the titles of their companies to Christian friends and continued to work. The Jews of the ghetto couldn't afford to go anywhere, so they scraped and scrounged to get by.

People suspected I was Jewish because I was not off fighting with the Italian army, from which all Jews, including several generals, had been expelled. I also took the precaution of adopting a pseudonym—I chose Sandro Weltman—and wrote freelance cultural pieces for various Fascist publications to earn a few lire. I had false identity papers drawn up just in case OVRA reappeared in my life, and asked my friend Livio Lippi (the one who extracted the fish bone from Prudence's throat) to write me a medical disability certificate before he departed with the medical corps for Somalia. Apparently, the poor eyesight or flat feet that had saved me from doing military service after university wouldn't work anymore, so Livio afflicted me with epilepsy.

Now and again, I wrote poetry and some pages of a novel but didn't try to publish much. Mostly, I translated Richard Wright's *Native Son* and some stories for an anthology of American literature Elio was putting together despite the censors' increased vigor. When I could, I visited Castiglioncello, where my mother had moved permanently. My social life was curtailed with Tullio gone, but there was a wide selection of lonely women in the city, some of whom I saw regularly. Over time, though, I became conspicuous as a healthy man not in uniform, and when in August, 1942, all able-bodied Jewish men were forced to perform manual labor in the city, I sensed that it might be time for me to leave Rome. The final decision was made for me the following Sunday, when I ran into Tullio's father in the gardens at the Villa Borghese. He was with another man and both wore the Fascist uniform. At first he pretended not to know me but about fifteen minutes later I felt his firm grip on my arm.

"I am sorry to see you," Tullio's father said, "and if I see you again you will be very sorry to see me. Your file is inactive because I fixed it so OVRA still believes you went to the United States. If they find out you are here, not only will I be unable to help you, I myself will be in danger." As he spoke, he glanced around our vicinity several times.

"How is Tullio?" I asked.

"He's fine." He let go of my arm. "His mother and sister are with him in California, but small talk must wait. Leave Rome tonight."

The next day, after some hesitation, I did as I was told.

In Castiglioncello, my mother and I led a quiet life for about a month. After the English bombarded Genoa in late October, the Mother Superior from next door sent a note asking if she could send the overflow of refugee children to stay with us in Aunt Pia's villa. After the children arrived, mother was always yelling, but I never saw her happier. And later, when I joined the Resistance, the children provided the perfect cover for the Action Party cell I ran from the villa's attic.

During those years, I did indeed lie very low. I never left the villa during the day, sneaking out only at night to blow up something or somebody. My comrade in arms was a Genoese named Pier Maria, whose wife and children had been killed in the allied bombing of his city. I didn't know much more. In case of capture, it was best to know as little as possible about others in the Resistance. He was younger than I, in his mid-twenties, short and stocky, with bulbous eyes that darted around like billiard balls. He killed people with efficiency and precision. Often he did the dirty work with me as backup, and that was how he wanted it. The one thing he did not do willingly was women. He refused to place bombs in brothels. If a woman was with a Fascist in a car we were about to demolish, he would hand the job over to me, and I didn't mind in the slightest. To me there is something feminine about the nature of violence in war. It assumes the power of the inevitable and has a logic all its own, no sooner establishing a rule than dismantling it, only to immediately reinvent it with some new twist.

On what was to be our last outing together, Pier Maria's foot was blown off by a German mine as we made our way to a bridge near Pisa that we planned to destroy. Pier Maria had gone ahead on reconnaissance and I was to bring up explosives at his signal—the call of a nightjar. I heard a blast, followed by the high-pitched yelping of an animal, the dreadful sound emanating from Pier Maria. Sniper fire cracked just as I neared where he lay. Blood gushed from his stump. I had to get a tourniquet around his thigh or he would bleed to death. Instead, I began a mad search for his foot. It was not far off, the shoe mostly destroyed—bits of leather and sock clung to flesh, but the foot seemed remarkably intact. I stood staring at it, unable to decide if I should collect the foot. Would Pier Maria want his foot? Would a doctor ever succeed in reattaching it to Pier Maria's leg? Where in hell would I find ice to keep the foot fresh until we found a doctor who could perform such an operation? The sniper fire came faster and closer. Pier Maria howled for me to get him out of there, and even lifted himself to his knees and began crawling toward the trees. Yet, all I could do was stare at his foot, the filthy toes, their brown overgrown toenails. I thought of all the toes I had kissed, sucked, licked, tickled, had wiggling up my ass. Would I ever love a toe again? *Pick up the fucking foot,* I told myself as I watched Pier Maria drag himself over the ground, leaving a trail of blood. *Pick up the fucking foot.* I picked up the foot, cut the smoldering sock from it with my combat knife, and put it in my jacket pocket. I tied up Pier Maria's leg and pulled him to a camouflaged foxhole we had dug for just such purposes. We lay there, Pier Maria gripping my arm and biting a cloth so hard his mouth bled, while I thought of nothing but the foot in my pocket.

Later, when we finally made it to the house of one of our doctors, most of Pier Maria's leg had to be amputated, and then he died anyway. When I got back to Aunt Pia's villa, I hid the foot under the dinghy in the corner of the garden. Soon there was a foul smell and my mother and the children complained. "A dead animal," I said. "It will decompose soon enough." They didn't ask about the smell again. When next I checked on the foot, the maggots had cleaned away most of the flesh. When they had finished their work, I brought the foot into the attic and wrapped it in a piece of lace I got from my mother. Like Thomas More's daughter, who kept her father's skull in a velvet sack always within her reach, I still possess Pier Maria's foot.

⌒

I woke up on *La Speranza* the next morning with a hangover so severe my phobias would have come as a welcome relief, which was probably why Fausto had gotten me smashed. I looked for Prudence in her stateroom but she was already gone. I put on my robe and emerged from *La Speranza*'s bowels to a resplendent day, although the waves seemed to roll faster. Besides the various clanging and ticking and banging sounds coming from our boat, I distinguished other buzzing and horn blowing and noticed there were quite a few vessels passing by in both directions.

"All these boats must mean we are nearing land," I said hopefully to Pino. He had laid a breakfast of black coffee, toasted bread, and blood oranges for me at a small table on deck. Prudence was there, fresh-faced and energetic, without a trace of the previous night's debauchery.

Pino said, "The Tyrrhenian hasn't seen this level of activity since the Bronze Age. We've watched vessels of every size go by carrying bizarre cargo—big spotlights in one; pillows and mattresses in another. One yacht transported a group of men all wearing identical berets and sunglasses."

"*On fait du cinema*," I said, then sat down to attempt breakfast.

Prudence pointed off *La Speranza*'s bow to a landmass on the horizon. "There's Stromboli," she said.

It appeared as a dark and fuming cone rising abruptly out of the sea and looming ever larger as we approached. It could easily have been a set constructed for *King Kong* or *Dr. Cyclops*. It occurred to me that both Rossellini and Magnani were mistaken in their choice of setting. This was the scenery for science fiction or fantasy pictures, not for melodrama. Human strife would not only be upstaged by this landscape, it would be rendered laughable.

"This is where," said Pino, "Odysseus stopped on his way to Ithaca and Aeolus gave him all the bad winds of the Mediterranean in a bag, warning him not to open it. When his ship had almost arrived home, his sailors, hoping for treasure, opened the bag. The winds escaped and blew them all the way back here. It took them many more years to get back home."

Fausto came out from the pilot bridge. "The Greeks believed that there were caverns connecting Stromboli, Vulcano, and Etna," said Pino, "and it was in these pits under the sea where the one-eyed giants Brontes, Steropes, and Arges made the gods' weapons."

"Where I come from," Prudence said, "the world began with the Kinetoscope. Everything else is backstory."

We sailed past Stromboli near enough to witness red-hot lava fly from the volcano's mouth like the blood-laced spittle of Emma Bovary's cough. Every inch of land that wasn't a sheer drop was terraced and cultivated in defiance of gravity. Deep caves punctured the shoreline, each suggesting the words, "Abandon all hope, you who enter here." Long black sand beaches ribboned the coast and great twisted boulders rose out of the sea like skyscrapers. The overall impression was one of precariousness, and I imagined that the inhabitants of Stromboli must possess an enviable disregard for fate.

On our way from Stromboli to Panarea, lying next to Prudence, I made another attempt to read over my manuscript. She wore a navy-blue-and-white-striped two-piece bathing suit, cat's-eye sunglasses and a wide-brimmed blue straw hat. I decided she had been right after all: no creature who looked as she did then could possibly have farted.

Reading, I was nauseated yet again. I tried concentrating on apples, but the impulse to wretch only became stronger. Then I felt myself uncomfortably exposed. I had neglected to put on my swimming trunks and was covered only by the flimsy cotton of my bathrobe. At moments like these, I envied the inherently defended nature of a woman's vagina. A woman's fundamental protection meant she need not invent all sorts of absurd defenses, as a man did, to shield his intense sense of vulnerability. And yet this odd and wizened appendage hanging between my legs ensured privilege and power in the world. I pulled my bathrobe farther over myself and tightened the belt. It was not the first time I found myself mulling over my penis while reviewing my manuscript pages.

The edges of the pages fluttered in the wind and a sudden gust tried to rip the sheets of paper from my hand. It would be difficult, but not the end of the world, if these pages were to fly up and away like so many seagulls. I had another copy at home—granted without the scribbled bits of genius I had made so far. A great writer was he who could chuck his manuscript to Aeolus confident that he could sit down and write a better one. Hemingway wrote a novel and, after reading it during a transatlantic crossing, ceremoniously dropped the manuscript into the sea, then composed *The Sun Also Rises*. And John Steinbeck's dog ate half the manuscript for *Of Mice and Men,* making it a shorter, and, according to the author, a worthier effort. I clutched my novel to my chest and went below, putting the pages out of reach of improvement.

When I came back on deck, we were passing through a weird conglomeration of islands and clusters of contorted columnar rocks suggesting the urban architecture of a distant galaxy. From his map, Fausto read us their names as we passed: "Panarelli, Dattilo, Lisca Bianca, Bottaro, Lisca Nera, Le Formiche." Basiluzzo, an island solely inhabited by sheep, was starboard. Panarea, covered with fields of flowering chamomile and a scattering of small white cubicle houses, was port side. I imagined myself Odysseus having survived Scylla and Charybdis only to find myself wondering if I weren't mistaken and were actually in Elysium.

Finally, the white pumice slopes of Lipari appeared before us, the rock face immense and blinding white, a movie screen for the gods.

Pino said, "They say of Lipari that it is a slice of the moon that has fallen into the sea."

As we approached the island, a debate I had been having with myself since we set sail from Civitavecchia returned: Which sailor, I wondered, would Gladys go for? Fausto was the obvious choice, which made me place my bet on Pino. But it would be hard for her to resist Fausto's brawn and fiery good looks.

We sailed along Lipari's eastern coast within spitting distance of its shores. Capers, their fruit the size of grapes, grew everywhere, as did juniper, figs, olives, clumps of prickly pears, palms, sea pines, spearwood, apricot, lemon, and pomegranate trees. The volcanic rock faces of the mountains shifted in color from black to yellow to white to red to orange and the sea did the same: indigo, emerald, turquoise, violet, cobalt. Prudence stood close to me, both of us leaning against the railing near the bow. The sea was now the color of India ink and white pumice rocks bobbed in it like the turds of angels. Prudence's hair tickled my nose and strands stuck to my lips. Fausto called out more place-names and landmarks, "Monte Pelato, Capo Rosso, Spiaggia della Papesca." This last was a beach of red and black obsidian pebbles.

During our nautical tour, I realized two things: First, Gladys would not choose. She would go for both. And second, I had missed her more than I had expected to. It was not as if I didn't go for long stretches of time without seeing Gladys, but there was something different now. Perhaps I was just associating Gladys with my deliverance from the sea. If we made it to Gladys, we had made it to the solid ground of Lipari, where I could get off La Speranza, and, at least temporarily, relax.

Fausto announced that we were coming around Lipari's Monte Rosa. We crossed the bay to Marinacorta, the island's only town of any size, where we weighed anchor in the shadow of an enormous castle perched on a bluff over the sea. We rowed the dinghy to the pier at the end of which sat the Church of the Souls of Purgatory. We mounted her stairs and made our way into town.

Marinacorta had the feeling of a place that had just been invaded by aliens. Doors were left open; half-smoked cigarettes smoldered in ashtrays; the eyes of the inhabitants were wide, their clothes disheveled, their actions accomplished in slow motion. The intruders, on the other hand, moved about with the swift purpose of conquerors. Everything about them appeared superior—the creamy smoothness of their skin, the style of their hair, the neatness of their clothes and fingernails. Even their postures made them taller and domineering. We stopped one of the invaders—he wore dark glasses and a beret—and asked him where we might find Gladys Godfrey. Glancing at us, the man replied, "She's staying in the Villetta Russo but you won't find her there. The German has us on a tight schedule—'verk, verk, verk.' They're shooting at the pumice quarry at the north end of the island. There's an observer's area if you want to go watch. It's an hour's walk that way or you can hire a skiff."

I begged Prudence to make the walk with me, but I had to admit the heat of the day was daunting. Prudence appeared cool in the white sundress she had pulled over her bathing suit, but my shirt had been drenched with sweat for some time. Fausto had told us there was a heat wave in southern Europe and that we were lucky to be where there was plenty of breeze. He said in Lisbon the temperature had reached 158 degrees for two minutes. Still, the last thing I wanted to do was to get back on that yacht. I considered taking the path by myself, but in the end Prudence prevailed, arguing that since we still had the entire trip home to look forward to, I would be better off maintaining what sea legs I had managed to develop already.

Returning to the boat, I felt like a child who had fallen off his bicycle and barely had a chance to enjoy his bloody knee before having to get right back on. During our twenty-minute ride to the small port of Acquacalda on the northern side of the island, I noticed just beneath the surface of the water among the floating pumice rocks thousands of tiny jellyfish, weightless and ethereal, like soap bubbles, with long hair-like strands trailing behind them.

Pino said, "The winds from Africa, the *Scirocco*, brings those things out. Touch one and you'll have a large red welt that burns for days."

When we disembarked, the air was so dry I thought I might suffocate. A dark path zigzagged up a white slope like a scar. To find Gladys we would have to follow it. After a few minutes up the steep incline, there was a dip in the terrain where we came upon a small crowd standing under a canopy at the edge of the set. The spectators were looking in the direction of a tall man dressed in white trousers, a white seersucker short-sleeved shirt, his head covered by a white cotton Bedouin headdress. His hands were sheathed in cream-colored suede gloves, William Dieterle's trademark. A man with sun-streaked hair and leathered skin was talking to the director. He wore nothing but swimming trunks, and still he looked aristocratic. This was Renzo Avanzo, Rossellini's betrayed cousin.

My heart, already quick from the climb, increased its beat when I saw Gladys sitting in her folding canvas-and-wood chair, G. *Godfrey* stenciled across its back. Dieterle's and Magnani's chairs were nearby but empty. Gladys wore a ragged cotton smock dress and had a bandanna tied about her head, her face smudged with dirt and sweat. The bedraggled yet alluring peasant look had the desired effect on me. I couldn't have dressed her up better myself. She did not look in our direction. Not far from her were two donkeys tied to the front of a large wooden cart half full of pumice rocks. In front of the donkey cart, a big black box sat on a wooden tripod, which in turn sat on a trolley on fifteen feet of track. The cameraman's arms hung around the camera in the manner of an adolescent boy with his new girlfriend. He was flanked by a number of men, mostly shirtless and wearing white cotton shorts. All wore hats of some sort—berets, straw fedoras, bandannas. I wondered how many of them Gladys had fucked. I recognized the photographer Federico Patellani clutching his Leica and leaning up against the camera trolley. Patellani had become a fixture on Italian movie sets, and, it was said, a pain in the ass to the official set photographer. Directors and actors, however, liked to have him there as his work pushed whatever film he was documenting a little closer to that holy grail: Art. He also was an excellent, Tullio-level gossip. Reflector panels, like hurdles in a relay race, encircled the set.

A group of women and children, hot and bored but obedient, milled about near Gladys but far enough away not to disturb the hierarchy. From their faces and dress, they must have been extras culled from the local population. On the far side of the camera trolley stood four more donkeys saddled with large straw baskets. A few skinny goats nibbled at an electric generator on wheels. A boy threw pumice pebbles at them, but the animals remained unperturbed. A long-haired wolfhound with a dazzling white coat with black spots lay panting in the shade of three large umbrellas outside the entrance to a canvas tent. I assumed this was Micia, Anna Magnani's dog. Anna herself was not visible.

A production assistant waved us under the observers' canopy and signaled for quiet. Among the group I identified the journalist Max David, who nodded to me, and the actor Errol Flynn, an old friend of Magnani's, whose nose, I never realized until then, was as pronounced as hers. The rest were women of various ages and beauty, wealth and nobility, including the Baroness Avanzo and her daughter, the Countess Kechler (and lady of the lagoon in the Veneto, another of Hemingway's conquests), the Marquess Carrego, and Princess Esmeralda Ruspoli. I knew two of them, biblically speaking, but that was no competition for Gladys's tally.

The director, Dieterle, made a motion with his gloved hand and a young man trotted over to the large tent and knocked on the canvas flap. Anna Magnani appeared immediately. Like Gladys, she had on a smock but wore the apparel with her singular lustiness. My eye, however, did not stay long on her clothes, rising swiftly to that notoriously strange face of little beauty but extraordinary power. It was a tired face, her dark eyes circled with black, her olive skin pale, almost ghostly. It was an eminently recognizable face, but as I watched her perform I noticed that her face was also very changeable. At one moment her expression was young and angular, the next haggard and bloated, the next soft, maternal, and adoring. Much of this was due to light. The arrangement of her features caused light to play across her face in the most illusory way, absorbing and refracting in the manner of a prism.

The cast and crew took their positions for the scene—a bitter exchange between the sisters over the Brazzi character—and Dieterle said something to Anna in English, which was then translated by Avanzo. We watched Dieterle say, "Quiet on the set," followed by "action," seven times. After each take, he altered some small detail—a word, a gesture, the position of an extra. It was fascinating and boring. Anna seemed to take it all in stride, while Gladys seemed impatient. The art of being an A-level B-actress, Gladys had told me, was the art of being unflappable. Perhaps Gladys was rehearsing for the big time.

Again, Dieterle started and then stopped the action. He calmly explained to Avanzo that a child in the background of the scene of women and children working the pumice quarry was eating his lunch ration too delicately. He nibbled on the bread and pretended to chew instead of devouring the bread as if he were starving.

Avanzo said, "You give them too much food. They are not used to eating so frequently. The children are stuffed."

Dieterle ignored the remark and pointed out that the water jug the boy was drinking from had no water in it. Avanzo conferred with the child, who nodded at the instructions. Avanzo then told one of the production assistants to fill the jug with water and to wet the outside of it as well. The action began again, only to be stopped. In practicing how to eat the bread the boy had finished the loaf and someone had to return to the town to get another. "This time," Dieterle said calmly to the designated bread-getter, one of the few young men present who wore a shirt, "come back with more than one loaf." The lack of bread meant an hour's break.

The first thing Gladys said to us was, "I've met someone." She kissed us each while Prudence and I exchanged a glance. We heard these words more than a few times from her lips. Yet each time they elicited in me a set of archaic emotions, the most fundamental of which was the fear of being replaced.

"This one is for real," she said.

"For real," I repeated, and she nodded.

We followed her up another path and came to a set of long tables covered in white tablecloths under a series of white canopies. I understood what Avanzo had been referring to when he said there was too much food. Bottled water, fruit, cookies, pastries, and sandwiches were in abundance on the tables, covered in a fine layer of volcanic powder. Most of the extras were already there, eating and drinking. Everyone wore sunglasses.

"His name is Kirk Dixon." She picked up a tangerine, peeled it, and tossed sections into her mouth like popcorn.

"American?" I asked.

"Australian," she said, and I was relieved because Australia was not her country and far away. The relief was temporary.

"Occupation?" Prudence asked.

———

"Extraordinary lover," Gladys said. Without looking at me she added, "I have known one or two in my time. He's also nice and I'm never bored."

"How did you meet?" I asked, not wanting to.

Between tangerine sections, Gladys said, "Anna and I are staying in one of the few habitable structures on the island, a gothic-style villa owned by an islander who made his fortune in Australia. Kirk has been the caretaker since the end of the war. Anna doesn't speak to me, and Rossano and his new wife never leave Selznick's yacht, so Kirk was Perseus to my Andromeda, chains and all." Gladys brushed the dust off her arms and dress with appealing vigor. "I don't understand this obsession with location. Give me a studio any day of the week. This heat, this whole place is a nightmare."

"Some say it's paradise on earth," I said.

"Who?" she said, and bit into a banana.

After that we talked about everything but Kirk. Gladys seemed to understand and didn't press the issue. We were well attuned, the three of us. I thought, gloomily, what a terrible shame it has to come to an end. The loaves of bread arrived and Gladys was called back on set. We arranged for her to come to the yacht with Kirk for dinner.

"It will be late," Gladys said. "Dieterle shoots until there's no more sun. And Anna is more eager than Dieterle to finish this picture. She hates it here, too, but more because of them." She pointed in the direction of Stromboli. "We'll finish ours first, I'm sure," Gladys went on. "Patellani goes back and forth between the islands and he says to us—not to her, of course—that it's such a love fest over there they hardly ever shoot a thing. To Anna he says that Ingrid is completely miscast, that she's terribly unhappy and uncomfortable, that she's too tall, that Roberto is obviously fed up with her, and that both the relationship and the picture are sure to be a disaster. God knows what he's telling Ingrid."

When we reached the dock in Acquacalda, Fausto was knee deep in the sea thrusting his arms toward something submerged. The water lapping at his legs turned a rich black and he raised an arm in the air enveloped by a writhing and slimy octopus. He repeatedly pulled the octopus's grasping tentacles off his skin, making a nasty ripping sound. No sooner had Fausto detached one or two or three of the legs than they slapped themselves back on again. If Fausto hadn't had a beatific expression on his face I might have yelled for help.

Prudence was awestruck. "I've never in my life seen such a thing."

Fausto continued this peeling off of tentacles for about five minutes until in one quick smooth gesture he used his free hand to yank the body of the octopus off his arm and with both hands turned the animal inside out. He then brought the beast to his mouth, bit something out of it, and spit it into the water. He later explained that he had excised the beak. "They say doing this keeps the flesh from getting rubbery in the pot."

On our way back to Marinacorta, clouds streaked the sky and the sea turned aluminum. Pino, who had stayed behind in Marinacorta, had procured us a beautiful piece of grouper, which he later grilled with capers and olives. He also served sautéed octopus, tomatoes and olive oil, and Liparese goat cheese melted over bread—the same kind Dieterle had made the boy chomp on with gusto. We drank the local white wine, which tingled on the tongue. But I enjoyed none of it, so pre-occupied was I with the guest of honor.

"Gladys has told me all about you" were his first words to me.

His accent was even more twangy and loopy than Gladys's. He was reasonably good looking but Gladys had had better. He was of average height, solid build, with reddish-blond hair, freckles, wide-set gray-blue eyes, and full pink lips. *Boyish* is the word that came to mind. In fact, he couldn't have been much older than twenty. Gladys had had innumerable lovers, some of whom I had met and even known well, so my anxiety about this Kirk (which rhymed with jerk, shirk, quirk, and perk, while his last name, Dixon, spoke for itself) was strange. Perhaps it was Kirk's arrant likeability that made me nervous. Perhaps something was different about Gladys. His introductory remark was banal, but so often a cliché meant more than the cleverest turn of phrase. If he had been lying I would have been comforted by the situation, but he was telling the truth. As the meal unfolded, my sense of foreboding eased as I watched Gladys checking out first Pino, then Fausto, both obviously appreciating her as well. Kirk made no signs of being disturbed by this interaction. He appeared relaxed and not in the least bit overwhelmed by Gladys or by his good fortune to be her lover.

When darkness was complete Marinacorta disappeared, save for a dim glow here and there. Around the bay, though, bright light, voices, laughter and the pealing clarinet of Benny Goodman ricocheted from yacht to yacht. We had finished eating and had started in on the Courvoisier. I said to Kirk, "A stranger in a strange land—how exotic you are."

Kirk said, "Many of the people who live here aren't from here." He pointed toward the monolithic sixteenth-century castle, a great dark shadow over us. "That's a prison. The Fascists sent a lot of people there. The police escorts hadn't finished pulling away from the docks before the Liparese were letting the prisoners out of their cells. One of them, a guy named Curzio Malaparte, who was sent here for a year in the mid-thirties for criticizing Mussolini's neckties, started a library. It has your books. I read them. I've read all the books. Not much else to do here." He laughed. "Before I met Gladys that is."

"According to Gladys, you should never meet the author of books you have read," I said.

"I was afraid of that but Gladys told me not to worry, that you were nothing like your books, so it didn't matter."

"Was she right?"

"Gladys," he said, "is always right."

During the evening, I tried to conceal my growing dejection over Gladys's new love. Perhaps it had been Gladys all along that I was in love with and I had been using Prudence to shield myself from the truth. I spun out a succession of scenarios, which included my declaring to Gladys my undying love and forcing her to choose between me and young Dix. But I had always known that the precariousness of our ménage is what allowed us to have it. Sadly, it was not meant to last. I would

———

soon lose both Gladys and Prudence. The root of my despair had nothing to do with them. And the root of my despair was: that it had nothing to do with them. If I hadn't known this I might have risked everything and fallen on my hands and knees before Gladys and begged her to renounce Kirk and marry me. Or I might have married Prudence with the secret intention of continuing to pursue Gladys. Or I could have decided that Prudence was indeed the woman who would make me eternally happy. There were all sorts of vectors I might have followed, but in the end I would have been no happier, and I would have dragged my beloved Prudence and Gladys deeper into my muck.

Gladys did not have to work the next day because they'd finished shooting at the pumice mines and were relocating the set for the underwater murder scene. I was keen to see the great crater where Anna Magnani would plummet to her death. And so, the next day, as it happened, into the muck we went. Gladys, Prudence, and I sailed for Vulcano on *La Speranza*. Serendipitously, Kirk could not join us, having been hired as a handyman to help relocate the set.

Fausto brought us to the black beaches of Porto Ponente, where we were immediately accosted by the sickening smell of carbonic gases. White steam from fumaroles shot up out of the lunar landscape like leaks in a radiator ready to blow. A few children met us on the beach and asked if we were movie stars. They offered to guide us to the miraculous mud baths, which would not only heal all complaints but fix us so we would live forever. We accepted their services. It was said that

Vulcano was the gateway to hell, and on the way to the shallow pools of stinking mud I thought it possible. The volcanic rock was tormented, the smell of the air fetid, the colors of the earth offered the reds of fresh and dried blood, the yellows and browns of rot and excrement, and obsidian's shiny black of death.

When we arrived at the place the children called Acqua di Bagno, I picked up a fistful of yellow sludge and flung it at Gladys, accidentally hitting her smack on the nose. She lost no time in throwing two balls of mud back at me and soon Prudence and the children had joined the fight. We had a grand time, the only sounds our own laughter and the occasional burp from small cones in the ground, from which borax-white, alum-yellow, selenium-green, and tellurium-red vapors escaped, followed by a geyser shooting mud into the air. We then swam in the bubbling sea, heated by underwater fumaroles.

After the three of us had played long enough in Vulcano's mud to ensure our immortality, Fausto took us back to Lipari by sailing around the island in the direction opposite to the one from which we had come. The coast was a continuous wonder—as if Vulcano's three volcanoes had mounted an exhibition of the sculpture they had been working on for millennia. In the half-mile-wide strait between Vulcano and Lipari, we made our way through sea monoliths frozen in misery after having stared deep into the eyes of the Medusa. We could have been in heaven or hell. It didn't matter. I was for another moment as happy as I could only be with Prudence and Gladys near me.

The next day, I told Prudence that work on my book was not going well and that I needed to return to Rome. She said she understood. We said goodbye to Gladys and Kirk and headed back toward the mainland.

nine

Rome

When Gladys and Kirk returned to Rome from Lipari in mid-August, they announced their engagement, with a small wedding to follow as soon as possible. I was not surprised. Since leaving Lipari in June, I had been preparing myself for this eventuality. It had been apparent for some time that Gladys was restless, our triangle inadequate, and she would soon be making a move to change the configuration. Sometimes I thought Gladys married off would be a relief; sometimes I thought a married Gladys would be a *divertissement*; much of the time I thought her defection to the land of matrimony calamitous.

As their official witnesses, Prudence and I accompanied the betrothed to the various bureaus and offices they needed to visit in order to execute the inscrutable deed. Surely Gladys's real purpose in having her secret lover come along was to transform tedium into titillation. Since giving my manuscript to Astolfo Falsetta, I had been unable to write, so I agreed to play the chaperone. When we weren't busy with things marital, I read the newspapers cover to cover—something I had never done much of. When denied the privilege in prison, I had fallen completely out of the habit. Generally I found the news to be at best a sorry attempt by journalists to pawn off their obsessions onto the rest of us. I preferred to stay focused on my own. But, at this particular moment, I appreciated the distraction. The war in Israel seemed over, and the Pope had excommunicated Communist Catholics, a bold move given their numbers. Giovanni Gambi had swum the seventeen miles from Naples to Capri, and there was an earthquake in Japan—the tally of the dead tripling and halving depending on the newspaper.

These stories, however, weren't the ones that absorbed me. I devoured the obituaries. Margaret Mitchell's untimely demise, for instance, mowed down by a speeding taxi while crossing Peachtree Street in Atlanta on her way to see the Powell and Pressburger picture, *A Canterbury Tale*. Her husband was holding her hand when the cab driver picked the novelist off like a sniper. Mr. Mitchell might spend the rest of his life wondering why he had always let her take the lead, following like a faithful puppy at her heel. His devoted but pusillanimous behavior had killed her. Or had he plotted his escape from a domineering and famous wife by hiring the cab-driver to hit and run, Mr. Mitchell assuring the cabby that if caught the most he would get was manslaughter and Mitchell would see that the driver's family received further handsome compensation. I did try to learn more about the driver, but all I gleaned was that on the evening in question he was deep in his cups.

The obituaries confirmed my impression that life consisted of a series of deaths, little and large, that came with the predictability of one's next breath. And each time someone died, he or she took away a piece of us. No wonder I had become so attached to Pier Maria's foot. I wanted to keep a chunk, dead as it was, from leaving this world. Like obituaries, wedding announcements had their own section in the newspaper that contained the particulars of those who had fallen. If Gladys would allow her single-self to perish, I would attend the funeral.

From a bureaucratic standpoint, marriage, in the case of Gladys and Kirk, was especially daunting; neither party was an Italian citizen, nor were they citizens of the same foreign country. Something about all those necessary pieces of paper, stamps, and signatures reminded me of writing—so many precise details essential to masking the underlying chaos.

The first item on Gladys and Kirk's list was an *Atto Notorio* affirming that they were who they said they were. This was procured from the Ordinary Tribunal in viale Giulio Cesare. The *Atto Notorio* then required certain stamps that could only be bought from certain tobacco vendors who held odd hours and were located in remote corners of Rome. Accomplishing this alone took us several days.

The next item was a *Nulla Osta*—a document proclaiming "there are no impediments"—valid for each party. These were secured at the Consular Section in via Veneto and had to be signed in front of the American Consul and the Australian Consul. At the American Consulate, a pretty blonde functionary from Ohio asked Gladys if she and her fiancé were intending to go back to America any-time soon. When Gladys said she thought it likely, the blonde suggested they wait and marry there, because the paperwork to legalize the marriage in the United States was equally unnerving, and some states didn't even recognize an Italian marriage.

"We'll just have to get married everywhere we go," Gladys responded. "I think marriage, like a politician, should have a term limit. A couple should be required to remarry every two years or the marriage is automatically over. Then after ten years the marriage is finished for good, no renewals, no extenuating circumstances, term ended, finito."

"Not a bad idea," said the blonde, her broad smile appealing. "But what about children?" She asked.

"Ah," said Gladys, "there's the rub."

At the Australian Consulate, we were helped by a clerk from Perth with the shoulders of a rugby player. As we left, Gladys offered him her telephone number in case there were any unforeseen contingencies.

How I would miss her.

Once both *Nulla Osta* documents were signed, along with the *Atto Notorio,* the documents had to be legalized at the Legalization Office on viale Ostiense. This was followed by a trip to the Marriage Office on via Petroselli to procure a Declaration of Intent to Marry, which entailed the posting of a Civil Ban for at least two weeks, including two consecutive Sundays. Only after the ban was completed and no objections to the union were made could a date then be scheduled for the civil marriage ceremony.

During this stroll down the road to Calvary, I amused myself by imagining Kirk's future as a Thoreauvian man leading a quietly desperate life in a drab American city. I pictured him a horned man, cheated on in perpetuity by his almost beautiful wife. As time passed in his fictional future, he would find a remedy in drink and become Ray Milland in *The Lost Weekend*.

Prudence, meanwhile, amused us all along our journey by reading aloud sections concerning the institution of marriage from Simone de Beauvoir's immensely popular treatise *The Second Sex*.

At the Ordinary Tribunal she read:

There is exaltation in beginning an enterprise, but nothing is more depressing than to become aware of a fate over which one has no control.

At the American Consulate:

A single woman in America, still more than in France, is a socially incomplete being even if she makes her own living; if she is to attain the whole dignity of a person and gain her full rights, she must wear a wedding ring.

At the Australian Consulate:

The jealous wife regards the male member as an article providing pleasure that belongs to her and of which she is as niggardly as she is of the preserves stored in her cupboards—if the husband is generous with a neighbor, none will remain for the wife; she scrutinizes his underwear to see if he has squandered the precious seed.

In the Legalization Office:

Kinsey states that there are many wives "who report that they consider their coital frequencies already too high and wish that their husbands did not desire intercourse so often. A very few wives wish for more frequent coitus." But as we have seen, woman's erotic capabilities are almost unlimited. This contradiction clearly indicates that marriage kills feminine eroticism in the effort to regularize it.

In the Marriage Office:

Eroticism is a movement toward the Other, this is its essential character; but in the deep intimacy of the couple, husband and wife become for one another the Same; no exchange is any longer possible between them, no giving and no conquering. Thus if they do continue to make love, it is often with a sense of shame: they feel that the sexual act is no longer an intersubjective experience in which each goes beyond self, but rather a kind of joint masturbation.

Gladys enjoyed the de Beauvoir readings enormously. Kirk seemed to admire the spectacle. I found Prudence's readings endearing. If Gladys's marriage made me feel something like Humpty Dumpty after falling off the wall, Prudence was doing a good imitation of Chicken Little dodging pieces of fallen sky. And then there was the question hovering around the two of us tacitly and obnoxiously like an unclaimed fart: Why were Prudence and I not marrying as well? By reading de Beauvoir, Prudence was answering the question. But Prudence couldn't comfort me—nor I her—regarding Gladys's new found love. Our precious instability had been transformed into an emotional quicksand. Any attempt at help from either of us meant sinking deeper into our mutual disquiet. We had seen each other relatively little since returning from Lipari, and she rarely stayed the night. When we were together, I felt Gladys's absence acutely. And since Gladys's return, I had no idea how to discuss with Prudence her sister's apparent need to marry with such speed. Worse, I could not complain to Prudence about my greatest lament in all of this: Gladys and I had not had sex since she met Kirk.

Gladys and Kirk were married on September 23, 1949, at the Palazzo du Conservatori on the Capitoline Hill. It was another beautiful day, the sun cashmere, soft and warm, never stifling. Gladys had on a leafy thin dress of pale green silk, the color of Prudence's eyes. I had helped Kirk buy a suit—brown silk shantung—and he looked fine. We began the day with a champagne breakfast at Babington's Tea Room. Such early drinking caused us to ignore the hour and we were late to the Capitoline Hill. We ran up the many steps to Michelangelo's complex of buildings—much maligned by the Marquis de Sade but praised by Goethe as one of the most perfect places on earth. I was inclined to agree with the Marquis, especially on that particular day. We saluted the equestrian statue of Marcus Aurelius in the center of the square and then breathlessly made our apologies to the impatient magistrate, who did his duty in what must have been record time. We all signed the many requisite sheets of paper while Prudence read:

> Marriage gives rise to fantastic comedies and play-acting between the partners, which may threaten to destroy the boundary between appearance and reality; and indeed in extreme cases definite perversion does appear.

We were ushered swiftly out of the room—the next bride and groom waiting nervously beyond the doors.

Gladys said, "Let's have a gay time all day." She grabbed Kirk's hand and pulled him toward another set of stairs leading up to Santa Maria in Aracoeli, a medieval church adjacent to and just above Michelangelo's famous square. Prudence and I followed them inside, where everything went dark and we were inundated by the smell of mushrooms. As our eyes adjusted, Gladys led us down a row of columns to a small crowded chapel. About twenty or so pilgrims had gathered around a young priest with bushy black eyebrows. On the priest's knee was a babydoll, its pink waxen face smiling mischievously as if it were possessed by some less than holy spirit. The doll was dressed in silk and gold lace and covered with sparkling jewels of every color—sapphire, amethyst, topaz, ruby, jade, turquoise.

"The *bambino Gesù* meets Tiffany," Gladys whispered. There was something peculiar about her expression as she gazed upon that bizarre object of idolatry. It had never occurred to me that Kirk and Gladys's wedding might have something of the shotgun to it, but I let the thought go as fast as it had come. Prudence read:

On the whole marriage is today a surviving relic of dead ways of life, and the situation of the wife is more ungrateful than formerly, because she still has the same duties but they no longer confer the same rights, privileges, and honors.

Soon we were tripping down another monumental stairway into Piazza Venezia, where we stood before the giant, gleaming Victor Emmanuel monument, appropriately nicknamed the "Wedding Cake." Also known as the "Giant Typewriter," it reminded me for an instant of an imminent event in my life—the publication in a few months' time of my novel. I had long since gotten used to the extravagant flights of fancy such an emergence brings with it—the delusions of grandeur followed hard upon by the delusions of despicability—all tools used for avoiding the truth of the thing.

We meandered through Rome's heart toward the Pantheon. In Piazza Minerva, we ran into Walter and Betsy Pope, the American couple we had met on the train to Venice almost a year before. Upon hearing the good news, they insisted we celebrate with them at the Cupole bar in the Grand Hotel de la Minerve, where they were staying. Walter had grown fatter and cut his hair short. Betsy had a new hairstyle—longer, straighter, more Lauren Bacall than Rita Hayworth. The Popes were accompanied by an Englishman, who was introduced to us as Lord Birdon. Gladys and he exchanged a look I knew well, a look I had once enjoyed myself. Walter ordered a bottle of Dom Perignon.

Kirk thanked Walter and said, "Gladys has told me so much about you."

I remembered how Gladys used to describe to me in detail her sexual encounters with other men.

Gladys invited the Popes to the reception Tullio had arranged that evening in the rooftop restaurant of the Hotel Hassler, on the Pincian Hill.

"Where are you going on your honeymoon?" Betsy asked Gladys.

"Niagara Falls," Gladys answered.

"The Great Barrier Reef," Kirk said.

"*Ça commence,*" I said.

"I have always thought Lisbon frightfully romantic," Lord Birdon said. "Of course, it lacks the primitive drama of the places you mention."

Prudence read:

But further, even when sexual love exists before the marriage or awakens during the honeymoon, it very rarely persists through the long years to come.

———

"You guys are so literary," Walter said.

Gladys said, "Dante is about to publish a new book."

"I have to confess I don't really read books," Walter said. "I feel kind of silly sitting still to read about someone else's adventures when I could be having my own."

"Imagine how I feel writing them," I said.

Walter threw an arm around me in one of those awkward manly embraces Americans wield to express affection. "I guess someone has to do it," he said with a laugh.

I wanted to ask Walter and Betsy if they knew anything about Margaret Mitchell's accident, but, after ordering another bottle of champagne for us, Walter announced that they had to get ready for an afternoon audience with the Pope.

"Don't let the last name fool you," he said with a wink. "We're not related."

We left the Minerve bar sometime later and headed for Alfredo's, a restaurant in via della Scrofa that, according to *Babbitt*, served the best fettuccine in the world. On our way, we passed Borromini's elaborately contorted little church, Sant'Ivo alla Sapienza. I had always admired the eccentric, mean-spirited, deeply rivalrous, and outrageously imaginative baroque architect who, like Cato, committed suicide by falling on his own sword in a fit of pique. After lunch, we had ice cream at Giolitti, meandered through the tiny, smelly, crowded streets of the Field of Mars, drifted through the shops in the Galleria Colonna, bought roses from a gypsy, and finally made our way to the Trevi Fountain.

The baroque style always seemed to me to be a parody of itself, having much in common with film sets for biblical epics, a self-conscious exaggeration, an expression of the part of us that always yearns for more, better, greater, stranger, curlier, straighter, richer, shinier, more immortal. But this fountain in particular—with its fake rocks, tritons, sea horses, and marble monsters pissing and spitting hundreds of tinkling jet streams into many staggered pools—parodied the parody and became the epitome of baroque. Wandering around that day in Rome, I felt myself to be the epitome of a parody, the rejected lover turned sycophant, a dog hoping to be thrown a scrap, my longing so acute that its satisfaction could only lead to despair.

I watched Gladys laugh with delight as she and Kirk threw coin after coin over their shoulders into the fountain's foaming waters, making very sure, as the Roman superstition dictated, that they would return to the Eternal City.

Over the roar of gushing water, Prudence asked, "Aren't you going to throw in a coin, Dante?"

"I'm not going anywhere. No need to ensure my return."

"Sometimes you are terribly literal," Gladys said.

"Don't you mean literary?" I asked. "In Hawthorne's day, the tradition was to take a sip from the miraculous fountain fed by the waters flowing from Agrippa's aqueduct, but too many travelers must have gone home and died of dysentery, so now you use coins. Three cheers for Capitalism."

Gladys threw a coin at me and it bounced off my shoulder into the water. We drank Campari and soda and ate pistachios at a caffè in the piazza while watching a burlesque of lovers and children and tourists throw coins, kiss, argue, and play before the celebrated fountain. Finally, we made our way back to Piazza di Spagna and up the steps to the Hotel Hassler, where the wedding festivities were getting under way.

The restaurant was overflowing with white roses and waiters carrying trays of champagne glasses filled to the brim. Tullio rushed up to us and gave Gladys a long kiss on the mouth. "Please don't take this the wrong way," he said, shaking Kirk's hand, "but I had hoped she would fall for one of us and be forced to live out her days on our soil. But as Dante is always reminding us, we are an old and tiresome lot, while you two come from places that still have a chance for survival."

To which Kirk, genuine and disarming, responded, "If we do leave, you could come with us." He looked at Tullio, then me, then back to Tullio.

"Dante and I tried to leave once," Tullio said. "Some things are just not meant to be. But other things are." He put his arms around Kirk and Gladys, kissing them both on the cheek.

While I was making a toast to love and destiny, Tullio was called away to the telephone. To the drone of a light orchestra, Prudence read:

It is a commonplace to say that in modern families, and especially in the United States, woman has reduced man to slavery. And this is nothing new. Since the times of the ancient Greeks males have always complained about Xantippe's tyranny.

Tullio returned and said, "President Truman just announced that the Soviets have exploded an atomic device."

Many conversations I overheard that night were a variation on a theme: the end of civilization. Armageddon had been predicted so often for so long that the yearning for it seemed natural. We had all become exhausted by the activity of living.

"Leave it to Gladys, " I said with true admiration, "to go out with a bang."

The dinner menu included oysters Rockefeller and lobster stuffed with pigeon, Tullio's idea of new world cuisine. I didn't eat very much. Gladys was ravenous, using her fingers and teeth to get into all the nooks and crannies of the lobster carcass. Kirk was describing the glories of the Outback to a very attentive Tullio. Prudence was asked to dance by Rocco Pompei, who, having sold his production company to MGM, was headed for Hollywood to direct musicals for Dore Schary.

"Let's all spend World War III in tinseltown," Rocco said, as he headed off with Prudence. "Can you sing, Dante?"

Tullio said, "I tried that once already. In the advent of the next holocaust, nuclear or otherwise, Kirk here has sold me on Sydney."

I asked Gladys to take a turn with me. We spun around among the guests, greeting them warmly, then whispering nasty things into each other's ears. When we came back into view of our table, we watched as Tullio and Kirk made their way quickly out of the room.

Gladys said, "I was wondering when Tullio would catch on."

I said, "You mean Kirk . . ."

"We all have our secret needs," she said.

I said, "I can't fathom why you are marrying this guy."

"Because you're not to be counted on in any permanent way," she said, biting so hard on my ear that I pulled my head away.

"Let's go somewhere," I said, bringing her back toward me, my hand tightening over her breast.

"Another time," she said. We had neared Prudence and Rocco on the dance floor. Gladys freed herself from me and tapped Rocco on the shoulder. "May I cut in?" she said.

Prudence and I made our way out to the terrace, the city before us a glittering expanse of urban constellations.

"She's pregnant. It was a mistake, but she couldn't bear another abortion."

"He'll be a good father," I said, remembering Germana and Vanni and feeling very tired.

The celebration continued late into the night. Tullio and Kirk spent most of it in each other's company. At one point, Rocco and Gladys disappeared for a while. When Gladys did finally return, Prudence read:

The wedding night transforms the erotic act into a test that both parties fear their inability to meet, each being too worried by his or her own problems to be able to think generously of the other. This gives the occasion a formidable air of solemnity, and it is not surprising if it dooms the woman to lasting frigidity.

I awoke late the next morning and began randomly poking at the keys on my Olivetti MP1, given to me by Germana when the model was brand new. I could never bring myself to get a new one. After a while, I looked at the page of meaningless characters, random letters that had gotten me through the better part of a day. It didn't matter that they spelled no words. The page was no more incoherent than the rest of my life. That I had recently resumed my involvement with Ilda proved it. I couldn't fault chance. I didn't happen to run into her. I sought out Ilda upon my return from the Aeolians and she had come to me faithfully nearly every afternoon during my sacred writing time, when Prudence stayed away. Her hesitant little tap, tap, tap on the front door right then irritated me and I realized that I would have to end it with her yet again. I stood up, but sat back down. Long ago, I had given Ilda the key to Aunt Pia's apartment, but I knew she would never use it, then or now.

I had met Ilda in the fall of 1938, just after my release from prison. She worked as a tailor's assistant on the Corso Vittorio Emanuele where Tullio had his shirts and suits made. After Tullio had convinced me to go with him to America, he took me to the shop so I would be well-dressed for our tour. Even before I was near enough to smell her, the sight of Ilda measuring a man's neck, the width of his shoulders, the length of his arms, drove me wild. She parted her caramel-colored hair on the side and it fell in gentle ripples to her shoulders. Her little tongue ran over her raspberry lips, leaving them shiny. Her skin was as smooth as eggshell. Her eyes—one cobalt blue, the other brown as chocolate—were her most compelling feature, their incongruity impossible to miss. She must have been sixteen years old. I was nearly thirty then, not especially drawn to young girls but by no means stuck in my ways, and, besides a few whores, I had not been with a woman since before Basilicata. When it was finally my turn to be measured (Ilda did the shirts, her boss, alas, the trousers), she started with my wrists. Up close, she smelled of cinnamon and rosewater. I don't remember what happened after that, as all my attention went toward the delicate task of concealing my rising desire for her.

A few days after my first visit to the shop, I went to pick up my suit, and possibly Ilda. To my great disappointment, she wasn't there, my final fitting taken care of exclusively by her boss, the tailor. The next day I waited outside the shop just before closing time and followed her as she walked home.

"I was just on my way to see you," I said, showing her the package with my suit in it.

She blushed, and I knew I was in.

"My suit does not fit quite right and I'm leaving tomorrow for the United States." I paused, giving her the opportunity to state the obvious.

She said, "I'm sorry, but the shop is closed and my boss has gone home by now." She wet her lips as she had in the shop.

I said nothing, assuming a grave and pathetic expression.

"I have with me a needle and thread, but where could we go?" she said, trying to lift my spirits.

I looked around us, as if I had her same dilemma, then said brightly, "I live just a couple of streets from here. Would you mind coming to my apartment to see if the suit can be mended before my departure? I would very much appreciate it."

She hesitated, but only as a formality. Once in Aunt Pia's apartment, I put the trousers on and told her the cuffs seemed uneven. As she knelt before me examining them, I said, "I can't keep my secret from you any longer."

She looked up, interested and a little alarmed.

"The first moment I saw you," I told her, "I knew I had to have you for my very own."

The confusion animating her face told me that it had not been the same for her, but that she liked the idea of someone wanting her so precipitously and so passionately.

I pressed on. "The sound of your voice, your sweet scent, your enchanting eyes have me at your feet." In truth, it was she who was at my feet. I put one hand under her chin and lifted her to me. She dropped the needle and thread as I kissed her. It never crossed my mind she was a virgin until it was too late.

Afterward, she said, "Are you Jewish?"

I shook my head.

"It doesn't matter," she said. "I am only half Jewish myself."

A small crimson stain marked the sheets. Embarrassed, she apologized and attempted to launder them for me, which I would not permit. I then told her that I would cut out the piece of cloth stained with her blood and take it with me to America.

She said, "We are now married in body and soul. When you return we will marry before a judge."

I nodded, and kissed her, certain that given a little time she would realize I was too old for her, and she would forget about me. I walked her home, murmuring to her that I would live on the memory of her tender kisses until I returned from my trip (I didn't specify when). On my way back to the apartment, I swore to myself I would never touch a virgin again as long as I lived, not because I felt them to be sacred but because the sexual experience had been rather dull. She had had no thought for me, only for what was happening to her, and though her desire and curiosity were palpable, she had been more afraid of what I might do to her rather than craving what I might do to her.

Just over three years later, in January, 1942, on a bitter cold day, rare for Rome, I ran into Ilda, this time without pretense, in Piazza Navona. She had changed only a little since I last saw her, the lines of her face slightly sharper, and she had a new confidence in her bearing. But she was still more girl than woman.

"With the war," she said, "I thought you must have stayed in America, but then I saw you once on the street and knew you had come back."

I didn't feel the need to explain myself and she didn't seem to be asking for an explanation. I was fully benefiting from the mass delusion brought about by war. The constant tension, the rationing, the destruction and death that saturated our daily lives were countered by our near-complete rejection of the reality we were living. We were adamant about continuing our lives as normally as possible and in order to do so became deaf, dumb, and blind, not only to the tragedies but to all the minor sorrows and discomforts of wartime existence. And time had come to a standstill.

Taking Ilda's hand, I led her into a caffè in the piazza, an unlikely place for a Jewish girl and an ex-convict to openly dawdle, but we both took great pleasure in doing it. I asked her how she was getting along and she told me that her mother had lost her job but because her father was Catholic she and her siblings were allowed to continue working. Her family, she said, was doing better than most. She went on to tell me more about her family than I wanted to know: births, deaths, marriages, the various illnesses and ailments of grandparents, aunts, and uncles, gossip about cousins, and so on, as if we were married and she was catching me up on family business. I listened patiently, our hands clasped tightly together, all the while devising a plan for getting her back into my bed. I knew that what I was about to do again to this young girl was unconscionable, but I found her love for me too absurd to deny myself the experience of it. And, of course, this was war.

Finally, I kissed her on the lips to stop her from talking. I told her to come by my apartment straightaway after work the next day. I was not entirely sure she would show, but she dutifully appeared at the given time. I had decided in the interim that if she did come, I wouldn't fuck her. Since she had a predilection for patience and duty, I brought her into my study and took off her clothes, removing each garment with care, instructing her to fold each item neatly and then place it in a pile on the floor next to my desk. When she had finished, I sat her down at the foot of my chair and placed her head in my lap and told her not to move until I gave her permission to do so. I then typed on my Olivetti, sometimes pausing to stroke her neck, or breasts. She would moan and I would press her face into my groin but I did not open my trousers, nor she her small but surprisingly competent mouth, until it was nearly time for her to leave. I asked her to return in a couple of days' time. If she visited every day, I explained, her parents might become suspicious, but if we saw each other only every few days she could always find an excuse—she had to stay late at the shop, she met up with a friend—for the missing couple of hours.

She arrived again two days later, and we repeated the ritual, as we did from then on. Sometimes I varied it by feeding her pieces of fruit I cut up with a stiletto, given to me by Ubaldo not long after the incident in his shop, and then making her lick the blade clean. Or I put clothespins on her nipples, her nose, her tongue, then later I soothed the sore spots with kisses. Believe it or not, I managed to get some good work done in this fashion. The whole setup functioned beautifully for a time, but eventually became oppressive. Ilda was required to be silent while I worked with her at my feet, but afterward she would prattle on about all the things we would do when we were married, the furniture we would buy, the children we would have, the holidays we would take. When she began making plans for when I would meet her family, I became irrationally angry at her for something trivial—a broken teacup or a misplaced book—and nearly threw her out of the apartment. When I next saw her, I made her swear that she would tell her family nothing about me, not a word or even a hint to a sister, cousin, aunt, or friend. I impressed upon her that if our relationship had even the slightest chance of continuing, it had to be secret. I told her if I heard her mention marriage again, I would disappear from her life forever. She looked at me with her funny eyes, which I now found disconcerting, even eerie, possessed of a special vision for discordant souls.

After my outburst, only rarely would the word "husband" escape her, but it did with enough frequency for me to know that I should have stopped the whole enterprise then and there. I did not, mostly out of laziness. It was not long before I began missing our appointments. Or when I did deign to be at the apartment when she came, I wouldn't let her near me, but watched as she cleaned and dusted, mended my socks, or cooked me a meal we would not be sharing. By the end, we rarely spoke to each other and almost never had any sort of sex, as if we were indeed married. I loathed this creature's unconditional love for me and I reveled in it. Like a little boy who tested his mother relentlessly to see if his bad behavior could push her to abandon him once and for all, I tested Ilda, only Ilda was but a girl herself.

This mock marriage took place amid the stench of anti-Semitism fouling the country. Rumors about what was happening to Jews in Germany and eastern Europe spread like pollen in springtime. No one in Rome wanted to believe they were true. Some even tried to construe as hyperbole the Nazi deportations of Jews from the Warsaw ghetto and Slovakia to concentration camps in Germany. Many insisted that Mussolini would never allow this to happen in Italy. Of course, the same thing had been said of the racial laws, which had only increased in severity. Ilda ran about as if the laws did not exist, and as someone with a Catholic father she was still exempt, but for how long?

Our liaison finally came to an end after I ran into Tullio's father in the gardens of the Villa Borghese, when he told me to get out of Rome. The morning after his words of warning, with my bags packed, I remembered that Ilda would be coming in the afternoon. I wrote her a note saying I had been called away indefinitely, and intended to leave it for her with my concierge, but on my way down the stairs, suitcases in hand, I stopped and could go no farther. I barely made it back to the apartment.

The early September day was warm. Sharp beams of sunlight penetrated every crack and hole in the shutters I had closed a short time ago. I sat on the couch and watched as the light gradually shifted direction. I knew I should take Ilda my keys in the eventuality that she and her family needed to elude the Nazis. I would inform the concierge—a good man and an anti-Fascist who had been devoted to Aunt Pia—and leave him money to make sure he helped Ilda. Instead, I sat on the couch in the shadows, absorbed by my own wavering: If Ilda had to hide with her family in my apartment, how would she explain to her parents who I was? Would she finally tell them I was her "husband"? If I gave her my key, would she take it to mean that I wanted to marry her? When I eventually returned to Rome, would I find her ensconced there?

I sat ruminating, light jabbing all around me like the arrows that perforated St. Sebastian's body. Only I was no martyr. I held no consistent beliefs. One's life could be seen as inevitable or purposeful, probable or random, and all were, in my mind, sustainable. We made choices—to believe or not to believe, to act or not to act. The shape of a life could be described by the curlicue of choices one makes. I could leave Ilda the key, and one sequence of events would be set in motion, or I could not leave Ilda the key, and another sequence of events would be set in motion. And either choice could lead to identical events. Consequence, a product of love and hope, was something from which I had always felt myself exempt.

My reveries that autumn day in 1942 might have continued indefinitely if not for the soft tap, tap, tap on my door. Ilda had come as scheduled. The light had softened into the gray of early evening. She saw my suitcases, the closed shutters. Without a word, I handed her the key. I thought she might ask why, but she said nothing.

"The concierge is aware that you and your family might be coming," I said. "If ever you are asked to explain about the apartment, do not mention me. I will only bring you trouble. Say you used to work for my aunt Pia, who owned the apartment, and you held on to the key when she died. The concierge will back you up."

I didn't say where I was going. As we parted, the fading light made her pied eyes appear uniform in color. Suddenly, she looked so much older than her twenty-one years.

Seven years later, I did not answer the door when I heard Ilda's meek tap. We had been repeating the same ritual as before, only now I blindfolded her, bound her in various positions, always at my feet. She tapped at intervals of five minutes before she gave up and went away. During the war, Ilda never did use the apartment. She and her family had fled Rome soon after I did—to a relative's villa in the countryside. The concierge hid another family in Aunt Pia's apartment and they were all arrested and deported to Buchenwald. As the sound of Ilda's footsteps receded, I telephoned Gladys. How unpleasant need was. Gladys's desire for me would hardly be stimulated by my pleas. Yet still I called, desperate for a chance to have her again. I wanted to be assured that we were still comrades in lust, that marriage and pregnancy, no matter how unorthodox the situation, could not annihilate our attachment. She answered the phone and I couldn't bring myself to speak.

"You're sulking again," she said. "I'll be right over."

When she arrived, the first thing she did was to open all the shutters, creamy light pouring into the apartment. She was dressed in a sleeveless white top, a long red skirt, and white open-toed pumps. She headed straight for the bedroom, continuing to talk as she took off her clothes.

"You should get to know yourself better, Dante. You are between books. It's always a bad time for you, and you think my getting married has changed things irrevocably." She shed her slip, her panties, her bra. She wore no stockings. Her belly was as perfectly flat as it had been on the night I met her, only her breasts were slightly swollen. "Well, it has. And change is good. Without it, we would get bored."

"With you," I said, "boredom is impossible."

She came up to me and draped her hands around the back of my neck. "Do whatever you like," she said, "something I'll never forget."

"Put your clothes back on," I said.

"But . . ."

"Now."

She did as I said. "That's my girl."

I got my combat knife with a blue blade and a leather-washer hilt, the one that had slit so many throats, spilt so many guts, the one that had cut the sock from Pier Maria's foot. I grabbed her right breast and gathered the material of her shirt in my fist, slicing through the fabric so that a chunk of it remained in my hand leaving a jagged hole. I did the same thing with the fabric over her left breast. I then more carefully and meticulously cut holes in her bra so that her nipples, now very erect, were exposed.

"Bored?" I asked.

"No, sir," she said, watching me closely.

I then bent her over the back of the armchair and with the tip of the blade slit the red material of her skirt upward from mid-thigh to the center of her ass.

"Now I am," she said. "That's Kirk's preferred territory and even so he somehow managed to get me pregnant."

I seized her hair and yanked her upright. Holding her head still, I lay the knife blade an inch above the hollow of her throat. "Tell me the child is mine."

"It's not," she whispered. "But go ahead, do us a favor."

I groaned and fell back onto the bed.

She took the knife from my hand. She said, "You and I are both cowards. That's why we get on so well." She took a handful of her hair and with a swift motion, cut off a lock. "Here's a piece of me," she said, "keep it. Kirk and I are going back to California just as soon as *Vulcano* premieres." Using the knife, she began to slowly cut away what remained of her clothing. "You better get yourself ready, because Prudence will say she wants to stay, but she won't be able to. Remember, she's damaged goods, so try to make it easy for her."

"You think of everything," I said. She was now completely naked, except for the knife.

"Dante, I know you're terribly fond of us," she said, touching the tip of the blade to the middle of my chest, "but there's no room in there for anyone else, not really. Besides, I'm twenty-eight and Prudence is twenty-nine. We've done the picture thing and we've had a lot of fun. But neither of us wants to be selling used yachts to Tullio in twenty years. Even Silvana, who really could be the next Rita Hayworth, says she's going to marry the first viable man who'll have her. It's time for the backup plan—marriage, kids, a house with a backyard. Kirk got the job for two reasons: he'll devote himself to taking care of me and the kid, and, whatever I get up to, he'll never be jealous since I'm not his heart's desire."

"And what's my backup plan?" I asked, although we both knew what it was, mine just as resigned and clichéd as hers.

"That blade is impressively sharp," she said, handing the knife back to me.

I nodded.

"Well, then," she said, lying back on the bed. "Use it to make me look as I did when I was a child."

I did as she asked. She arched a few times so abruptly that the knife nicked her and she bled. My horror was as great as my rapture, but mostly I was awed by how vividly she lived.

Afterwards, she lit two cigarettes, handing one to me, and said, "I always like to save the best for last."

"Gladys, was that your idea of a sympathy fuck?"

She laughed. "You should know by now that every time I fuck it's a sympathy fuck," she said. "Sympathy for myself."

She was silent for a while, inhaling, exhaling, wrapping herself in a veil of smoke. Finally she said, "You ought to collect things—stamps, lead soldiers, butterflies—something you can obsess over but that won't ever really hurt you. If you can't find that stamp from Bhutan after years of searching, you'll be less likely to kill yourself over it."

She kissed me hard on the lips, found some clothes to put on, and left.

ten

Castiglioncello

The sea in winter is a study in rejection. The water ice cold, the air bitter, the wind slapping you away with its wide blustery hands. "Don't come near me," the sea commands. Yet, from the safety of the shore, I finally gained an inkling of Melville's claim for the sea's hypnotic powers. I have sat for hours, until my feet and hands were numb from cold, staring at the rolling waves, listening to the swish and gurgle of water washing over rocks. I have remained undisturbed for long stretches of time, neither seeing nor hearing another human until a trawler chugged by in the distance or a nun silently appeared. Mostly, I have stayed alone with the gulls and their rejecting sea.

Despite its perpetual rebuff, the winter sea had sustained me since I arrived at Aunt Pia's villa nearly a month ago, in early December. I ventured out to the beach both morning and afternoon, no matter what the weather. I had a favorite boulder, sculpted and softened by the sea into a grand seat. "The

Throne," Ubaldo's boys had dubbed it when we were children and many battles had been waged to claim it. But as monarchs knew, gaining the throne was one thing, keeping it another, especially if you preferred swimming or climbing rocks or doing nothing at all. Eventually, we found defending The Throne more trouble than it was worth and the rock was abandoned. But now I had reclaimed it, my thoughts bleak and boring as they had been then, feeling trapped by having won what I did not want. I had always been one of the successful—successfully dead while alive—the body continuing on, like the sea, with an infinite will.

The new year and a new decade were only a few days away and I was still in what Gladys had rightly described as one of my "in-between" periods. I had begun two translations—one of Ann Petry's *The Street*, the other of Dawn Powell's *The Locusts Have No King*—but stopped both after only a few pages. I hadn't done anything since and had spoken to no one from Rome or Milan. There was nothing new about my imposed isolation. I would come out of it eventually, when I tired of myself. It was either that or the option I had so far failed to execute.

My novel was published to relentlessly positive reviews, leaving me once again the nude emperor. How was I able, sea-like, to hypnotize all those people into seeing something not there? I was a prestidigitator—and should have been proud. Pulling the wool over everyone's eyes was an artist's dream, the writer just another con man, master of disguise, impersonator, seducer, and betrayer. Yet I longed to be exposed. I was convinced that being objectionable would prove my worth. Gertrude Stein said that an artist who seeks criticism is not an artist, the true artist only hears praise. I heard only my failure loud and clear in the applause. The weight in my chest day in and day out was not solely due to the vicissitudes of accomplishment but also due to the solidity of regret. I had let Gladys and Prudence slip away from me.

I remembered reading the Henry James novella *The Lesson of the Master* when Vanni, Germana, and I were living together. The story described a famous writer named St. George, who was happily married to a devoted wife. He insisted to Paul Overt, a young writer, that an artist of genius must remain celibate in order to achieve greatness, a wife and children necessarily making one willing to compromise. I had used this story to justify my choice to resist all commitments. In reality, I wanted to sleep with as many women as possible, and a steady girlfriend, not to mention marriage, was an unnecessary bump along that road. Germana had pointed out that at the end of the novella St. George, having been widowed during the course of the narrative, lived happily ever after by marrying the young, exceedingly intelligent and beautiful girl Paul Overt had decided to abandon after talking to St. George. As was once true for me, St. George was having his cake and eating it, too.

My hours on the beach were permeated by a sense of yearning. I hadn't wanted to marry Prudence. I hadn't wanted to have a child with Gladys. Yet I was dismayed by the thought of the two of them without me as a part of their lives. It seemed such a peculiar human affliction to long for things we could not stand to have, more difficult to fathom than murder or suicide. I could be driven to distraction by this yearning and yet the thing I was yearning for was clearly not what I was after. I craved the yearning itself.

Today at breakfast I received two wires. One from Prudence, the other from Astolfo Falsetta.

From Prudence: *Arriving this afternoon.* Upon receipt of which the yearning immediately ceased.

From Astolfo: *Novel short-listed for the Bagutta Prize, the Viareggio Prize, and the Prix Medicis Etranger.* In the Henry James novella, St. George convinced Paul to renounce love in pursuit of artistic perfection by saying, "But try, try all the same. I think your chances are good and you'll win a great prize."

Soon after reading these missives, I headed down to the beach, feeling gleeful at my indifference to them, and I had been resting on The Throne ever since. The sea was neither rough nor placid. The sky was clear, the sun high, its white light catching on withered weeds jutting out of cracks in the stone wall that kept the shoreline from spilling into the sea. The gulls were in hysterics over something I was not privy to. I spied no nuns but they could have already come and gone. I knew I had to get back to work, or not, but I couldn't remain as I was for much longer. A decision had to be made, a step taken, however small. Perhaps I should have done as Gladys suggested and begun to collect things. One needed to be obsessed with something other than dying. I knew a woman, Liana, who had a sprawling apartment just off the via dei Condotti—it must have had eleven rooms but she lived exclusively in one. All the other rooms were packed full to the ceiling with magazines and newspapers waiting to be read or reread, piles of clothing to be mended, appliances in need of fixing. I had heard of others with this compulsion but the extraordinary thing about Liana was that she knew precisely where everything was, and down to the last needle and pin, what she owned. I used to tease her by asking if by any chance she had a certain issue of *Prospettive* or *La Voce di Aretusa* and she would disappear for twenty, sometimes forty, minutes and reappear with it. I would look at it and toss it aside, and from that moment on she did everything in her power without being blatantly rude to get rid of me so she could put the magazine back in its place.

"Just put the magazine back, Liana," I would say.

She would protest. "You must think me crazy. I don't mind a little disorder now and again. I'll put it back in good time." But she couldn't sit still until it had been done. In every other arena of her life, Liana was sparklingly clear-headed.

I had considered taking up chess. Lately, Ubaldo and I played chess during the evenings and I enjoyed myself but did not find the activity dire. We were well matched and I liked to watch him wanting to win while not wanting to upset me. Mostly, we played to see who was more skilled at letting the other win without his knowing for sure that the game was being conceded. Though diverting, it was hardly the material of obsession.

The question was: Can one's obsessions be changed midstream? Everything was possible, but the comfort I had always taken in thoughts of suicide, along with my numerous fears, had kept me going year in and out. Fear of writing, fear of not writing. Fear of failure. Fear of success. Fear of heights, depths, small spaces, big spaces. Fear of women, friendship, commitment, children. Fear of going crazy or not being crazy enough. And, my worst fear, mediocrity. For anyone but myself, I celebrated mediocrity. My Gladys and Prudence were shining examples. They took the world as it came, sought out the new, and appreciated the old. They never looked far enough in any direction to despair. They had their share of rough knocks and conquests, and they might have desired more from the world, but they did not expect it. I, on the other hand, had never been able to tolerate *good enough.*

Vanni used to say, "Better to do something badly than to not do it at all," and I would argue with him until dawn about how dangerous that idea was. Something badly done, I would say, was an affront to human potential. To encourage the second-, third-, fourth-, and fifth-rate to exist was ultimately pushing ourselves down the path to self-destruction. Standards would fall. We would evolve toward stupidity, rather than greater intelligence. I quoted Nietzsche: "We have art so we shall not die of reality." If our art, I argued, were some banal reflection of our reality, a soporific instead of a true and worthwhile escape, we would all surely expire. Vanni's response was that the objectively great could not be known—what was great to some now would be drivel to others later. Therefore, all creation—good, bad, and middling—must be encouraged.

Even mediocrity didn't terrify me anymore, though. Nothing did, and I didn't miss the trembling, the panic, the nausea.

My existence without them these past weeks had been illumi-
nating. I found myself concentrating on actions and thoughts
I was actually involved in. When I felt thirsty, I walked to the
kitchen cabinet, placed my hand on a glass, and went to the
bottles of well-water Ubaldo kept stored for me in the pantry. I
poured the liquid into the glass. I drank from the glass. Sometimes it took more water and sometimes less to quench my
thirst. Sometimes I drank even if I wasn't thirsty. Sometimes I
poured the remainder of water into the sink after I had drunk
my fill. I rinsed the glass and set it on the dish rack to dry or I
left it for Nerina to clean later.

For the first time in my life, I did not anticipate the next
sexual encounter, though I still engaged in sex. I masturbated,
and there was Nerina. Nerina came to me as she always had,
but there was a worry in her dark eyes I wanted to avoid. I
started to make up lies for why it was inconvenient for me to
see her such as, I was finishing an epic poem that had taken me
a decade to write and could not be disturbed.

Sound had altered for me. I heard the world differently.
Nothing was background noise. Each sound was registered
with equal intensity: a voice, a footfall, the shriek of a gull, the
wind in the trees, the gnawing of an industrious insect. I found
the sensual presence of these things painful, the repetitive murmuring of the sea a relief.

This morning after Ubaldo brought me the two wires, I noticed from my window that he was dawdling in the garden. He
cleaned up some twigs and dead leaves and checked the shutters to make sure they were in good working order. He then

stood around shuffling his feet and looking nervous. I was impatient to get down to the beach but didn't feel I could just walk off and leave him, though I certainly had done so plenty of times before. He took care of Aunt Pia's villa with a scrupulousness and attention I never gave it myself, and he was often there repairing a leak or fixing a crack in the floor while I read a book or took a walk. There had never been any monetary exchange for the work Ubaldo did for me at the villa. He had his vegetable garden on the land, but that too seemed to be more for my benefit than his, all the best produce coming my way when I was around. Whenever I could, I gave him a bottle of whisky or a cured ham. Although he made his gratitude clear, he always seemed slightly offended. My relationship with Ubaldo was unconditional in a one-way direction—my way. I was unsure exactly why, but I suppose it had something to do with his belief that I had saved his life. In an act that had more to do with detachment than beneficence, I had recently made a visit to a notary in order to draw up a will in which I left Aunt Pia's villa to Ubaldo. Afterward, I felt bad about it, afraid he would think I was paying him for something for which he had always wanted nothing in return.

When I couldn't bear another minute of Ubaldo's loitering, I finally went outside and asked, "What is it, Ubaldo?"

"I'd like to fix up the dinghy and the sailboat for my grandchildren," he said.

Ubaldo's youngest son, Risveglio, had loved to row and sail when we were young. My aversion to boats had begun early, and at first those boats were never used. Finally, Risveglio, for whom my mother had a special affection, petitioned her to use them. Ubaldo was horrified when he heard of his son's forward behavior, and came to the villa to apologize to Aunt Pia, who initially had no idea what he was talking about.

When finally she understood the situation, she said to Ubaldo, "I am not a Socialist. I firmly believe in ownership. But I also admire efficiency and despise waste. If Risveglio will put those boats to good use, I will be content to see it happen."

As with so many things from the past, Ubaldo and I hadn't spoken about any of his sons for a long time, but it was clear that Risveglio was on both our minds just then.

"Of course, Ubaldo," I said. "It's a wonderful idea. And, if you are able to make those vessels seaworthy, I wouldn't mind trying one or the other out myself one of these days."

By the fall of 1943, Anelito and Congedino, Ubaldo's elder sons, had been killed while fighting at the Russian front. Eteocle, his third boy, had been hanged by the Black Shirts for desertion, his body left dangling for days as a preventative measure. And Risveglio, barely sixteen years old, had joined the Third Garibaldi Brigade of the Cecina Valley, a clandestine anti-Fascist group mostly made up of workers from the Solvay chemical plant in Rosignano, the town immediately south of Castiglioncello. Our particular stretch of coast was lined with enormous villas built by Germans at the turn of the century to look like medieval castles, and given its strategic position as a port city,

Livorno became an obvious stronghold of the Third Reich after their occupation of Italy in early September.

On the 8th of September, the Third Garibaldi Brigade spearheaded a simultaneous attack against several enemy posts. The action failed, and Risveglio was captured by the Germans. After some frantic investigation by Ubaldo and his wife Duella, it was determined that Risveglio was to be sent to the Regina Coeli in Rome and then on to a prisoner-of-war camp in Germany. Since the German occupation, massive deportations had already gone into effect. Six hundred thousand soldiers would be sent to Germany as conscripted laborers, a technical term for slaves, and over seven thousand Jews would be sent to death camps.

A few days after Risveglio's arrest, Ubaldo came to me and my mother late one evening to ask if we knew of anyone who could help keep Risveglio from being deported. It was a well-known fact that if he were kept in an Italian prison or sent to one of the camps in the south his chances for survival would increase exponentially. My mother, who had never concealed her favoritism for Ubaldo's youngest, said she would immediately send a note to her priest in Florence. I just shook my head.

When my mother left the room to make coffee, Ubaldo said in a conspiratorial tone, "We want you to take Risveglio's place in the brigade. I told them I would ask you. I told them you had been in prison for three years for crimes against the state. They knew about you."

"Who are 'they,' Ubaldo?" I asked.

"It's best not to know yet," he said. "They just want to know if you are willing."

I had been hoping, having secured my official diagnosis of epilepsy from Livio, to avoid any full-fledged participation in fighting. In Rome, I had been happy to lend a hand here and there, but my only genuine commitment was that I had none. I had little regard for Fascism, the Fascists indulging with such frequency in our natural tendency toward ignorance and cruelty. At best, however, I considered myself an observer who watched and recorded without trying to determine the outcome.

"Even if I were willing, Ubaldo, there is my mother to think about. I am all she has left."

I invoked my mother, but I was not really worried about her. I was worried about me. I loved my mother, but I hated her more. I hated her, just as I had hated my father, for never getting over the death of my brother, Giovanni. He had hardly lived, after all, before he died. And I hated them for not giving me another living brother (my mother had suffered two subsequent miscarriages). I was convinced that they had wanted to remain in mourning for Giovanni—for all he could have been, for all that I was not. Lost potential was more comforting than real loss. They became attached to the dead child in lieu of me, so they would never have to suffer such deprivation again. I had always felt that both my mother and my father were terrified of me. Initially, the only explanation I could imagine for what I had done wrong was not to die as my brother had. Still, I never stopped hoping that she and my father would one day realize that my not dying was a triumph and they would be proud of me for it. I know mine was a childish interpretation, but it was one I had devoted myself to early on and maturity had done little to change it.

"Of course, Ubaldo, I will take Risveglio's place. And forgive me my hesitation. I am a coward. It is why I write poetry."

"There is no need to apologize, Dante. It pains me greatly even to ask you. You are like a son to me and I feel like Abraham sacrificing another of my boys to a God who is Himself horrified by my actions."

My mother came back into the room carrying a tray with the coffee service on it. I could see in her eyes that she had heard our conversation and was pleased, not because I had agreed to join the Resistance but by my expressed concern for her.

Less than a year later, on July 9, 1944, Castiglioncello was liberated and four days later Rosignano, after such long and bitter fighting the allies called it the "Battle of Little Cassino." Since Pier Maria, I had been paired up with several men whom I had watched die. For this particular battle, Ubaldo and I fought side by side until he was hit in the leg with mortar fire. I was then teamed up with two Americans, Sergeant Howard Urabe and Akio Mishikawa, a medic, of the 442nd Regimental Combat Team from the 34th Division. It was an all-Nisei Army Unit, most of whom were from Hawaii. Many of their family members were in internment camps back in the U.S. On our first assignment, Howard, who was studying to be a social worker when the Japanese attacked Pearl Harbor, and I crawled on our bellies to reach a position in front of an enemy machine gun. Howard stood up and fired a rifle grenade into the nest, killing the machine gunner and destroying the gun. He then picked off the two other members of the gun crew as they started to run. Another machine gun fired on us, and he knocked that out with a second grenade. I stood there sweeping my M-1 rifle across the landscape as if on a birdwatching expedition, while a sniper put a bullet through the middle of Howard's forehead. Two days later, Akio saw one of his friends from the 442nd go down amid concentrated artillery and mortar shellings. He said, "Gotta go," and ran a hundred yards through a storm of metal to administer first aid. Both men died.

Alone the last day of the battle, I watched men, women, and children dying like flies swatted on a summer afternoon. Ubaldo was ashamed of himself for thinking it, but he was glad Risveglio was far away, safe in a POW camp. I survived the entire four days with barely a scratch. The number of decomposing bodies was so high that Rosignano had to be quarantined to contain infectious diseases—smallpox, influenza, plague, malaria, cholera, typhus—from spreading. Let the dead bury their dead, I thought, and stayed to help.

A week later, when the quarantine was lifted, I left Rosignano and walked the several miles along the beach to Castiglioncello. I climbed the stairs to the villa, looking forward to seeing my mother and the children. But even before I reached the house I knew something was awry. The front door was wide open, which made sense due to the stultifying heat. But that was the last thing that made sense to me for some time. Inside, mats covered every inch of the stone floor and on these mats were bodies. About half were children, the rest were women, nuns I figured, and most were dead—their eyes and mouths frozen open, in expressions of despair or surprise but mostly exhaustion. Flies were everywhere—buzzing, crawling, emerging from between lips, blackening entire faces. The stench burned my throat. Apparently, we had failed to contain the scourge of cholera. I heard a noise coming from the floor above. I climbed the stairs to the drawing room. More bodies, and the Mother Superior trying to get those alive to drink from Aunt Pia's silver pitcher.

"Where is my mother?" I said.

The nun looked at me, her eyes brimming with tears, and shook her head.

"Where is my mother?" I yelled.

She said nothing and continued to pour water.

"Speak to me, you old whore." I went over to her and shook her. She was thin and brittle. If I had exerted the slightest additional force, I could have snapped each bone in her body. "Tell me where she is."

I knew where she was, but I wanted the nun to break her goddamned vow and tell me herself. We stared at each other for several moments, I in my rage, she in her martyrdom. I thought of raping her and knew she would silently forgive me while I ripped up her insides. What kind of place was this, I thought, where the only response to violence was more violence, the only antidote for pain, worse pain? I threw her down, spilling precious uncontaminated water all over the drawing room floor. I ran up to my mother's bedroom where she lay on her bed, her body covered with a sheet. I fell on top of her, howling. Everything I had done in my life I had done for her, including staying alive, yet I was sure all she ever felt from me was my distance and disappointment, my bile and venom, my blaming her for having brought me into this world that I scorned, and where I was now alone.

I don't know how long I was there before I felt a hand caress the back of my head. I sat up, startled. It was the Mother Superior and she spoke to me, her voice without melody, her accent flat and common, sounds the world could easily do without.

She said, "Her last words were, 'Tell Dante I loved him the best I could and better than he knows.'"

None of the children survived the cholera outbreak at the convent, and only a few of the nuns. Ubaldo was fine and helped me and the Mother Superior bury the bodies on consecrated ground within the convent walls. Wanting to get the hell out of there, as soon as I could I returned to fight. In only a matter of days Livorno was liberated by a division of the American 5th Army. The Germans retreated fifty miles to the heavily fortified Gothic Line, leaving behind their Schu-mines and booby traps, and even more died that summer. Ubaldo never tired of trying to find out where in Germany Risveglio was, hoping to somehow get him home. When Cardinal Spellman came to Rosignano to say Mass in mid-July and when Winston Churchill stopped overnight in Castiglioncello in August, Ubaldo made sure both leaders received letters, translated by me, pleading for help in locating Risveglio.

———

The Germans surrendered in April, 1945. Weeks, months, a year and more passed, Ubaldo and Duella waiting for Risveglio to return home. Ubaldo stopped waiting after Duella died, having poisoned herself with belladonna root. Risveglio had never made it to a German POW camp. He was shot to death while trying to flee the train taking him there. Just before Christmas of 1947, when Nerina and her mother had been living with Ubaldo for some time already, he received a letter from a woman in northern Italy telling him she had found Risveglio's body still warm in a field in January, 1944, and had, with the help of her priest, laid him to rest in the town cemetery. She was sorry she had been unable to locate his family sooner.

⁓

Now, on December 25, 1949, it had snowed on the beach in Castiglioncello. Christmas had never meant much to me, even when I was a boy. My parents would take me to the Duomo for Mass in the morning, followed by a large and interminable meal with various relatives who doted upon me. As a child, I preferred to be ignored, which would happen eventually, but not until every last adult had pinched my cheek or made some inane comment about my growth rate for the sheer purpose of assuaging their guilt from the fact that they couldn't care less about me. Christmas was a celebration of birth, and birth had never been a very happy occasion in our family, as far as I could discern. I'm sure my own had been happy enough for my parents, but I, of course, had no recollection of it and it had never become part of the family drama in the way that my brother's birth had. If I were to feel any self-pity for being alone on a holiday, it would not have been on Christmas Day, and as it happened that Christmas I was surrounded by nearly the entire town of Castiglioncello, nuns included.

The day had been overcast, not too damp or cold. I was on the beach as usual, succumbing to the rhythms of the sea, when I felt the gentlest touch on my cheek and then my nose. I thought it might be a raindrop or sea spray. I had turned my attention back to the sounds of the sea when I heard a child's voice cry out, "Look, it's snowing." I did look, and indeed the sky had turned white with snowflakes coming down fast and thick. It was not a flurry but a dumping such as they regularly got in Turin or Milan, but almost never here. Soon children were running up and down the beach yelling and throwing snowballs at each other and into the sea while the rest of the town's citizens gradually made their way down to the shore. Ubaldo was there with his grandchildren. Nerina and Beppe were there, arms linked. Rainieri's sons Edamo, Iliade, Norge, and Goete all came with their children. Before long, a cluster of nuns arrived in their white woolen habits and white woolen caps. They were such a vision through the curtain of snow that everyone, even the children, fell into awed silence, as if a troop of angels had descended from heaven. They gathered at the far end of the beach and began to sing St. Francis's Christmas hymn *Psalmus in Nativitate*. Everyone joined in, even I, and we sang hymns and carols until the snow stopped some time later. Afterward Ubaldo insisted, as he had for days, that I join them for Christmas dinner, and even Beppe didn't seem to mind my presence at the table.

Today, the sun, though devoid of warmth, was too bright for there to be snow. I had no idea how long I had been on the beach leaning against my rock throne, my eyes closed, when my awareness was drawn to the sharp crackle of footsteps on the stone stairway descending from the villa to the beach.

"So you're here, Dante." I listened to the dulcet tones of Prudence's voice. "I have been waiting for you in the house for over an hour. I had no idea you would be down here in this cold."

I opened my eyes, crusty with sea salt and tears, and felt the searing pain of penetrating light. I tried to stand up, but much of my body was paralyzed from cold or sleep or both.

"Wait," she said, "let me help you." She appeared very warm in her white cashmere coat and her rabbit fur muff and hat. She put her strong arms around me and tried to lift me, but I was a big man. She kneeled down before me. "You're frozen," she said.

"Just numb," I said. "Pound on me a bit and the circulation will come back."

As she massaged my legs and arms, she recited Emily Dickinson:

This is the hour of Lead—
Remembered, if outlived,
As Freezing persons, recollect the Snow—
First—Chill—the Stupor—then the letting go—

"I missed you," I said, feeling a sharp tingling in my limbs, then heaviness as my blood began to flow.

"I've missed you too, Dante," she said.

With my newly animated arms I pulled her onto my lap, and put my face into her hair.

"Your nose is like a piece of ice on my neck," she said, shivering. "Let's go up and sit by the fire a while."

"If we do I will melt into a big puddle on the floor. The cold is what keeps me in one piece."

"Then I shall scoop you up, pour you into a bottle, and keep you in my pocket." She stood up and pulled on me to do the same. "I've come because Gladys, Kirk, and I are going to Lisbon to celebrate the New Year and we want you to come too."

"The city of longing," I said.

"Have you been there before?" she asked.

"No," I said. I stood up and we made our way slowly over the rocky beach and up the stairs. Lisbon, I thought, would be as good a place as any to finally prove that what I was after had nothing to do with Prudence or Gladys. When we entered the villa, I saw that my bag was packed. She was not usually so presumptuous, but she was not usually anything.

"Our train leaves in an hour," she said. "We meet Gladys and Kirk at the airport in Fiumicino tomorrow morning."

If I had any hesitation about going to Lisbon, it all dissipated with this news. I had never flown in an airplane. I could barely conceive of the many fears that might be triggered by such a journey, which, as my beloved Prudence surely knew, might just be the step I was in need of taking.

———

1950

eleven

Lisbon

*The active life has always struck me as the
least comfortable of suicides.*

FERNANDO PESSOA

I was quite sure the poet Fernando Pessoa, whose city I,
like an arrow, was whizzing toward, never had the experience
of flying. Poet Gabriele D'Annunzio, on the other hand, had
certainly soared the skies, believing, along with Mussolini, that
aviation was by definition a Fascist activity. Lindbergh had fit
the bill, hobnobbing with Goering and declaring his admiration
for Nazi order. Ever since I read D'Annunzio's line, "To fly is
necessary, living is not necessary," I had been curious to find
out firsthand what he meant.

Flying was like being in an enormous womb with propellers, suspended in midair while being jostled to and fro, nothing about it plausible, and yet there was an atavistic rightness

to being up there, as if, in fact, we were born to fly. How like chickens we had been for all these centuries! From my window, the houses, cars, people had shrunk to details in a diorama. The surface of the earth was organized into shapes, some repeated, some discrete, some with angles, some circular or oblong or blobbish, all of which fit together perfectly like a puzzle. From that perspective, the world did seem to have a pattern to it, a hint of God. My overall sensation of upness led me to the conclusion that Howard Hughes's use of airplane technology to build a better bra for Jane Russell in his film *The Outlaw* was divinely inspired.

The aircraft belonged to Lord Birdon, the Englishman we had met with Walter and Betsy Pope at the Cupole bar on the day of Gladys and Kirk's nuptials. He owned vineyards near Oporto and was England's largest importer of port wine. Gladys had evidently pursued Lord Birdon's suggestion of Lisbon as a honeymoon spot—how far she had pursued *him* I couldn't be sure, but Gladys rarely stopped short of all the way. That morning, the air was crisp, the sky bright blue and cloud-dappled. At the airfield, Lord Birdon had told us that we would be flying in a De Havilland Dove, equipped with two Gipsy Queen six-cylinder engines driving three-bladed propellers. It had a raised flight deck, and a separate ten-passenger cabin. "One of our most successful projects," he said mysteriously. He also informed us, after Kirk asked, that there was a Lady Birdon, but she rarely left Kent and did not like to fly. The two sisters were wearing their matching white coats and hats, their hair once again shoulder-length and mouse brown. They looked much as they had when I first met them.

Once on the plane, Gladys sat next to Lord Birdon, Prudence and I opposite them. Kirk was seated behind us next to Lord Birdon's secretary, Lewis from Liverpool, who served us drinks. It took us over three hours to fly from Rome to Lisbon and yet I felt we had barely risen into the air before we were coming down again. I didn't mind the bumps or the sudden dips that made my stomach leap and my heart flutter. I would look out the window to try to identify the disturbance and inevitably could see only blue sky or white cloud. Who or what was shoving the plane around was invisible.

Being inside a cloud was the physical equivalent of being inside a book, the rules of space and time overturned, mortality only an idea. Many times I looked out the window and we were simply hanging in the air, as solid and still as Brunelleschi's dome. Yet we were moving, and fast, otherwise we would have fallen back to earth like another piece of Chicken Little's sky. Prudence appeared unimpressed by this intimation of heaven.

During the flight you had to yell to be heard by anyone, so I tried to read. Before leaving for Lisbon, I had made a quick visit to Liana at her apartment in Rome, wanting to take on the trip anything she could find in her stacks written by Fernando Pessoa. It was a tall order in any case, but in Liana's, I was asking her to disrupt her perfect ménage for me. She disappeared for nearly forty-five minutes and then reappeared with a neat pile of literary magazines. Overcoming the enormity of her sacrifice, she said cheerfully, "Have a good trip."

In the vast colony of our being there are many species of
people who think and feel in different ways.

—FP

Pessoa had mostly published under the names of three of
his "heteronyms"—Alberto Caeiro, Álvaro de Campos, and
Ricardo Reis. Their writing appeared in Lisbon's more obscure newspapers and magazines, two of which were actually
founded by Pessoa personas. The heteronyms wrote about the
others, praising and criticizing their work and ideas. They explained and commented upon the latest European literary and
cultural trends: Futurism, Cubism, Orphism, Surrealism, automatic writing, psychoanalysis, and phenomenology. Extended
and vitriolic polemics between them erupted in print and
became the talk at dinner parties of the cultural elite. After
Pessoa died, in 1935, friends and scholars slowly began sifting
through the 25,000 scraps of writing—essay fragments, bits
of poetry, aphorisms, maxims, horoscopes—left in a wooden
trunk in his rented room and written by one or another of his
heteronyms, which turned out to number more than seventy.

I came across the writing of Fernando Pessoa during my
early days in Rome, when I was hanging around the artists and
writers in via Cavour and doing odd jobs for the editors of the
journal *L'Italia Letteraria*. Whenever I would find something
in translation by this unfathomable poet from Lisbon, I would
run home and read it to Vanni and Germana. As the three of us
devoured all the Pessoa we could find, I knew I had uncovered
a great love. After Germana died, I read him only rarely.

On the plane, I became too involved with being out of control to enter the highly controlled environment of literature. A reader was, in fact, never in control of anything he read, but the act of reading allowed him the illusion. At the very least, he could put the book down in an instant. Up there, if I wanted to suddenly stop flying, go down, get off, it would mean death. I had quite literally given up and I had never felt more at ease in all my days. I wondered if it would be possible to stay up there for the rest of my life. Could I buy a plane, hire a couple of pilots, and move up there permanently? Many had chosen to make their domiciles on boats. Could I live on a plane?

Some have a great dream in life and fall short of it. Others have no dream and also fall short of it.

—FP

If Mussolini prevailed, he planned to keep whole segments of the population living in the sky. Instead, he was shot by a firing squad and dumped in Milan's Piazzale Loreto, his dead body beaten, lacerated, and urinated upon by an angry crowd before they strung him by his feet over a gas station, his semi-nude and equally bullet-ridden mistress by his side. Was this too a preventative measure? The populace sending a message to itself: BEWARE PEOPLE OF ITALY! LET US NEVER AGAIN BE RULED BY A DICTATOR.

At the Lisbon airport, Lord Birdon and Lewis, guests of the English ambassador, disappeared into a waiting car. We were staying at York House, a former convent recently converted into a hotel, and, according to Gladys, the preferred accommodation of writers and spies. We rode along the Tagus Estuary in a black taxi identical to the ones I had seen in London in 1938. On our left flowed the wide, silver river and on our right rose a fragile city built on hills and covered in gleaming, colorful ceramic tile. I thought of Genoa, Naples, Dresden, Berlin, London, and absorbed the miracle that Portugal had managed to stay out of the war. We circled the enormous Commercial Square, lined with elegant arcades. The plaza pullulated with Austin Sevens and Ascots, Bentleys, Morris Eights, Lagondas, Aston Martins, Daimlers, and double-decker buses. Apparently, it was a country of Anglophiles. Pessoa, who spent his youth in South Africa, had translated many works of English literature into Portuguese, had written and published two books of poetry in English, and had worked in Lisbon as a translator of commercial correspondence for import-export companies.

I turned to Prudence and said, "What a perfect place you have brought me to."

Kirk said, "On the plane Lewis told me about *fado*, music that has the saddest words and melodies he's ever heard."

Prudence said, "I once saw a film about Maria Severa, the first great *fadista*. She lived a scandalous life and died young."

"Let's live scandalous lives and die old," said Gladys.

The taxi stopped in front of a building with a facade of bright-blue-and-white tiles depicting scenes from the New Testament. We went through a tiny doorway, up a dank and unlit winding staircase, and into a courtyard jungle of plants and flowers, where several tables and chairs encircled a small marble cherub, water gurgling from his puckered lips. Even now, it was warm enough for us to sit outside and have tea while our rooms were prepared. I was mildly concerned that I would be shown to the sparse, cold cell of a nun whose silent suffering would permeate the walls. I was eventually led to a grand room on the top floor with a wide four-poster bed made up with crisp white linens, a large writing desk, and an eiderdown love-seat under the window. The porter opened the drapes, and the mahogany furniture went from dull brown to russet.

"The Mother Superior's room?" I queried the young man.

"No," he said, "this room was for visiting priests or monks." I tipped him and he added, "During the renovation, they found a secret passageway leading up here from the novitiates' quarters." He pointed to an uneven patch of floorboards in the corner of the room. "It could still be used if there was the wish."

"I'll let you know," I said, and followed him to the door.

The walls in the room spoke of all things, including suffering. Outside the window, the river and the late afternoon light were engaged in a mating ritual, a dance staving off the darkness creeping steadily toward us from just beyond the horizon. The lambent yellow-red light caused every object in its glow to declare authenticity. I turned away from the window and lay on my bed to read until it was time to go to dinner.

What I achieve is not the product of an act of my will but of my will's surrender. I begin because I don't have the strength to think; I finish because I don't have the courage to quit.

—FP

I met up with my party in the hotel restaurant, a rectangular room at one end of the courtyard that was once the refectory, where a mural in painted tiles of the Last Supper dominated one wall. The long communal tables had been replaced by smaller ones, set with immaculate white tablecloths and a porcelain dinner service. All were occupied. In the far corner, a gorgeous toffee-skinned woman sat with a much younger man, also beautiful, who looked exactly like her. Two attractive women of a certain age ate their dinner, each engrossed in a French novel. A man with a mustache—wearing spectacles and an incongruous red bow tie—dined alone. An English couple instructed their two young children on table manners. A Portuguese pair, well into their eighties, whispered furiously at each other and barely touched their food. Every one of the diners looked at us, discreetly and less so, when we entered, and their glances were not of mild curiosity but of prurience. I watched Gladys and Prudence take reassurance in their ability to ignite a room.

"I'm starving," Gladys said. A timbre in her voice made me look at her and notice for the first time that her belly had rounded.

"They can't possibly know who you two are here," Kirk said. "Why does everyone always stare at you?"

"It's the angles," I said.

The waiter brought us water and bread, informed us that because it was Friday we would be served fish, and offered us a choice of salt cod mixed with scrambled eggs or grilled red mullet with cockle rice.

"You missed both of Prudence's premieres in Rome," Gladys said to me. "It was very rude of you. Rocco Pompei called you a cad."

"The last one to call me that was a fair sight prettier than Rocco," I said. I then turned to Prudence. "Did they go well?" I asked.

"Rocco's film won't do much," Prudence said. "*Bitter Rice* stands a chance because of Silvana. Premieres are the worst part of filmmaking. Probably like publishing a book. Just make sure you don't miss Gladys's premiere on the first of February."

"I promise I'll be there," I said.

"Somehow," said Kirk, "and I haven't known you that long, I get the feeling that if you had said 'Sorry, I can't make it' there would be more of a chance that you might show up."

Both girls broke into laughter and Kirk and I joined in. The waiter brought us our fish.

"Since your new book came out, everyone in Rome has been talking about you," Gladys said. "I had no idea you were *that* famous. It was rather selfish of you to go off like you did."

The waiter suggested a bottle of *vinho verde* to accompany our dinner.

"Writing all day long must be very isolating," Kirk said. "It seems unlikely that a man so alone could make meaning out of life."

"I don't," I said. "I subvert meaning. Or that's what I thought I was doing, but really either way it's the same thing."

"Your crises of *meaning* are so tedious. You should have been a spy," Gladys said, lowering her voice, "like Lord Birdon.

He's here on a secret mission to officially offer Salazar unofficial US and British support. He actually said to me, 'better a Fascist dictator than a Communist dictator,' as if the war never happened."

"Gladys, one truth about dictatorships is that walls do have ears," I said. "If you are not more careful, you might lose us our ride home."

"You should have thrown that coin in the Trevi fountain," she scolded. "Who knows if you'll ever get back now."

After dinner, Gladys, Kirk, and Prudence went out in search of *fado*. I pleaded exhaustion and retired to my room to read Pessoa. Now that I had had the extraordinary experience of flight, I didn't quite know what I was doing in Lisbon with these women whom I thought I loved but who were destined to be memories. Longing, I concluded, was to experience nostalgia in the present.

> *To love is to tire of being alone: it is therefore a cowardice, a be-trayal of ourselves. (It's exceedingly important that we not love.)*
> —FP

Vanni would have said that it was ridiculous to make pronouncements on greatness, but I had nothing against being ridiculous. In a hundred years' time, Fernando Pessoa would be considered one of the greatest literary minds of the twentieth century. And the bulk of the product of that mind—stored in a trunk and recorded on napkins, envelopes, company stationery, scraps of paper—could easily have been tossed into the garbage. How many Pessoas have there been? How many figures of greatness have come and gone, never to be known, all traces of them having disappeared into dust? A great many was the answer, yet indifference on such a mighty scale was a hard thing to fathom, like sudden death, or life itself.

> *I'm nothing.*
> *I'll always be nothing.*
> *I can't even wish to be something.*
> *Aside from that, I've got all the world's dreams inside me.*
> —FP

Sometime in the night, I heard a creaking of wood—was it the door or the floor?—followed by a soft rustling, then the warmth of skin and silk and hair, the smell of Prudence's honied breath, of Gladys's nectarous perfume. Like mermaids swimming around a ship that had sunk to the bottom of the sea, I felt them rippling about me, exploring me, as if they were looking for treasure. I heard them whisper my name, together, separately. I turned to Prudence, then to Gladys, then back to Prudence. I reached out to her and she was not there. When I opened my eyes, I was alone, the morning sun streaming through my window.

Over breakfast in the garden, plans were made to go to the Moorish Castelo de São Jorge in the Alfama district, a Romanesque cathedral called the Sé, and to the Elevador de Santa Justa, a wrought-iron elevator tower built by an apprentice of Gustave Eiffel. I was enthusiastic about the itinerary and imagined a wonderful day wandering the city, but when it came time to go I was unable. As I came down the staircase from my room to the reception, I began to sweat profusely. The day was warm but by no means scorching, yet perspiration was pouring off me with even the slightest movement. I could not possibly walk anywhere or I would have been drenched in a matter of seconds. I was also having trouble breathing. I felt as if all the air had gone from my lungs, the room, Lisbon, the earth. I thought of calling for a doctor but I suspected that if I returned to my room and lay down for a spell, I would be all right.

Through a window in the stairwell, I saw that Gladys, Prudence, and Kirk were waiting for me in the courtyard. They made a fine trio. Prudence carried a book and Gladys a parasol. Kirk wore dark glasses, white trousers, and a navy pullover. He looked like a sailor or a tennis player. I couldn't face their disappointment, or my own, so I made my way back up the stairs to my room, water trickling down my temples and along the ravine between my shoulder blades. I asked a chambermaid to take a note to them. I returned to the stairwell, and watched Prudence read the piece of paper and sigh. She looked upward and I jumped away from the window.

For most of the day I slept, read, and brooded.

The Poet is a faker. He
Fakes it so completely,
He even fakes he's suffering
The pain he's really feeling.
            —FP

My depression, my panic, so crippling and consuming, always had a quality of deception, which kept me interested in it. The apathy I had been feeling, however, was simple. I was losing any sense of urgency. I was not even particularly sorry that both Prudence and Gladys would soon be gone from my life.

There are departing sunsets that grieve me more than the deaths of children.

—FP

In the evening, my companions came back to the hotel to have supper with me. I was, as much as possible, happy to see them. They were full of the enthusiasm of discovery that can be infectious but to which I had become immune. According to Gladys, Lisbon was the most romantic city she'd ever been to. According to Prudence, it was the most exotic. And in Kirk's view, the city had the greatest number of bookstores per capita in the world. They had lunched on pork and clams with Lord Birdon, as guests of the English ambassador and his wife at the state dining room in the Palácio Cor de Rosa. Their plan for the next day, New Year's Eve, was to drive out to Monserrate, an estate on the sea just up the coast from Lisbon, famous for its wild gardens described by Byron in "Childe Harold's Pilgrimage."

"You will come with us?" Prudence asked me, though her voice told me she knew I would not.

"I wouldn't miss it for the world," I answered. Catching Kirk's expression—boyish, sly, empathetic—I added, "Let me clarify. It is more likely that hell will freeze over than I will accompany you to Monserrate tomorrow."

"Now that's what I call hope," Gladys said.

Late the next afternoon, they returned to the hotel and began to get ready for a New Year's Eve gala we were invited to at the embassy. Prudence came to my room, still dressed in trousers and a cardigan. She lay back on the bed next to me.

She said, "Dante, if you want me to stay, I will."

"No," I said, "go. I have only coagulated gloom for you here and it's New Year's Eve."

"No, I mean stay in Italy with you."

"Prudence," I said, "if you stayed, you would stay out of fear for me, not out of desire for me."

"I don't know what I fear or desire, Dante, but I know what I love."

"In that case, Gladys is your better bet," I said. "If you remained I might stick around for a few more years or I might not. This is the way I live, and it is no way to live."

Prudence rose from the bed and went over to the window, her face bathed in the pink light of a consumed sun.

"I was hoping I might change your mind, which is also no way to live," she said.

When Gladys came to get us for the party, she saw that we were not in our evening clothes. She said nothing and left the room. After a half hour, she returned with Kirk and several waiters carrying trays of caviar and langoustines and half a dozen bottles of champagne.

"I am the party," she said, "and tonight it will happen here."

She had been the party for me. We had been to the edge, peered in, sounded its depth, taken its measure, but into it I would go alone.

On the roof of the hotel, we greeted the New Year watching fireworks explode over the Tagus in a spring of colored light.

Kirk said, "I will miss living in Europe."

Gladys said, "If we hate it in L.A., we can always come back. We might even fly."

I said, "You'll be back if the Trevi Fountain has any self-respect." A white missile whistled into the air, burst into a bright white spider, its legs long and dangling, then vanished.

"I don't want to count on superstition," Prudence said. A series of pinwheels spun over our heads like the wheels of Apollo's chariot.

Gladys said, "Why not? It'll do as well as anything else, *ce n'est pas vrai*, Dante?"

I said to Gladys, "I've always been impressed by your knack for the truth."

When the sky was again dark, Gladys and Kirk left for the embassy and Prudence and I returned to my room.

I had barely closed the door when I decided to have my own bout with the truth. "Prudence," I said, "I've been fucking your sister since the day we met."

"Dante, don't bother," she said. "If this is a ploy to get me to go away, you can relax. I have no intention of staying, probably never did."

"I thought I wanted you," I went on, "but I see now that it was Gladys I wanted all along."

She came close to me. "You're saying these things so you can wallow deeper in your self-pity."

"Perhaps," I said, "perhaps not. But if I had my way tonight, Gladys would be standing where you are."

She backed away. Her eyes were red, her mouth twisted. "Well, then," she said, smoothing her hair and face with her hands before looking straight at me with her chameleon eyes. "You're the writer. Use your imagination."

I did, and mine, of course, was a sewer.

"All right, slut, undress."

She slowly started to unbutton her shirt but I intervened and stripped her myself, throwing her clothes in a messy pile on the floor. Her discomfort standing naked in front of me spurred me on. I said, "Down on your hands and knees." She did as she was told. "Stick your ass up in the air." I left her there while I took off my clothes. I then walked around in front of her. I put my hand under her chin and lifted her face. "Spit on my hand." She did and I asked her to do it again. "Now stick out your tongue and don't put it back." I walked back around her. I grabbed her hair and pulled so that she arched even further, pushing myself inside. She cried out and I told her to shut up and keep her tongue out. I slammed into her until she collapsed onto the floor and I fell on top of her.

We lay there for a while until finally she crawled out from under me and put on her clothes.

"How could I do this to you?" I said.

"No matter how much we'd like to believe otherwise," she said, "we've been headed here all along. Now maybe we can start to get on with our lives."

As she left the room, I silently wished her all the luck in the world.

The ride home in the De Havilland Dove was three hours of what was described to me by Lord Birdon as "extreme turbulence but nothing to worry about." Jejunely, I wished the plane might crash, my body forever lost on a mountaintop or deep in a forest or at the bottom of the sea. I had always known, though, that I would not die by accident but by my deliberate choice, and I was nearer to accomplishing that than ever before. I did, however, spend a lot of that flight wondering if fate had suddenly decided to take the situation out of my hands.

Twice the pilot considered landing in order to wait for better weather, but Lord Birdon would have none of it. He had been invited to a shooting party in Maremma the next day and refused to miss it on account of a few bumps. Kirk's complexion had turned the color of a lima bean and he was gripping the armrests with such force that he seemed, Atlas-like, to be attempting to hold the plane up in the sky. Gladys, who again sat next to Lord Birdon, seemed oblivious. While the plane was at the height of its pitching, she and Lord Birdon made their way to the bathroom at the back of the plane, passing Lewis from Liverpool, who, when he wasn't vomiting into a bag, was picking up broken pieces of glass from cups and dishes that had toppled from a cabinet. As Gladys and her latest trophy entered paradise, I watched Prudence, who was somehow sleeping through it all. Since the night when I made her endure being touched with violence and scorn, our hold on each other had, in fact, loosened.

twelve

Castiglioncello

Prudence and Gladys Godfrey departed for the United States on a transatlantic liner out of Genoa on St. Valentine's Day, 1950. I had known them just about two years. For all the wreckage created and revealed among the three of us, for all the moments of dream-like horror, there were more moments of transcendent joy, and if I had a chance to do it all over again I wouldn't hesitate. As deviant as the venture was, I had found a way to love a woman by loving two. Happily, the women in question had arrived safe and sound in Los Angeles, and from the letters I had just received from each of them, they were still surprising me.

I had come to Castiglioncello on a late April morning, the air smelling of newly blossoming flowers—oleander and bougain-villea—and faintly of brine. I soon learned that Ubaldo and his family, including Nerina and the children, had gone to a cousin's wedding in Grossetto and wouldn't be back for several days. As usual, the villa was in good order, waiting for me. It was not long before I made my way down to the beach. I sat on The Throne, turned my face to the sun, and listened to the chiming of the rocks jostled by the waves. Every so often an inland breeze would carry the odor of burning brush. Aunt Pia used to sing the praises of rocky beaches as opposed to the sandy ones of Viareggio and Rosignano. Her first claim to superiority was that no tiny grains of filth were ever hidden in odd corners of your shoes or bathing suit, only to appear at some inopportune moment. Aunt Pia's second claim was nostalgic. One could watch the evolution of a rocky beach and become attached to certain boulders such as The Throne, or The Great One, a huge rock twenty meters from the shore that had been the ultimate destination when I was learning to swim, the pinnacle of achievement when first diving. Year after year, the rocks endured, lending to one's life a sense of continuity. It was impossible, remarked Aunt Pia, to become attached to a grain of sand. It occurred to me that Aunt Pia and Prudence would have gotten along famously.

After returning from our trip to Lisbon, I had done as promised and attended Gladys's opening night. As Ingrid Bergman gave birth to a son and Anna Magnani was being consoled by her pets, having refused to attend her own premiere, I walked down the red carpet, a tongue uncurling from the mouth of the luscious Cinema Fiamma. Gladys and Prudence poised on each of my arms, we made our way on that crisp February evening to the first public screening of *Vulcano*. Light bulbs flashing, the crowd cheering, I decided that what aroused humankind most of all was the truth, and on that red carpet all shades of truth were on parade, the atmosphere bacchanalian.

My spirits had lifted considerably since Lisbon, and knowing time was short, I had seen Prudence and Gladys frequently, though never separately. Our triangle had been forever torn apart, but that had been apparent well before the trip. My monstrous behavior with both Gladys and Prudence went unheeded, as monstrous behavior is wont to do. The premiere was bittersweet, a taste of what had been, what could have been, what could never be, played out in an atmosphere of the sublimely absurd. That evening the sisters looked ravishing wearing matching strapless gowns of vermilion satin, white sable stoles, and long black gloves reaching just shy of their shoulders. Their honey brown hair, longer than usual, tumbled down their backs. Gladys was visibly pregnant and adorable. Rossano Brazzi had made the stroll before us and stood in his corner posing for photographers while being interviewed by the gossip columnist Teodora Bora Bora, whom I had once prosaically made love to during an air raid. Brazzi was without his wife, and Gladys was without Kirk (they were already inside), since red carpet rules allowed spouses only if famous in their own right. I was granted admission due to the continued delusion of picture people that my profession added heft to their product. And though my fame on their scale had the weight of an American girl's fart, enough of them had heard my name at dinner parties to deem me fit for display. I watched Gladys and Prudence for what seemed like an eternity as their faces shifted with perfect timing from excited to a tad bored, to grateful, to magnanimous acceptance of the tedium of it all. They were consummate professionals.

Finally, it was our turn to be interviewed by Teodora. Her stream of obvious questions—"Aren't you just thrilled to be here? Was Anna Magnani inspiring to work with? What is it like being an American actress in Italy? Is there truth to the rumor you're heading back to Hollywood?"—were mitigated by a few of her infamous knife thrusts.

"Remind me, Gladys, have you ever actually had a leading role in a picture?"

To which Gladys responded, "I'm still young, compared to some."

For Prudence she had this: "Pushing thirty and still unmarried? You must be so happy that you'll soon be an auntie."

To which Prudence responded: "I'm planning on having at least five husbands and a child with each."

And for me: "We writers are positively dwarfed by all this, don't you think, Mr. Sabato?"

To which I responded: "Now, now, Teo, as you well know, when alluding to me *gigantic* is the more appropriate adjective."

Once inside, we found Kirk standing next to a replica of a volcano erupting Campari from its cone. Waiters dressed as deep sea divers, complete with helmet and air hoses, served raw oysters and clams on the half shell to film people, members of the aristocracy, government officials, and a posse of shelf-breasted women with thick red mouths. And, of course, there was the press, who mimicked seagulls following a loaded trawler. Tullio was chatting with a senator, a countess, a minister, and a couple of ambassadors.

"I can't believe this is for real," said Kirk, handing us champagne flutes of Campari and soda. "Those guys must be dying in those suits."

"I'm sure they're not wearing the genuine item, darling, but something from the costume department," Gladys said. "Let's go talk to the German." We headed over to where the director, sporting the white gloves, was standing alone, his wife not far off having a tête-à-tête with the actress Giulietta Masina.

"Selznick," Dieterle told us, "sends his regrets. He had a last-minute change of plans and went to Paris to broker peace between Marcel Carné and Jean Gabin. Their squabbling has stopped the shooting of a Simenon novel and the delay has already cost David a mint." Dieterle shook his head, his expression one of sorrow at yet another instance of his industry's gross inefficiency.

On one side of the volcano, Luchino Visconti, Federico Fellini, Vittorio De Sica, Cesare Zavattini, and Dino De Laurentiis were all crowded around the exquisite Silvana Mangano, whose head was tilted so far back it looked as if her neck might snap. Her long red-blonde hair hung down like the tail of an Arabian horse. Against her full lips, Fellini held an oyster shell. The live animal slid off its pearly home into her mouth, and she shivered and laughed and begged for more. De Laurentiis, her fiancé, warned her against hazardous side effects, then grabbed a tray from a waiter and held it while Federico fed her a dozen more.

Gladys leaned over to me and whispered, "That should be me." Nothing in her voice indicated envy. She was simply stating a fact. This was her premiere and, given Magnani's absence, she should have been the center of attention. Gladys was getting plenty of play, but not of that caliber. And you couldn't say it was because she wasn't pretty enough, or didn't want it bad enough, or wasn't talented enough, because she could have gotten around all those things one way or another. "In this life," she said to me, "it isn't going to be my turn."

Tullio sidled up to us and, nodding appreciatively toward Silvana, said, "No offense, Gladys, but I believe the best cinema we'll see tonight is happening in front of us now."

He was right, of course, and even more so when the rest of the evening disintegrated into the tragi-comic. After we had drunk our fill of lava, we settled in our seats, the lights went off, and the screen lit up with the formidable visage of Anna Magnani. In a matter of seconds her face revealed all the passion and bleakness the world could muster, her dark, hollowed eyes suggesting a life that had known only desperation and despair. The projector spluttered, the cinema went dark, and the lights came up. The audience waited patiently, as this was a regular enough occurrence at the cinema. Renzo Avanzo strode back and forth between the projector room and Dieterle, who was sitting with us at the back of the cinema. It seemed an amplifier fuse had blown and its replacement was missing. A Fiamma employee was sent running to the nearest cinema to borrow one. He had arrived back with the new fuse just as two replacement fuses miraculously reappeared in the exact spot where they were normally stored.

Gladys whispered to no one in particular, "I told you this picture was doomed."

We sank deeper into our plush crimson seats before the great blank screen as the room again went dark and the large and luminous image of Anna filled the emptiness. She was soon joined by Gladys and Rossano and the whole theater seemed to relax. But then the sound began to slip out of sync and we were watching Gladys's lips move while hearing the deep tones of Rossano's voice. A crescendo of giggling swept through the audience. The lights went up, the giggling turned to polite coughing, the problem was fixed, the lights went off, the audience still showed all signs of good sportsmanship. Rossano and Gladys's scene continued. Her performance was tender and natural, but, before the scene had finished, the amplifier fuse blew a second time. The audience now refused to contain their incredulity. The hum in the room was loud. Whispers of sabotage ricocheted about the theater, necks craned to a rumor that Anna herself had shown up to try to save the evening. (She hadn't.) Several people—mostly political types—walked out of the theater. Tullio, who had been sitting with them, came over and sat with us.

"They're afraid this might be leading up to some sort of attack," he said.

Dino and Silvana snuck out on the heels of the politicians. I watched as Prudence's eyes met Silvana's and she sheepishly shrugged while pointing at Dino, indicating that their leaving was his fault. Naturally, the critics all stayed. Renzo Avanzo took to the stage and apologized with humor and grace. Those left were convinced that something fishy was going on. Many speculated that Roberto Rossellini had hired thugs to ruin the launch of his ex-lover's film. Others suspected disgruntled Yugoslavians unhappy about Trieste becoming a Free Territory (the evening was a benefit for a Trieste-based orphanage). By the time the theater went dark again, a good half of the audience was gone.

I whispered to Gladys, "You have never been better."

She whispered back, "Better to be bad in a good picture than good in a bad picture."

Prudence said, "Better to be good in a bad picture than bad in a bad picture."

Tullio said, "All publicity is good publicity."

Kirk said, "We are very lucky. Because of tonight's fiasco, no one can tell how bad the picture actually is."

We watched the end of the film without much pleasure. Dieterle had taken off his gloves and was wringing them like a wet towel. The dinner following the film with the actors, director, wives, husbands, and a few others like me and Tullio was a dismal affair and we all went home early. The papers over the next few days barely mentioned the film, reporting instead on the potential scandal surrounding the opening night events. No culprit could be found, however, and attention soon fizzled. About a week after the picture opened, the Vatican announced, "All Catholics throughout the world are forbidden to see the film *Vulcano*." But even that endorsement couldn't save it. It was not the send-off I would have wished for my Gladys, but she was laughing about the whole thing by the next day, and the story was destined to have pride of place in her repertoire of anecdotes.

Two weeks after standing on the red carpet of the Cinema Fiamma, I was standing on another red carpet leading up the white marble stairway into the ornate lobby of the Principe di Piemonte, Viareggio's finest hotel. A bellhop was unloading our bags from Tullio's rose-petal-white Alpha Romeo 1900. We stood watching the boy struggle with our things while we smoked and stretched our legs after the three-hour journey from Genoa. Gladys, Prudence, and Kirk had sailed the evening before on the *M.S. Italia*, one of the few liners left in Italy not owned by Achille Lauro. The parting had been jolly, full of champagne and talk of future plans.

Tullio said, "Before I left Rome, I took a few bets and the odds are 2 to 1 in your favor. Moravia and Gadda are 3 and 4 to 1 respectively. You're the obvious choice, so you won't win. Gadda may be a genius but he's unreadable. I put my money on Moravia because his wife won a couple of years ago and male pride is at stake. You want to make a bet?"

I tossed him a 10,000 lire note. "Unreadability should win but I'll bet on myself."

I had been put up for a variety of prizes in my career, won some, lost others. During the Fascist years, literary prizes were in such abundance that even my pseudonym, Sandro Weltman, won several for his essays but never turned up to claim them. The one I was presently vying for, the Viareggio Literary Prize, had been established as a way to bring people to a seaside resort during the off-season. Though the prize had become one of the most prestigious in Italy, it had yet to thaw the town's frozen economy.

In Viareggio's newly built Teatro Bussola, I would be competing for my prize later that evening by giving a public reading. After we three contestants had all performed, a carefully screened audience would vote to select the winner. I was reminded of Shirley Jackson's short story "The Lottery," which I had read during the trip to Venice with Gladys and Prudence and had forgotten about until that moment. I had the distinct sensation that I was about to be chosen for something dreadful.

I was grateful to Tullio for having offered to come with me, both to Genoa and then here to Viareggio. I suspected he had been persuaded to do it by Falsetta, but I was done with being suspicious of Tullio, and what did it matter anyway? He always happened to be there. Though Tullio was the most loyal friend I had, over the years I had devised all sorts of reasons why he had to be kept at arm's length—after Vanni I never wanted another close friend, Tullio was not to be trusted, Tullio had shady connections, Tullio was an opportunist. These, of course, were all the things about Tullio that drew me to him. I sought out no one's company as often and as willingly as I did Tullio's, which was auspicious since we would be, as sodomite and suicide, spending all of eternity together.

In truth, Tullio and I hadn't spent more than a few hours at a time together since I left London to go to my father's funeral and he sailed for America on the *Queen Mary*. I sometimes wondered what would have happened if I had gone with him to America. Would I have come back? Could I have been absorbed into that great idea of existence without a past? Would being able to say "I am American" have changed me forever? I thought not, but the possibility of such a thing had nourished millions of imaginations and once had nourished my own.

"Tullio," I said, lighting another cigarette, "what was it like in California?"

He looked at me and in his eyes I watched him consider lying, then decide on the truth. But I could have been wrong. He was still very beautiful, perhaps even more so, his youthfulness now dashed with the tangible signs of wisdom.

"In retrospect, it was atrocious," he said, "but at the time I just felt lucky."

"Atrocious?" I repeated.

"It was the war. Our country was already in very low regard after having dumped so many of its citizens on the brave new world. And it didn't help to be from the side that produced, as the newsreels put it, 'the greatest evil yet known to mankind,' so it was all very awkward for me. Ironically, I found myself dropping into every conversation I could the fact that I was Jewish."

"So you never thought about staying?"

"I wouldn't say never. But it became clear to me that by staying I would be swapping one set of foibles for another. I

was more familiar with my own." The bellhop motioned that
he was ready to accompany us to our rooms. "But who knows.
Perhaps if you had come with me, it would have been different."

"Maybe. I used to wonder what it would have been like if
Germana had lived, but I don't anymore."

"She loved you, of that there is no doubt," Tullio said. "But
would that have changed anything in your life?"

"In mine, nothing; in hers, everything."

After smelling the soaps and testing the mattress, I knocked
on Tullio's door and suggested we take a walk along Viareggio's seaside promenade. The bright bathhouses on the wide
sandy beach were nestled up against each other like dolls on
a child's bed. Across the *viale*, Liberty-style hotels with pas-
tel-hued facades, cupolas, archways, balconies, tiled roofs, and
arabesque ornamentation sat beneath groves of towering sea
pines. Our destination was the mythical Gran Caffè Margherita, an impressive establishment resembling a Mughal palace
with a bar, restaurant, tea room, and a large rooftop terrace
from which the eye could meander over the sea, among the
Apuane Alps, and down to the parade below. Aunt Pia used
to bring me there from Castiglioncello once or twice during
the summer, and I looked forward to those trips all year. We
would drive an hour or so to Viareggio for the afternoon and I
would watch as she tried on dresses and hats and shoes at the
fancy boutiques that lined the promenade and she would ask
me what I thought. I always told her she was the most beautiful
woman I had ever seen, which initially was true, but in time

I repeated these words for the sheer pleasure it gave her. We would then go to the Gran Caffè Margherita, where she would order her pink martini and I would drink Coca-Cola and we would have an early supper of pasta with clams or fish stew, wiping our plates clean with Viareggio's salty flat bread.

The weather that day was not ideal for my stroll with Tullio. The air was cold and the sky overcast but as the sun began to fall behind the mountains the clouds dispersed, granting us a view of a crenellated sky. Despite the efforts of the prize organizers, the promenade was hardly teeming with pocket-lined life. Most of the shops, including a new department store called Forty-Eight, were closed, even boarded up, for the season, and the seafront, so crowded in the summer months with the aspiring middle class, was now virtually abandoned. On carts outside the few open restaurants were skimpy displays of shellfish atop mountains of gray ice. Through small gaps between bathhouses, we glimpsed the expanse of rippled sand truncated by the green sea. In summer, the beach became invisible under the thousands of sun umbrellas and deck chairs, concession stands, and bodies taking up every inch available, even beyond the water line. But now it was a big, open, empty space, with a few bundled children running around in circles pulling along a kite that refused to fly. It was as if Viareggio in the winter and Viareggio in the summer were two entirely different cities: one a little sad and soulful, the other boisterous and rich in superficiality.

"Did you know Gladys and Prudence very well while you were in California?" I asked Tullio.

"Not well. I ran into Prudence now and again because of her thing with Billy Wilder."

"I never understood what happened with him," I said. "I mean why it ended."

Tullio looked at me and shrugged. "The story was he left her for Jane Russell. But another story was that he knocked up Gladys. After the abortion, Prudence secured from him an all-expenses-paid trip here, and then made him find them work."

"Ah," I said, "of course."

"Those two sisters," Tullio said, "are like Siamese twins. You're never sure which one is in control, and, if you ever tried to separate them, one or the other or both would surely die."

It was another of Tullio's instant assessments that had taken me two years to understand. We continued walking along slowly. We tried to spot who might be in town for the prize, with a keen eye for the other nominees, both of whom had written better books than I, ensuring my victory, but we spied no one we knew. To amuse ourselves, we read aloud the names of the bathhouses as if they were lovers—Alice, Irene, Dora, Nora, Giuseppina, Gabriella, Alfea, Annita. And for Tullio—Amadeo, Artiglio, Maurizio, Florindo, Guido, Ermanno.

After a while Tullio said, "Are you all right?"

My answer surprised even me. "Do you love me, Tullio?"

"Dante," he said, his expression one of great relief, "I have always loved you. Let's go get drunk before your reading."

We went into the bar at the Gran Caffè Margherita and drank Manhattans until neither of us could say an entire sentence without slurring. At some point, I looked at my watch and realized the readings were scheduled to begin in a quarter of an hour. I began to cry.

"What's wrong, old boy?" Tullio said, putting his arm around me.

"I am going to lose," I sobbed.

Tullio howled with laughter. "I hope so," he said. "I have quite a bit of money riding on it." He helped me to my feet and we both fell back onto a chair that in turn crashed to the ground. A waiter ran to help us and Tullio told him to bring two quadruple espressos on the double.

As we pulled ourselves together and prepared to make our way to the Teatro Bussola, Tullio's face blanched. He said, "I suddenly have a terrible feeling that you are going to win."

And win I did.

When I got back to Rome, I filled the void left by the Godfrey sisters with work. I started a new sonnet cycle and a novel. Two of my books had been optioned for films by Rocco Pompei, now in Hollywood, and he had hired me to write the screenplays. For *Cinema*, I was reviewing Graham Greene's *The Third Man* and was in the midst of a translation of Raymond Chandler's *The Little Sister*, which I hoped to finish soon. In short, I was a bundle of activity. But when the letters from Gladys and Prudence arrived, I abandoned all writing projects and took the next train to Castiglioncello.

From The Throne, I spied six nuns filing onto the beach, already in their summer habits of white linen and winged headdresses. While staring at this string of saltwater pearls, I glimpsed the dinghy and the sailboat, looking brand-new (Ubaldo, too, had been busy), perched on the rocks above the tideline and securely fastened to iron rings cemented into the stone wall. I pondered taking the dinghy out for a spin. I thought it time for me to get beyond my antipathy for boats. I looked over at the small vessel and tried to collect my nerve. I caught the eye of a nun who seemed to know exactly what I was plotting and relished the prospect of a spectacle. I couldn't do it, I decided, with anyone looking on. I would have to delay my nautical adventure until later, when the beach was empty of all divinely inspired observers.

I closed my eyes and let my mind drift, lamenting the fact that I would never know what it was like to be a bank robber. Two redoubtable thefts had occurred recently in the United States with a combined take of over three million dollars, expanding my definition of "prize." The heists had been a comfort to all, restoring faith in America's pioneering lawlessness at a time of otherwise profound paranoia and persecution. The first jet passenger flight had successfully crossed the Atlantic, and I considered, one of these days, availing myself of this leap into the future to go visit Gladys and Prudence. My new book had as its central protagonist a poet, a device I had sworn to avoid, but my act of rebellion excited me. When I told Tullio about my misgivings, he said to me, "Dante, if it's not autobiographical, it's plagiarism. *The Divine Comedy* was an embellished diary and Shakespeare was a consummate thief. Write what you know, old boy, or write what you don't know, it's all the same to the rest of us."

The sun had long since begun its journey to the other side when I went back up to the villa to have a cup of tea, sit by the window, and read the letters from Gladys and Prudence yet again.

Los Angeles
April 5, 1950

Dear Dante,

I know Gladys has written to you about Beatrice but I also know she won't have told you what a perfect beauty that little girl is. She makes the world seem an entirely new place.

Yet, in many ways, sadly, the world is the same repetitive place, as you like to point out. My good friend Olive Dearing has been taken to task by Ronald Reagan, head of the Screen Actors Guild, because of her friendship with Edward Dmytryk. She's managed to get Edward G. Robinson and Cecil B. DeMille to write letters on her behalf. Supposedly there are ways to clear one's name. Unlike Bogie, Olive can't write an article confessing her sins because she's too small-time to interest a magazine. But she would do anything to keep working, anything but name names, which is really all they want.

We very much miss you here in dusty Los Angeles. We're living by the sea so the grit is mixed with salt and somehow more tolerable. We eat terrible food and yearn for any indication that the world began before 1920. I managed to get a good part in a Darryl F. Zanuck picture and whenever I can, I bring Beatrice with me to the set. I am glad for the distractions, otherwise I would only think of you, which I do anyway.

I have been trying to see a way to come back to Rome and to you. In spite of all the pain we have caused each other, it is what I want. But I cannot leave Gladys just yet. Our father died recently, so I am hoping that his horrible specter will finally fade from our lives. Until then, I need her to feel as protected as possible, something I didn't do when we were children.

I have heard your book is winning all the prizes. Please don't let those silly things put you in too foul a mood. I hope you have begun something new, though writing seems like such a sad business—a string of love affairs, each destined to end in irreversible loss. I couldn't bear it myself.

your Prudence

The letter from Gladys came the day after Prudence's, though it had been written a few days before.

Los Angeles
April 1, 1950

Dear Dante,

She looks just like you, prunish and wizened. Luckily, she has red hair like Kirk, Prudence's green eyes, and my nature—she screams bloody murder every evening for four hours straight, otherwise she's a doll. In honor of you we have called her Beatrice, poor dear. I am still fat as a suckling pig, and they tell me I will never get my figure back. Like Scarlett O'Hara, I feel resentful enough never to have another child. The birth itself was horrendous but I won't bother you with the details. Suffice it to say that giving birth has led me to believe in God. Only a Man would punish a woman so perversely, n'est-ce pas? One more week and my obstetrician says it will be safe for me to mate again. He's first in line.

For the moment, the four of us are living in a nice little house in Santa Monica near the beach. Prudence is looking for her own place but I think that's stupid. All she wants to do is go back to Rome. I've been too fat for the pictures so work for me consists of hand commercials and voice-overs for TV and radio. Kirk has found himself a job as a prop manager for MGM. My father died just before Bea was born and left us the house in North Dakota, so we're thinking of moving there for a while. Prudence, of course, refuses to come with us.

I miss you very much, Dante. We were such pals. I'll never find that again with anyone.

Love, Gladys

Day had turned to night without my noticing. Perhaps I had fallen asleep, the letters slipping from my hand to the floor. Out my window, I stared straight into the moon's stony eye. I remembered the newly repaired dinghy on the beach. The sky was a spectacular display, worthy of a Pino and Fausto oration, and I wanted to see it far from the lights of the shore. I put the letters in my pocket, then found a candle to light my way down the stone stairs to the beach. I left the house, then turned back, deciding to bring with me Pier Maria's foot, which I kept in a box on the windowsill in my study. I also brought the bottle of perfume I had failed to give Prudence on Capri, and the fishbone.

Once down on the beach there was plenty of light from the moon and the stars, so I blew out the candle and tossed it aside. Dragging the dinghy over the rocks to the water took a great deal of effort. I had worn rubber boots but my feet still got wet when I climbed in the boat, and then, as I put in the oars, it nearly capsized. A breeze had come up, the waves splashing against the sides of the dinghy, and I kept telling myself that at any moment I could turn back, give up, leave the boat trip for another time. But I persevered, impelled by the desire to lie down at sea, stare up at the sky, and find my place in the world's geometry. I thought it would be as good a way as any to end just another day.

AFTERWORD

After a screening of Giuseppe De Santis's *Bitter Rice*, as the credits rolled I was struck by the name of the supporting actress, Dorothy Dowling. I turned to my friend Myra Kamenetzky, better known as Lally, an Italian of Russian descent. She was a young woman in Rome during the war and postwar period, and is as knowledgeable about Italian film as anyone I have ever met. I asked her about this actress with a decidedly non-Italian name. She explained, "Dorothy Dowling and her sister Constance were American actresses who went to work in Rome after the war and became famous for a while, not so much for the films they were in as for Constance's affair with the writer Cesare Pavese just before his death." My research into the story of Pavese and the Dowlings pretty much ended there. Beyond the seedling of truth planted by Lally, and a few historical incidents and personalities to lend verisimilitude, Dante Omero Sabato, the Godfrey sisters, and most of the characters and events in this story, have sprung entirely from my imagination. Any congruence with reality is delightful.

——

Printed in the United States
by Baker & Taylor Publisher Services